# WIND DANCER

# WIND DANCER

*a novel*

JAMIE CARIE

Nashville, Tennessee

Printed in the United States of America

978-0-8054-4534-3

Published by B&H Publishing Group,
Nashville, Tennessee

Dewey Decimal Classification: F
Subject Heading: ADVENTURE FICTION \
ROMANCES \ UNITED STATES—HISTORY—
1775–1783, REVOLUTION—FICTION

Publisher's Note: This novel is a work of fiction. Although it is based on historical events, some of the names, characters, places, and incidents are the product of the author's imagination. In some cases, fictitious words or actions have been attributed to real individuals; these, too, are imagined.

1 2 3 4 5 6 7 8 • 12 11 10 09

This book is dedicated to my mother, Donna. How can I tell you what you have been to me and this family? I only know this—I would have never known Hope and her characterization without watching you live out your love for your family and for Him. I imagine getting to heaven and seeing you with all your crowns on your head. (Crowns that you have thrown at the feet of Jesus, He convincing you that they belong on your head in all their towering beauty). *Beauty.* That's it. That is what you are and will forever be.

# Acknowledgments

To David Webb, who helped make this story all that it is. I appreciate you as both an editor and a friend.

To Leo Finnerty, a park ranger at George Rogers Clark National Historical Park. Thank you for checking my work, believing in it, and praying for it. You said I gave "new life" to Clark's story. You helped in that. I am thankful God put you in my life.

And lastly to the citizens of Vincennes, Indiana. I hope you are as proud as I am to have walked the same soil as someone like George Rogers Clark. I hope we all can be so full of faith in our mission on this earth. You are a grand old city . . . one that I am proud to have called home.

***Sometimes that which takes the most faith to believe is the most true . . . to those who live in the truth.***

# 1

## *Illinois Country 1778*

He heard it again. Coming upstream and upwind, deep in the dark shroud of forest trees, the unmistakable crunch of autumn leaves. Samuel Holt crouched low over the tiny fire-pit of birch bark, hoarding the last wisp of warmth before the inevitable flight about to be demanded of him. He had discovered this means of keeping warm while giving the locals few clues to his presence. Now, after many a night's practice, he could sleep while squatting over a hole that gave off little smoke but enough warmth to keep a man through the cold, dark hours of night. His deerskin jacket hung tent-like from broad shoulders, trapping the heat. His position was small and blended into his surroundings, but his body held the easy suppleness of finely tuned muscle that could explode with power at a moment's notice. He knew with a fair amount of humble acknowledgment that he could spring up on legs that would carry him for miles at a run if need be; and judging from the tingling in his scalp, this might be one of those occasions.

Allowing himself some small movement of his head, he looked to the predawn sky, still and pregnant with the possibilities of any new day. He felt the last tendrils of sleep fall away and sucked the cold, damp air into his lungs to enliven him. In a matter of seconds, he had gone from sound sleep to full alert, every sense straining for advantage and, with it, survival.

His gaze scanned the tree line for movement. Mentally, he took quick accounting of his accoutrements. He could feel the steady weight of his knife sheathed at his thigh, a weight to which he was so accustomed that he had to think of it to realize it was there. His tomahawk hung from his belt, hidden by the fringed jacket hard won in a game of hazard and comfortingly close to his belly. His long rifle, loaded and inches from his right hand, lay on the forest floor, hidden among the brown curl of the leaves.

The buck he had killed at dusk the night before was stretched out next to the rifle, it too blending into the ground where all creatures eventually return. He hadn't wanted to gut it in the dark, so he had decided to camp during the deep part of the night and then, in the morning, clean the animal and carry it back to Fort Harrod where the people were in dire need of fresh meat. The wilderness fort had been under constant siege, forever at the mercy of native raiding parties. It had been four long days since anyone had ventured outside the skinny poles that formed the stockade—skinny poles that nonetheless meant the difference between life and death.

Samuel had come upon them yesterday, having returned to Kentucky and the Illinois country after traveling from Williamsburg with George Rogers Clark to drum up support and ammunition for the campaign. Theirs had been a mission of desperation, but Clark had his plans and the wherewithal to convince others that those plans were not only right and sound but just short of God-breathed. After hearing him speak, Samuel had been convinced as well. Convinced and ready to follow a man like George Rogers Clark to hades and back, which might be required by the campaign outlined in his leader's red head. Samuel was one of the few who knew the full of Clark's bold plan to take the British forts of Kaskaskia, Cahokia, and Vincennes. Success would mean much to the American cause, opening trade routes, the rivers, and the western frontier. What few others knew is that Clark also had his eye on Detroit, the well-fortified British stronghold of the Northwest. It was a bold plan all right. A plan to change history.

They were elated finally to receive permission from Patrick Henry to recruit a militia worthy of Clark's plan. Yet getting permission turned out to be the easy part. Clark and Samuel scoured the countryside, riding long hours on horseback through the backcountry of Virginia, talking to scores of farmers and tradesmen, stopping fathers and sons in open fields where the scent of tobacco reigned. They then traveled the cities and villages, from one smoke-filled tavern to another, then on to the docks and quays of the coastal towns. They soon discovered that recruiting men who were not already engaged in the Virginia militia was harder than finding seed in a chicken coop. It had taken them weeks to scrounge up even a few dozen men—and these were the most ragged, hard-bitten lot that even someone as toughened as Samuel had ever seen.

Finally, and though Clark had hated to, he'd sent Samuel back to the frontier to watch over the vulnerable forts. They had agreed to meet back up in May at the Falls of the Ohio River, just close enough to British-held Kaskaskia to spy and train. In the meantime Clark had commissioned Samuel to do just what he was doing: check on the forts, spread good news of support from Virginia, and keep his scalp attached.

It was a job Samuel had a knack for.

Upon reaching Fort Harrod, Samuel had found men with sunken cheeks, the women and children starving. The inhabitants were half frozen from lack of decent shelter and in a state of fearful paralysis, unable, mentally at least, to venture forth for fresh meat. He had been greeted by children with eyes as round as walnuts, women looking at him as though he was their savior, and men wounded or burying the latest dead. Samuel had immediately set out once more for provisions. They said it often enough: It was men like him who kept the territory open. Men like him who made it possible for brave souls to etch out a living on the frontier. And Samuel knew, deep in a place that stirred to life when on a mission of meat or war or peace even, that this was his place in the world. At least for now.

Now, with every fiber alert, he waited for the inevitable, anticipated it even. Suddenly, and with heart-stopping shrillness, a scream pierced the stillness of predawn. Samuel leapt up, rifle in hand, swung the massive buck unto his shoulders, and began to run. He was fast, had been fast since his boyhood days on a Virginia plantation where he raced and won against friends and foes, and that quickness had kept his scalp attached to his head for his twenty-four years. He knew, as sure as he knew his eyes were blue, that it would stand him in good stead now.

An arrow whizzed by his ear, and he turned, aimed, and fired. In the time it took him to turn back around, dodging trees and forest bramble, he had assessed the situation. Six warriors, two mounted and hot on his trail, one now dead, lying with a bullet lodged in his heart. Samuel had learned long ago the disadvantages of merely wounding an Indian, so now he left them little chance to plead vengeance oaths from their brothers. Not that his head wasn't held in high regard as it was. He knew of several chiefs who would give a daughter's hand in marriage for a bloody swatch of Samuel's golden hair. The Glorious One, he had heard them call him.

Reloading as he ran, Samuel cut a jagged path through the dense undergrowth where hidden roots and bramble might cause the warriors to slow. He shifted the heavy weight of the deer, wondering if he would be forced to abandon it. No, the fort needed this meat; he had to make it with the provisions intact. Otherwise, this excursion would only be a footrace.

He turned to the left where the pounding of the ponies hoofs were beating heedlessly into his ears, like the drumming of a nightmare, but a nightmare so familiar it no longer held any terror, only a sure outcome. He took aim with instincts deeper than his sight and fired again. Moments later he heard a sound behind him. Unable to reload fast enough, he paused, grasped his tomahawk with a tight-fisted grip, and swung it around. The head of the tomahawk lodged in the throat of a man whose fierce eyes would be added to the others that haunted him. As he whirled back around, ready to sprint the last distance to the fort, Samuel marveled at the excitement in his blood.

## *The Village of Vincennes*
## *May 1778*

Isabelle tapped her foot, up and down, up and down, on the church steps, waiting for Father Francis to join her. Whatever was the old priest up to now? She twirled a lock of long black hair around one finger, jerking on it in her agitation. It wasn't as if this was the first time. She should have known better than to wear rouge to Mass yesterday. But it was spring, and in the spring she always became so restless.

And that dress! He was sure to comment on the flame-red dress that she had designed herself, saving every cent for months to buy the fabric and then conniving old Josses, the local tanner, out of a nice bit of fur for the trim. She had looked like a gypsy, she knew. And she knew what arguments the good Father would use—so worn in the grooves of her mind that she feared she would go to her grave feeling guilty for the ostentatious bent to her nature. Why couldn't they understand that she had tried to tame the wildness beating inside her? That she had tried to conform to their notions of right and wrong but felt ready to burst within the steel cage of her own will. And her will was very strong. If she wanted to, she could do it. She could let herself drown in the nothingness and live out a life that conformed to the expectations of her friends and neighbors, but everything within her rebelled at the thought. Besides, when she tried, she was miserable and made everyone around her miserable. So here she was again, irritated but resolute that she would take her punishment, if a lecture from a gentle priest—and more her father than her real one—could be truly called a punishment. She would muster up some humility and listen, and then she would go on to the next infraction, and onward it went.

A clearing throat behind her caused her to spin around.

"Father Francis, how do you fare today?" She gave him her sunniest smile, not to manipulate but because it always made her heart glad to see him. His bald head was covered in brown age spots, and his skin wrinkled in soft folds when he spoke. But his clear eyes held a dear place for her that she always found solace in.

He smiled now, a bit distracted, and motioned her to sit on the wooden step next to him. He let out a sigh as his pale hazel eyes looked out at the village that was Vincennes. "My dear girl, I must say I have been better. The rheumatism, it does plague me today." His eyes found her face and he frowned slightly. "You have too pretty a face to paint, you know."

There it was. Straight to the point, and not without a certain amount of censure. Isabelle sighed. "Yes, my mother said as much, but . . . well . . . I thought Father might be back from Detroit. He has been gone longer than usual." She shook her head defiantly. "He would have liked the effect."

Father Francis nodded, laughing a little. "Yes, no doubt of that. You are peas in a pod, the two of you."

Isabelle's father was a French trader, a *voyageur*, with a charismatic flare that had blinded Isabelle's mother, Hope, to the darker side of him until well into their marriage. He traveled often and when at home could mostly be found singing songs and telling outrageous stories to the French inhabitants and a fair amount of Indians around a bottle of some sort of imported spirits. He was well liked—no, loved—by his neighbors and friends, and there wasn't much they wouldn't do for him or at his bequest. But when it came to settling into family life, there was a restless energy that kept him forever gone, both physically and emotionally.

---

A DEEP UNDERSTANDING came into Father Francis's eyes as he looked down at the pretty girl of nineteen beside him. He knew her motivations, but he hoped to temper them, to teach her the modest tact and taste that would compliment her so well one day.

"I have an idea . . . another way you might impress your father when he returns." He heard the slight hesitation in his voice belying his sure expression, not able to help his reservations. Was he loosening a fox in the henhouse to give her this job?

She looked curious but wary. "I'll not try teaching school again. You know those children won't listen to me, and it gave me headaches."

Father Francis laughed, slapping his thigh at the memory. Yes, that was certainly true. It had given him a few headaches too. "No, no child. This is quite different and much more to your liking, I think."

He saw the rush of anticipation in Isabelle's face and relished it. "Tell me," she demanded.

He hid his smile, fingering the folds of his cloak. "I have an errand that needs to be accomplished in the next few weeks. A letter arrived from Father Reginald in New Orleans. He writes that my books are on their way to Kaskaskia." The priest clasped his hands together in excitement, then looked down at her. "They are so close—at last."

"How wonderful, Father Francis! I know you had practically given up hope that they would ever come. But what can I do?"

He leaned toward her, as if to share a great secret. "I was going to go myself, but these legs do not travel as well as they used to. I want you to go, take Julian and a pack horse. The adventure should take a few weeks and provide you with a much needed outlet, yes?"

Isabelle's eyes grew round with disbelief. "Mother will never let me go, and she will certainly not allow Julian to go. You know how protective she is of him."

The priest winked at her. "I've already spoken with her. After a little persuasion, she agreed."

Isabelle stared at him, then gave out a whoop of joy and threw her arms around the old man's neck. Leaning back to look into his eyes, she said with conviction, "I won't let you down, Father. Truly. You shall have every last yellow-paged, dusty volume before summer is out. When do we leave?"

The old man paused, enjoying the radiance on her face. "Soon, child. Now tell me, how are your shooting lessons?" He had given up encouraging her in the gentler arts, as had her mother. Except for her clothing designs, Isabelle had little interest in feminine pursuits. She thrived in the woods. And seeing as how she always escaped into them at any opportunity, the family had finally decided it prudent to allow her to learn to shoot, not that they'd had much choice. She and her brother spent many an afternoon hunting the swampy woods near Vincennes, and Isabelle knew those trees like an infant knows her mother's face. Many times Father Francis had gone with them, yet he hid from Isabelle the jolt of admiring joy that flared in his heart when she displayed her skill. She was a wonder with a long rifle.

Once she was proficient with the rifle, she had begged a musket with bayonet from one of the British soldiers currently occupying Vincennes.

"The musket is heavier, but I am getting used to it, though I'll always prefer my long rifle." She gazed at the priest, warming to the subject. "The tomahawk, though, I should like to tackle that next."

He laughed and shook his head. "You are a blood-thirsty wench, my girl. What need have you of a tomahawk?"

Isabelle stood. Taking an imaginary weapon from her bright red sash, she leaned her weight into one leg and poised gracefully. Suddenly she spun around, "throwing" it with a dance-like movement. When she turned to face him, he inhaled sharply. There it was—that look in her eyes of fire and certainty and something else that always made the hairs on the back of his neck stand on end.

Father Francis looked heavenward.

*For what purpose did you fashion this one, my Lord?*

# 2

Hope Renoir stood on the front porch of what had been her home for the last ten years, an arm wrapped about one of the supports, looking toward the setting sun for any sign of her daughter. Whatever had she been thinking to give her permission for such an errand? Worry had not stopped its gnawing hold on her stomach since she'd given in to the Father's request. She bit one side of her lower lip, brow furrowed, reassuring herself that it wasn't too late to change her mind.

After clearing up the noon dishes, she had sent Isabelle to the priest, knowing how much joy it would give the old man to send her on the quest for his books himself. He had such a soft spot for anything of beauty, and Hope supposed she couldn't blame him. Against the rugged existence of this place, Isabelle stood out, always had, even as a little girl. It wasn't that she was beautiful, though Hope thought that was becoming more and more a fact. No, it was something within her—something that caught and held a person. Something that her father, Joseph Renoir, had given her.

*Isabelle, merciful God, that one needs a strong hand to curb her wildness!* Who would ever marry her? *Let him be strong, Lord, yet gentle enough to allow her spirit to flourish.*

The sounds of her daughter's singing caught her attention, and she smiled. Isabelle was just visible at the edge of the village, coming home and singing with the joy of her news. Her steps were light and graceful, her arms swinging with lively energy at her sides. When her face came into view, Hope felt the sting of tears in her eyes. There was a glow to her face that made it shine.

"I won't let myself be killed," Isabelle announced with delighted fierceness.

Hope let out startled laughter. "I should hope not! He told you then?"

"Yes, yes, and yes!" She grasped one of the columns of the porch and twirled around it. "Thank you for entrusting me to the task. It will be such an adventure!"

Hope looked into the excited green eyes of her daughter and took in a deep breath, knowing she had to let her do this. "You will watch over your brother? Without him realizing it?"

"Of course. You know that is second nature for me."

Hope grasped her daughter's waist and led her toward the front door. "I have hired a guide. An Indian named Quiet Fox."

"A guide? *Ma Mère*, we will not need a guide," Isabelle insisted, stopping her mother and glaring at her.

"Of course you will. I will not have you and Julian traveling that distance alone."

"Who is he? Where does he come from?" Isabelle's eyes blazed with the greens and golds of her ever-changing moods.

Hope lifted her hand, gesturing her impatience. "He comes highly recommended. Now come, let us plan what you will take with you. I want you well provisioned."

THEIR MISSION LOOKED impossible. Nine hundred miles of waterway behind them, George Rogers Clark and his motley group of woodsmen, farmers, a handful of criminals, and even a few of questionable sanity climbed up the bank of Corn Island at the Falls of the Ohio River. They would train here for a few weeks, then travel to their first target—Kaskaskia.

Clark looked out over his men and wiped the sweat off his brow with the sleeve of his buckskin jacket. They were industrious now, felling trees to build cabins as quickly as they could. Clark's planted rumor—that any man found unable to apply his muscle to the task of building camp would be left on this island with the women and children—seemed to be working. He would have to assign a small force, though, to stay and raise corn and provisions. The next few days should separate the chaff from the wheat, making his decision easy.

Clark took a long breath, watched two men nearly come to blows over who would wield an ax and smiled. Hard-bitten as they were, he was still thankful to have raised a fighting force of any kind. After months of passionate speech-making, he had managed to convince the politicians of Virginia that it was vital to the colonies' quest for freedom that they protect the territory west of the Allegheny Mountains. He had left Patrick Henry's office with a gleeful jump in his step, but after weeks of riding the countryside with Samuel Holt, he had not been so cheerful. Manpower in the east was so depleted due to Virginia's own need that Clark had been able to cobble together a militia of only about one hundred and fifty men between Williamsburg and Pittsburg, far short of the five hundred he had hoped for.

And the hundred and fifty he had . . . "God help me," he muttered. Stubborn, independent thinkers, and so cocksure of their prowess both on the battlefield and off . . . well, it was laughable. Where these men came up with such high-minded opinions of themselves he would like to know, given their motley appearance. Every one of them thought he could take on the British army by himself, and each seemed to envision himself raising the company flag over enemy territory with a gapped-toothed, bearded grin to the hearty hurrahs of the troops. Clark had overheard more than one daydream aloud of conquest against both the savage and the redcoats as they rowed the long miles west along the Ohio River. Still, they were able-bodied and, for one reason or another, eager for a fight. For that, Clark was intensely grateful.

His thoughts roamed back to men he admired, friends and compatriots from his exploring days. What he wouldn't give to have a hundred and fifty Simon Kentons or Samuel Holts. Simon and Samuel should be meeting up with him at Corn Island any day now. Both were excellent scouts and fierce in battle. And both were friends. They would provide a good example for the men and good companionship for him. And he was hungry for news on how the frontier forts were doing. Was there anything left to defend? It was all hanging on by such a delicate, blood-drenched thread . . . but a thread was enough. A thread was all one needed to weave the outskirts of a nation.

Clark took a deep breath and expelled it in a rush, feeling the fire in his belly flare to life. He didn't know why he cared so much, didn't understand where exactly this burning desire to see the birth of something new—a freedom that men had only dreamed about to this point in history—had come from. He didn't know why he was so certain of the importance of Illinois and Kentucky and the men and women who were trying to make a living there. He just knew. And for the last eighteen months he had done little beyond planning a campaign to take it all from the scalp-buying British and their dependent native tribes.

He thought of the British Lieutenant Governor, Henry "the Hairbuyer" Hamilton, sitting in his fort in Detroit, making deals with Chief Black Bird of the Chippewa and other tribes to trade settlers' scalps for rum and trinkets. His lips pressed together in a thin line. Hamilton was creating a dependent cycle that kept the Indians entrenched and entrapped. A new knife for a farming man's life, glass beads for his wife, and a bottle of spirits for their children—it was a bloody cycle that he, George Rogers Clark, planned to bring to an end.

Clark now stood on the brink of his campaign, just a few days' travel from his first target, and shuddered, his resolve strengthened, full of his own imaginings concerning a man named Henry Hamilton.

---

SAMUEL ABSORBED EVERY detail of his surroundings, judging and weighing the dense shadows of the forest while making his way down the weed-clogged hill to his canoe. His gaze swept the banks of the Ohio River, taking in the strong smells of rotting woodland and moss, the humming of insects and frogs, the buck a quarter mile to the east with ears perked at his passage, and most important, the dense overgrowth surrounding the water, making a fine lair for enemies lying in wait. Reports of recent heated attacks by the Shawnee up and down the Kentucky frontier made his body tense with constant watchfulness, his nerves as skittish as rattlesnakes.

Seeing nothing but the lush green of a June morning, mist still rising above the green-gray waters of the river, and hearing only the distant roar of the falls upstream, he pushed his canoe into the water, jumped aboard, and settled himself low in the bottom of the craft. He found the familiar, smooth handle of the paddle in his hands, grasped hold, and dipped it deep into the water, feeling the glide of the small vessel across the calm surface.

Sunlight glinted off the glassy top, a welcome glare only in the sense that it felt like a new adventure awaiting him. A soft breeze blew, caressing his hair that had become rather long and bleached further by the sun. Stirrings of excitement reached his belly . . . rising . . . rising into a deep breath of the morning air.

It didn't take long to paddle the distance. Corn Island and George Rogers Clark awaited him just ahead. Smoke was rising from the trees, the smells of breakfast cooking in the air. He'd been there before, a couple of years ago. Corn Island was just a small outcropping of land and yet could be, would be, the training camp for a small army with grand designs.

Sweat trickled down his back as he paddled faster, fishy-smelling water dripping onto his legs as he switched sides. He had not seen his friend in months, and he missed Clark's broad grin and wild dreams. Now they would train an army before attempting the impossible—taking a series of forts from the best military force in the world with just a handful of pitchfork-swinging farmers and sharp-shooting backwoodsmen.

Whatever the odds, there was an element to a fight that always felt the same to Samuel—the sure knowledge that all he imagined would come true. Clark had that too. And when men like that came together and agreed on it, something happened. He had seen it before and knew it was about to happen again. Samuel grinned. With no one to see him and no one to care, he grinned with presumptive victory.

A few more minutes of paddling and then he spotted Clark's tall redhead standing out in the field of greens and browns.

"Clark," he called out, waving from the canoe. He didn't wait for him to answer but banked, pulled the craft up onto the shore, and crossed dry land to greet his friend with a hearty clap on the shoulder that Clark turned into a bear hug.

"You've come, at last, my friend."

Samuel grinned. "How are you? Have you been here long? Did you raise enough men?"

Clark quickly walked with him some distance away and spoke in low tones. "I'm well and ready, Samuel. Glad you've made it. As to the men, not as many as I would like, that's the honest truth. But they are solid men—good enough, I think."

Samuel scanned the camp, noting the organization of the troops, seeing industrious men at their chores. "How many?"

"About a hundred and fifty. Hard-bitten, I'll admit," he chuckled, "but I have been training them." He smiled, his auburn hair shining bright in the sun and the wrinkles around his eyes attesting to many hours spent out in the elements. "You have checked on the forts? Kept the frontier free while I have been training these ragamuffins?"

Samuel laughed, then suddenly grew serious. "They're not doing well. All are weak, especially Fort Harrod and Fort Boonesborough. Lack of food and, worse, lack of hope plague them. The Shawnee are ever ready to torment them, keeping them penned in for weeks at a time, preventing them from spring planting. I don't know how they will survive the winter without a summer's worth of provisions. Most of the families haven't even been able to finish their cabins, and all of them are tired of living in the forts."

Clark's keen gaze said he understood. "That is why we cannot fail, Samuel. We win these British forts, we really take them, making the French and Indians our allies, it will change everything. Who's the worst off?"

"Fort Harrod is in real bad shape. The people are scared and were nearly starving to death six months ago, but I think they are recovering. Boonesborough, though, may be headed for a different kind of trouble. When I first got there, I was encouraged. More men, better provisioned, stronger fort." Samuel shook his head. "But now, I don't know, they fight and argue among themselves more than anything. Everyone wants to lead, and no one will follow. It doesn't look good for them."

"Is Daniel there?"

"Didn't you hear? Boone was captured by Blackfish himself. Adopted his white son, some say."

Clark pressed his lips together in grim contemplation. "If Boone was there, they would do all right. I feel bad for stealing you away."

Samuel huffed in frustration. "I couldn't lead those men. Do you ever want to wring their necks?"

"Sure, all the time. But keep in mind what's really going on down there."

"I wish I understood." Samuel shook his head. "Constant rumors and backbiting, jealousy, and competition for control. It undermines all they're doing and makes me spitting mad."

Samuel looked into Clark's eyes. "Don't they know? Don't they understand that the wilderness has no room for such things? That here they have to be more than they ever imagined they could be? But no, they crave the paltry power of a hollow square stockade. Kings over a barrier of upright posts. Fools, the lot of them!"

Samuel leaned over and spit the bad taste from his mouth, stalking a few steps toward the river and gazing out at its placid flow. "There was even talk that you had turned, abandoned them," he said quietly. "Sometimes I wonder if they're worth what you're planning to do for them."

Clark laid a hand on Samuel's shoulder. "Individually, they might not seem like it sometimes. But together, what they represent, *that* is worth it. They are Kentuckians and, God willing, soon to be Americans. Can you imagine it, Samuel? We are all going to be Americans someday."

The word sounded foreign to Samuel's ear. No more the title of Colonists; no more the swell of pride at being British subjects. They had turned rebel, independence screaming from their core. Samuel grinned in agreement and nodded. It was why they were there.

"Let's introduce you to the men." As they headed to the camp, a sudden commotion at the riverbank caused both men to turn sharply back to the river. A lone man, wearing worn Colonial army colors, was striding up the bank toward them. He bowed his head, then looked up at Clark. "Colonel Clark?" At Clark's nod, he presented a letter and stated in staccato, "News from Patrick Henry, sir."

Clark took the letter, pried up the wax seal, and quickly scanned the document. Samuel watched as a broad grin split his commander's face, then grinned himself as Clark gripped the letter, shaking his head in obvious wonderment. It must be good news.

"The French have agreed to support us, Samuel. They are joining our side in the war."

All the implications fell into place. They were about to take British forts inhabited by French citizens. Their job just got incredibly easier. Suddenly, it all seemed possible, what their commander in chief, George Washington, was doing back east and what they were about to attempt right here. The French were sending armies, trained armies, armies that had fought the British countless times over the centuries.

Armies that had won.

# 3

The darkening forest surrounded them, a living, breathing entity of creature noise and vegetation stirring, straining, it seemed, to snare them. Isabelle crouched down beside her brother, waiting and breathing in shallow gasps, buried almost in the dense underbrush. She watched the wind grow stronger with sudden gusts that sent showers of leaves twirling about them as it ripped summer's canopy from the branches overhead. Her gaze scanned the sky that was turning an eerie green. Tornado weather. Isabelle shivered, thinking of the one tornado she had ever seen. Of how her mother, her brother, and she had crouched down in the tiny, damp root cellar until it had passed.

There would be no hiding places here.

Their Indian guide stood a little away, motioning them to remain back and still. Isabelle watched Quiet Fox, watched the way he used every sense to assess their surroundings, to identify the cause of their uneasiness. They had all sensed it, that crawling sensation up the back of the spine that came with the sure feeling of being watched. And then they had heard a sound that sent them scurrying to cover—a swishing of the brush nearby, as if someone had passed near them. A sudden flight of birds winging away to safety had only furthered their disquiet. With sudden movements of his hands and an intense look in his eyes, Quiet Fox had backed them into this copse, then padded a few steps away and turned, his lean body taut with tension, his nostrils flared, eyes darting everywhere.

Isabelle shivered, thinking she was glad to have him with them now. She looked up to the wind whipping through the trees overhead, where the leaves made a sound like rushing water, and found her heart pounding like that of a trapped animal. Yet she could find no evidence of danger aside from the possibility of a coming thunderstorm. Leaning toward her brother, she whispered, "Do you hear anything?"

He shook his head, frowning at her for talking, which made her want to argue that she was quieter and more attuned to the forest than he, but she restrained herself with a silent huff. Everyone knew that Julian was the dreamer, the poet and musician of the family, and that Isabelle could outshoot, outrun, and outhunt him any day of the week. But now wasn't the time to remind him of that. Now, what she wanted more than anything was to prove to Quiet Fox, her mother, and the others shaking their heads in worry about this excursion, that she could successfully complete this mission and bring the old priest's books to him in perfect condition. Or at least in whatever condition she found them.

Thinking of her mother gave her a slight pang in the stomach region. Isabelle wanted nothing more than to please her mother, but she could never seem to understand what it was her mother wanted. She remembered the night before they had left. She had plopped herself on Hope's featherbed with a pleased smile and asked, "You will really let me go, *Ma Mère*?"

Hope smiled back at her, fondness and disquiet in her eyes. "Yes, I have despaired of making anything but a woodsman out of you, so why shouldn't you tromp through the forest for a few weeks and see if you get your fill." She shook her head. "For a time, at least."

"I shan't be a woodsman, mother," Isabelle corrected in annoyance. "I will be a *grande dame* in New Orleans and wear beautiful clothes and live in a fine house by the river with my handsome Spanish husband."

Her mother laughed and stroked Isabelle's cheek, a softness in her eyes that now brought a lump of emotion to Isabelle's throat. "And will the *grande dame* trade her long rifle for a *guitare* and pluck away at the strings, entertaining your many guests?"

Isabelle grinned. "*Non, Ma Mère.* This *grande dame* will fence with her guests in the morning, hunt with them in the afternoon, and throw the most outrageous balls in the evening."

"Oh, Isabelle, you are your father's daughter."

"And Julian? Is he more like you?"

"I think he has some of both sides in him. My mother is a wonderful artist, but your father is a poet." Hope shrugged. "I just hope he can keep up with you on the journey."

"I was surprised you would let him go."

The worried look increased in her mother's eyes, but she nodded firmly. "Yes, I surprised myself with that decision. But it will be good for him."

Her mother trusted Isabelle to watch over Julian, which was why she had been able to relinquish him to the supposed dangers of such a journey. But this—this was real danger. And Isabelle was suddenly wondering whether the task was beyond her capability.

Quiet Fox was motioning them forward. They moved toward him, Isabelle intent on being as silent as any Indian she had ever met.

*"Nous continueraient à se déplacer,"* he whispered when they arrived at his side. They would keep moving.

"Have you seen nothing? Heard nothing?" Isabelle insisted.

*"Non.* We walk, but go around." He motioned with his finger, around the clearing.

Isabelle nodded.

Quiet Fox moved out of the thicket, Isabelle and then Julian following close behind.

They were all tired, having hiked for two days in mud and muck with the heat and mosquitoes. They were tired enough that the marshy forest floor was looking as inviting as a featherbed, except now they were fueled with the inexplicable desire to put as much distance between them and this area as they could. They just didn't know why.

---

HEAT LIGHTNING PULSED bright behind dark, pregnant clouds while the air settled heavy and thick in Samuel's lungs. It was late afternoon and hot for a June day, leaving sweat marks on Samuel's white, linsey-woolsey shirt. He quickened his pace, making for a supposed farmhouse that one of the hunters they had captured last week told him about, just three miles from Kaskaskia, their first target.

A little later, hearing the distant rumble of thunder, his gaze swept the green tinged sky. No doubt about it—a thunderstorm was coming. He was walking in an open place, between one dark line of trees and another, scouting ahead of the army, per Clark's orders. He knew he should take cover, find shelter for the duration of the storm, but he wanted to reach the farmhouse on this side of the Kaskaskia River as soon as possible. It could be an invaluable place from which to launch their attack and set up Clark's field headquarters. And it was up to him to find it.

With renewed energy that came from long experience of trusting his instincts, he lengthened his stride and picked up his pace. The wind kicked up and began to howl as a sudden downpour beat on Samuel's head. He stopped, glad for the relief from the intense heat. Lifting his face, he let the rain run down his head and shoulders, sweet tasting and clean. He set his rifle aside and stretched out his arms, letting the shower soak through his shirt, sticking to his chest and back, taking with it some of the sweat and grime of the last few miles.

As suddenly as it had started, the rain changed form, from a pleasant shower to cold, tiny, needle-sharp shards. His hair blew into his face, and he turned to face the gusting wind. A jagged streak of lightning cut through the sky. Thunder rolled close by, chasing the lightning's tail and announcing its proximity.

"Aaaaggghhhh!"

Samuel turned as a scream pierced the wet air. He changed directions, running toward the sound, then sank into the cover of the brush, creeping slowly forward, feeling the deep rumble of thunder echo inside his chest. He inched his way deeper into the wood. There, in the distance, he could just make out the dark outline of a smoldering tree. The lightning *had* been close. The curling smoke above the sycamore told him it must have caught some of the branches on fire but was quickly extinguished by the rain. As he inched closer, he began to make out excited voices. He stopped and listened, sure they hadn't heard him.

Leaning to see past a thorny bush, he heard the voice of a woman and the lower tones of men—two of them, he thought—but he couldn't make out their faces in the dim light. Creeping closer, he strained to hear what they were saying.

"That was close! *Mon Dieu*, Julian, did you see it?" A woman asked.

"Yes, of course I saw it. But must you scream? You fear so little, why must you fear thunderstorms so?" The man sounded irritated, and Samuel found himself grinning.

Another flash of lightning lit up the area, giving Samuel enough light to see three forms under low, leafy branches. An Indian stood off at a distance watching the sky, while a woman stood at the side of the other man, their backs hugging a short, fat tree. Moving closer still, he waited for more clues as to their identity before revealing himself. They might never be so honest as when being unknowingly watched.

"I'm not afraid," she protested, "just startled is all. Why must you always exaggerate, Julian?"

The man called Julian huffed. "You were in mother's bed, hiding under the covers during the last storm. I saw you."

"Spying were you? I might have known. And I wasn't hiding, I was . . . comforting mother. She was alone again; the storms bother her."

"Yes, of course. It is mother who is afraid of thunder and lightning. Pray, forgive me, I should have known better."

Samuel nearly chuckled aloud. He had enough siblings of his own to recognize this squabble.

The Indian spoke. "Enough." He said it with quiet authority, and they both became silent until all Samuel could hear was the pelting of rain on leaves. The storm was diminishing, passing over like a great, dark bird.

A soft voice broke the silence. "I'm sorry, Julian. I *am* a little afraid of storms. I have never been cornered under a tree by lightning, at any rate." There was a smile in her voice that warmed it.

"Yes, well, neither of us has been nearly struck by lightning. The hairs on the back of my neck rose as well. We were lucky, eh, Quiet Fox?"

The Indian grunted.

Samuel squatted in the brush, letting the rain drip from the brim of his hat onto his back. He supposed he should make his presence known, but he didn't want to get shot at. The Indian was alert and ready with his long rifle. Maybe he could circle around and come up from behind them. The rain would make enough noise to cover him. It was a better plan than just stepping out of the trees into the middle of an armed party.

He stood slightly and backed his way into a clear section of the forest floor. It didn't take long to silently tread around the threesome. When he came to the tree where the two were standing, he found that Julian had left his post beside the girl and had joined the Indian looking at the clouds. The girl—woman, he corrected himself, now seeing her shapely silhouette clearly against the tree trunk—was alone and digging through her pack. He inched forward, hoping to glimpse her face in the light of the blue-green sky that was growing brighter as the storm moved to the east.

A sudden gust of wind moved the branches overhead, letting a shaft of light fall to the wet ground. The woman looked up, her face wet and beautiful in the strange light. Then, for no reason he could imagine, she suddenly turned and looked straight into his eyes.

She yelled again—not with fear this time but with challenge.

Suddenly, shockingly, he found himself looking down the barrel of her long rifle. *Where did that come from?*

"Come out, you skulking scourge," the hellion shouted at him.

Slowly, with his hands raised in surrender, Samuel stepped out of the brush to find two more barrels pointing at him from either side. If one of them fired, they would shoot his head clean off.

Samuel checked his irritation and controlled his facial expression. Carefully calm, he said, "I was walking by . . ." He looked into Isabelle's eyes, hardly believing this fierce creature with her wild, dark hair, long and swirling provocatively around her skirts, was the one he had just heard conversing with her brother. "I heard your cry—the lightning, I supposed—and came to investigate."

Isabelle eyed him like he had never been looked at by a woman before. He found himself both repelled and fascinated. A sudden image of her fierce and in his bed flashed through his mind, leaving him feeling as if a fog had invaded his brain, placing him under some spell. Worse still, he didn't know what to do next. Frustrated, he shook his head to clear it. Such things never happened to him.

"Come closer."

Was her voice huskier? Was she weaving a magic he was hopeless to resist? It made him angry and determined—to do *what,* he didn't know—but he found himself obeying, walking slowly up to her.

---

ISABELLE TOOK A deep breath as the man walked toward her. An odd sense of familiarity slammed through her as he moved out of the shadows. It was as though he was walking out of the pages of history. Yes, that was it, he was like a knight of old, or what she had always imagined one would be, except he was clothed in frontiersman's garb. A poem she had memorized flashed through her mind as she stared at him, unable to look away. She recalled the lines, speaking them just under her breath in smiling admiration.

*He sees his future*
*stretched before him,*
*cold as steel.*
*Sleepless, lonely*
*await the kill.*
*Going for to find the damsel,*
*dragon-slayer, crusade-warrior.*
*No choice of mine,*
*knight in shining armor*
*weighted heavy, silver-shine.*
*Tall and broad, he blocks the sun,*
*man of honor,*
*chivalrous Knight.*
*Great men tremble in his glory,*
*pay him homage, dread his plight.*
*Courtly manners, noble talk.*
*Not a prancing peacock, he.*
*His word of honor, binding truth*
*the truth of chivalry.*

"Are you mumbling, miss?"

Surfacing back to the real world, where this man could be a threat, Isabelle scowled at him. "Where are you heading?" she demanded instead of answering, rifle trained on his heart.

Samuel held out his hands. "I'd be happy to oblige your questions, miss, but could we dispense with the weaponry? I'm not generally given to harming women." He looked questioningly at the Indian, who nodded his agreement. Julian and Quiet Fox lowered their weapons but kept them easy and ready at their sides.

Isabelle kept the weapon trained at him in silent challenge. For a long, quiet moment, they just stared at one another. Finally she shrugged one shoulder and lowered her weapon. Then she laughed. "But you'd harm a man, I dare say." She stared at him, her chin poking out defiantly as she brazenly teased in a low voice, "You have harmed more than few men, I would guess."

He only stared back. This man would not be the easy conquest of a few batted eyelashes. Here was someone with more substance. How much more was still to be discovered, causing a thrill to rise inside of Isabelle at the thought of it.

He took a step closer to her. It was as if they were alone and neither of them could tear their eyes off the other long enough to see the reactions of those with them.

In a deep voice he responded to her needling. "Stories that would curl your toes, miss. Maybe you will be able to coax them from me . . . someday."

A slow smile spread across her face and coursed all the way through her body. "Perhaps our acquaintance will lend itself to such discourse, sir. Perhaps not."

Before he had time to respond, Julian interrupted their banter. "Isabelle, you have only just met the man." Stretching out his hand toward Samuel, he said, "Julian Renoir. We travel west from Vincennes to Kaskaskia on a mission of old books. Please excuse my sister's brazen manners. She is spoiled, I'm afraid. And you, sir?"

"Samuel Holt. Traveling to Kaskaskia also."

He shook hands with her brother, who was looking at the big man with the wide-eyed beginnings of hero worship. When Mr. Holt turned toward Quiet Fox, he paused. Isabelle looked back and forth between them. Their guide had gone very still and did not look Mr. Holt in the eyes. Did they know each other? Samuel seemed to recover first and turned toward her expectantly, as if waiting for her to explain her mystery further.

Isabelle had no such intentions. Let him wonder . . . and wait. But she relented enough to give up her name. Reaching for his hand as her brother had, she said, "Isabelle Renoir."

She found herself holding her breath as he reached out toward her. His handshake was firm, his grasp wrapping warmly around hers, making her feel small and trapped. She let go, wanting to break the contact, and stepped back from him. "If you are heading to Kaskaskia, then we should travel together," she said despite her misgivings.

Samuel seemed to consider her words, then replied in a voice so deep she felt it more than heard it. "Yes." He nodded. "I think perhaps we should."

# 4

In the aftermath of the storm, the air was mercifully cooler, the light kind and soft with the promise of summer's twilight. The four fell into line—Samuel leading, the Renoirs in the middle, and Quiet Fox, a brooding frown in his eyes and a tight grip on his rifle, taking up the rear. Julian trailed behind Samuel's long-legged stride, matching it the best he could with shorter legs and untried lungs, the combination of which quickly put an end to the questions he had attempted to ask Samuel when they started out. It was soon clear to all of them that Samuel moved faster and more efficiently than even Quiet Fox, who seemed to be stumbling along behind them.

Isabelle studied Samuel Holt with growing interest. He was dressed in the lean manner of the frontiersman, a loose-sleeved, linsey-woolsey shirt hanging with effortless grace from his broad shoulders. A slim cord of leather around his neck disappeared beneath the open collar of his shirt, hiding whatever hung on the end. Honey-colored buckskin leggings clung to his thighs and blended into buckskin boots, like long moccasins that graced his feet and calves. Weapons and ammunition hung everywhere on his person. A long, wicked-looking knife was tied down to his right thigh; another smaller one on his right calf was attached by a scarlet ribbon. A tomahawk was slung from his belt, which also held a water cask. To complete the picture was the Kentucky long rifle grasped like an extension of his right hand and appearing to weigh no more than the powder horn slung across his chest which hung to one side just above the shot pouch.

She couldn't pull her gaze from the way his body moved over the land, supple muscle climbing, striding, vigilant and protecting, pushing through the dense marshland in front of them, showing the way. But there was more to this man—some indescribable quality of strength that, for the first time Isabelle could ever remember, made her see him as more than a match for her own abilities. She was shocked by the thought, but instead of resenting him for it, instead of wanting to prove herself against him like any other man of strength she had met in the past, she wanted to trust in it, simply to rest in the knowledge that he went before. She found it . . . oddly comforting.

She smiled a little, her breath measured to match her footsteps, pacing her strength for this long endurance race, wanting to impress Mr. Holt. But she also knew that the moment she said she needed a rest, he would stop.

As they walked, every so often Samuel turned his head as if to judge how his traveling companions were keeping up, and at times his gaze would meet hers. She could sense in his eyes the same feelings she was experiencing, the interest and admiration. But something else lay deeper in his gaze—a disquiet, an old wound. Then he would turn from her and face the wilderness again and a danger known.

Just as darkness was settling over them they stopped. With trembling in her legs and a great sigh of relief, she sank down against the smooth, white bark of a sycamore tree. Samuel had pushed them until they found this small circular clearing and a wide stream to refresh them a short distance away.

Isabelle closed her eyes, breathed deeply of the moss-moist air, and allowed her thoughts to wander randomly over the events of the day. She drifted off, the feel of fringed buckskin almost real against her hand. The next thing she knew, Julian was waving a piece of jerked beef beneath her nose and saying in a singsong voice, "Wake up, sleeping beauty. 'Tis time to cook for us."

Isabelle slapped away his hand and the awful smelling meat, but a smile hovered around the corners of her lips. "In truth you are a better cook than I am, and you know it, Julian. Let me rest." But she opened her eyes a crack and studied the activities of the others. Samuel was building what looked to be a lean-to out of thin branches, some from the ground, some recently cut from surrounding birches and hickory trees, the leaf-filled limbs of which would create a break against the night air. Quiet Fox had still not returned from the stream, but Isabelle was used to his sudden disappearances and thought little of it. Someone had set up a trivet over a small cooking fire, and suddenly eager for some honey-sweetened tea and a hunk of crusty bread, Isabelle rose and dusted off her skirts.

Soon the three of them sat around the fire, eating the mostly cold supper, passing around a loaf of bread, some jerked meat, and chewing contentedly. Isabelle's tea was finally ready, and as they only had two cups between them, she offered hers to Samuel.

Samuel smiled up at her as she held out the tin cup. "There's plenty of fresh water at the stream. You keep it." He patted his water canteen. "I need to fill up anyway."

Isabelle shook her head, insisting. "I'm good at tea."

Samuel considered her offer for a long moment, then nodded, a smile in his eyes, taking it from her hand and draining it in one long gulp. He wiped his mouth with the back of his hand, then grinned at her, handing the cup back. "It's good. Thank you."

Isabelle frowned, a line pressing between her brows. "You couldn't possibly taste it like that." She took the cup out of his hand and walked away, hearing Samuel's small chuckle dog her heels. She refilled the cup from the small pot by the fire then walked back to him, sinking down in front of the frontiersman, the edges of her skirt covering his feet.

"Like this," she promised with a sly smile. She put the cup to her mouth and inhaled the steam. Looking over the metal rim, she tilted the cup slowly back, tasting the sweet honey, the rich, black tea her father had brought back from New Orleans just for her. She tilted her head back a little more with the next sip, showing him the long column of her throat. Then she lowered the cup and gave him a slow smile.

"You see?" She feigned sudden innocence as she held the cup out to him. Who had taught her this? She didn't know.

Samuel looked to be torn between trying not to laugh and remembering to breathe. He nodded at her though, took the cup in his hand, sniffed at the steam, and then took a giant gulp, nodding. "You're right, miss. That was much better."

She made an irritated noise and pressed her lips together, considering him with her head tilted a little to one side.

Samuel grinned suddenly and grasped her hand. "I'd rather watch you drink it." He said it in that voice—that low, silky voice that made her knees go to water. She found herself blushing, something she couldn't remember ever doing in her life.

Isabelle pulled her hand from his grasp, turning brisk. "Well, as you're such a slow pupil, I'm afraid the lesson was lost on you. You are a hopeless . . . male." She stood, wishing to retreat as quickly as possible.

Samuel nodded and grinned, biting off a hunk of the dried

beef she had given him. "I surely must be, miss, as you are the best teacher I have ever seen."

He was making fun of her! She turned her back on him and stalked over to her forgotten plate. Every time she glanced in his direction, he was staring at her and smiling.

"It is good. Did you dry it?" Samuel shouted over to her, holding up the beef.

A memory of her mother and Julian working in the smokehouse flashed through her mind. She had been target-shooting at the time. "I believe Julian helped dry that batch. I only brought home the buck."

Humor lit his eyes. "A worthy contribution."

She smiled back, softening a little. Not many of her acquaintances would praise her for that particular skill.

She covertly watched him finish his meal, watched him take long pulls on his water cask and wipe his mouth with the back of his sleeve, watched him brush away imaginary crumbs, then stand and stretch. He helped clean the dishes and pack them away, then directed Julian as to the finishing touches on the lean-to.

It was full dark when she decided she would speak to him again. "I am going to the stream. I could refill your water."

Samuel nodded while unwinding the leather strap from his belt. "Have a care. The woods are full of the spying ears, British and Indians alike."

She nodded, taking the strap tightly in hand with the two she already carried for Julian and herself. She picked up her long rifle and looked at him over her shoulder. "I can take care of myself."

---

AMID THE SURROUNDING stillness of night, the water tripped lightly over the river rock, each trickle melodious and calming.

Isabelle crossed, barefoot, to the grassy bank, then the water's edge. A nearly full moon reflected yellow on the rippling surface.

Squatting down, she submerged Samuel's cask, allowing it to bubble and fill, closing her eyes, enjoying the cool night air and the musical water. A song hummed inside her, growing, then straining to get out. Giving into it, she began to hum softly as she filled the other two casks.

It happened like this sometimes, rare moments that she treasured. She rose, the canteens forgotten on the bank, beauty bursting inside her. Swaying to the sounds of the water and the sounds within her head, she smiled and allowed the feeling to encompass her. The music soon took over, making her forget where she was and what she was doing. Eyes closed, head back, her hair heavy on her back, she drank in the wind song, the tree song, the water song, the song of living things, harmonizing with the rich tones coming from her throat. Her arms twined over her head, her hips swaying gently. Her feet moved with the natural, sweeping grace of a world-class ballerina.

Words came, unbidden. Words of praise. Words of wonder for the beauty of the night and the joy she felt within. "*O Holy One*," she sang, her feet flying, then her back bending until she faced the sky, her arms upraised, her hair touching the ground behind her. It was almost as if she could see the angels as they looked down from their place in the heavens. She could just imagine their voices joining in, giving her words and then taking them, taking her earthly attempts and combining it with their higher heavenly sounds to make beautiful incense that she imagined would rise up into the very throne room of God. Never did she feel so fully alive and complete.

It swept her away into another world, a world that she touched only on rare occasions such as this.

So she danced. In the light of the moonlight, in the reflection of the water and the moon. In the thick, heavy air of God's glory.

---

SAMUEL WAS ARRANGING his bedding crossways at the entrance to the lean-to where Isabelle and Julian would sleep when a sudden foreboding crept into his consciousness. He looked up from his squatted position into the trees, squinting his eyes, searching everywhere for the source of his uneasiness. He didn't know how or why he sensed these things, but he trusted his instincts. Standing, he noted Julian already asleep inside his bedroll to one side of the lean-to. The boy was worn through. Quiet Fox had wandered off without a word to anyone and still had not returned. Isabelle had not come back from the stream. He had assumed she had personal needs to attend to aside from filling up the canteens, but she had been gone much longer than that should take.

While he was taking in the surroundings, his hands were feeling for his weapons, finding his tomahawk on his belt, his knife sheathed against his thigh. Picking up the long rifle, he headed into the woods toward the sounds of the water.

He heard her before he saw her.

Was that singing? Slowing, he approached the bank, alert for danger but finding nothing. As he broke free of the woods, he saw her. There, in the pale glow of the moon, she twirled and sang, her arms upraised, her feet flying. There were wet tracks of tears on her cheeks, reflecting silvery in the moonlight. She was so engrossed, so . . . free. Samuel had never seen anything like it. What kind of woman was this? Nothing like Sara, that was for sure.

A crashing noise broke from the trees to Samuel's right. His senses, so caught up in Isabelle, took a moment to comprehend what was happening. A wolf, snarling and grunting, had leaped from its hiding place and was bearing down with full force on the dancing woman. She stopped suddenly, facing the animal, comprehension dawning on her face in stages, turning from rapture to alarm.

Without thought Samuel raised his rifle, aimed, and shot. A yelping sound tore from the wolf's throat, but it kept moving toward her.

Unable to reload in time, Samuel dropped the weapon and sprinted toward the now-enraged animal. He grasped the hilt of his knife as he ran, knowing he would not reach her in time. Knowing that the wolf had every intention of killing her.

He watched, as in a daze or a dream, as Isabelle crouched down, wondering why she didn't run. His throat wanted to yell, "Run!" but no sound would come. As in a nightmare, he watched as the bloody animal leaped several feet through the air to land on top of the woman. He heard a great cry tear from her throat.

As he came upon them, Samuel plunged his knife into the side of the animal's belly but quickly realized that the wolf was already a limp pile of dead carcass. Isabelle rose from beneath it, like an Amazon, a Joan of Arc, a legend of old. She kicked the carcass off her, yelling and bloody. As she heaved the animal over, Samuel saw to his amazement another knife sticking out from the wolf's chest. She had stabbed it.

She stood over the animal, shaking and wild-eyed, her breathing fast and hard. "Is it—is it dead?"

Samuel went to her and grasped both her arms, wanting Isabelle to focus on his face so that he could calm her, all the while checking for injuries. It was hard to tell with the wolf's blood smeared all over her dress and face.

"Yes, it's dead. Are you hurt?"

Isabelle stared at him. He could see reality return, taking the place of the shock as she stared into his eyes. Suddenly, she was laughing. Small and low, then building into a deep laugh. It was a victor's laugh. With a whoop she threw herself into his arms and against his chest. "I killed it! I did. I did it!"

She turned her face up to his, then grew suddenly serious. "We are meant for each other, you know."

Samuel gazed into her blood-smeared face and knew fear like he'd never known. His heart had yet to stop the wild pounding that had begun when he first saw the wolf. Now, as he looked down into her fierce countenance, he wondered if she wasn't a little mad.

Before he had time to respond, she had backed out of his arms. "He came out of nowhere. Did you see any others?"

Samuel looked down at the wolf. It was large and so gray that it appeared black against the dark ground. Its eyes were open and glassy. Pulling himself from the haze this woman held him in, he looked to the dark tree line where the wolf had entered the clearing. A frown creased his brow. Where *had* the wolf come from? It was strange to see one alone and attacking boldly like that. It didn't look particularly hungry either; it was large and well fed. A strange feeling assailed him, the same feeling that had made him come looking for Isabelle in the first place. Something was happening here, something he couldn't quite place, but it was sinister, and for some reason he couldn't explain, he was certain that whatever it was, it wanted to destroy this woman in front of him.

He said, "It *is* strange, his being alone." He walked back to where he had thrown his long rifle down, reloaded it as he talked. "I should check for others. I'll walk you back to the camp first. I don't want you alone at night anymore."

Glancing up, he saw a slow smile spread across her face, her eyes slanting provocatively at him. "Are you my protector now?"

How could she be flirtatious after such an ordeal? It was all he could do not to shake some sense into her. He contented himself with, "As far as you'll let me. But it seems obvious you know what to do when you have to." He finished reloading, then looked up from his rifle, their gazes locking in the silent moonlight. "You knew not to run, to crouch down. You knew just where to stab it, didn't you?"

"Yes. I knew. The position making me the most vulnerable was the only position strong enough to kill it. I didn't think all of that through, mind you." She smiled at him. "But something . . . something inside me knew." She laughed. "I must wash, though. If Julian sees me like this, he'll try to pack me off back home to mother, and that I will not allow."

Samuel nodded his understanding. "Jump in the stream then." He grinned his own wicked grin at her. "We'll say you tripped and fell in while dancing."

Isabelle gasped. "How long were you standing there watching me?"

"Oh, long enough, I think. I don't suppose you can complain. . . . I did slow him down a bit." He looked pointedly at the dead wolf.

Isabelle gestured toward her clothing. "If you were going to go and spy on me, you could have at least killed the thing and saved me the trouble of a ruined dress."

Samuel took a step closer, then another and another. Reaching out, he grasped the side of her face, wiping a smear of the wolf's blood from her cheek with his thumb. His voice lowered. "Next time, I will not fail your dress."

Isabelle tilted her head into his hand. "Why do I feel I know you?" It was a breathy thought, as if to herself. "As if I have found the place where I can finally breathe?"

Samuel inhaled as he heard his own feelings being put into words, feelings that were unheard and unsought and more frightening than any wolf or enemy or an entire army even.

Had he ever felt this connected to Sara?

"I shouldn't want to put you to sleep." He took refuge in teasing, trying to make light of the intensity between them.

Her lips curved into a provocative smile. "What should you want with me then, sir?"

He groaned. Did she know what she did to him? Did she really want the truth? "I should want to awaken something in you," he heard himself say.

Isabelle took a step toward him.

His heart began a steady drumming that he thought she must be able to hear. He wanted to kiss her. But he just stared at her, his gaze roving over each delicate feature, a face a moment ago that was so fierce in victory but was now pliant and open to him.

His thumb stroked her jaw, and then he realized what he was doing, reminding himself why anything with this temptress would prove as wrong as his first marriage, and he let his arm drop back to his side.

She stepped closer, not giving up, reaching for him, sliding her hands inside his jacket, touching his ribs. She traced a lower rib saying on a breath, "Here is where I was taken."

He drew in a sharp breath, felt the panic like a lance in that spot.

Backing away, his hands outstretched as if to ward her off. He turned from her passionate stare and did something he'd only done once before in his life.

He ran away.

# 5

Hope picked up a candle from the bedside table and quietly lit it, walking from the bedroom to the fireplace in her kitchen. She stretched as she walked, the ache in her low back more profound than usual.

She had been awakened by a nightmare. An apparition, ferocious and huge, had attacked her daughter, mauling her while several people stood by and watched. She had stood in that group, frozen and unable to help, her throat working with the effort to shout. Isabelle, her daughter, had been torn to pieces.

Still overwhelmed by the intensity of the dream, Hope crept out of the bedroom where Joseph quietly snored, home from his latest excursion, and went to calm herself with a cup of tea. While the tea steeped, the feeling that her children were in danger would not leave her. So she settled in to pray.

This had happened to her before. And she recognized it as a battle, something she had to pray through until the pressure lifted from her. As she walked around the living area, working the aches from her body, she knew that this particular battle had not yet been won. "What now, Lord?"

A memory assailed her. While living in the east, Hope had become friends with a Christian woman who could only be described as on fire with the zeal of God. The woman, Lydia, had spent much time with Hope, teaching her to understand and apply the Holy Scriptures to her life. And slowly her life had begun to change. She began to accept and love Joseph as he was. As she learned to trust God to meet all of her needs, she was able to allow Joseph and the others around her freedom to be who they were. She let go of her attempts to change Joseph so that she might feel stable and instead found stability in an intimate relationship with her Savior.

Hope and Lydia had spent many hours together in prayer, and as God chose to answer their petitions, they saw strange things, wonderful things, and sometimes frightening, otherworldly things.

Occasionally Hope was awakened at night and could feel the presence of God in the room with her. She would get up and begin to pray, often for an hour or more. Then, just as suddenly as it had begun, the burden would be lifted, and as tired as any soldier, Hope would climb back into her warm bed to sleep.

It had been a long time since this had happened, and as she thought about it, Hope realized that she still missed Lydia. In truth, it was harder to walk the road of the prayer warrior alone. Suddenly she understood that deep within she was still upset about being separated from her friend. Her whole life had been about moving away from people she cared about—about following Joseph's dreams instead of her own heart. A few still moments passed as she reflected on this revelation. Yes. In her heart there was still hardness, some bitterness, some loneliness she had not yet dealt with.

Then another revelation, and Hope took a sudden breath: She had allowed this resentment toward God to rob her of her prayer life. To rob her of what was quite possibly her reason for being on this earth. She felt her eyes well with tears. She might not be a great explorer like her husband, regaling an audience with stories of her conquests or holding people spellbound with her personal charisma. No, she was a warrior of prayer. A warrior in a realm more real than this flesh would prove to be, of that she was certain. And as God knew, she could carry this mission to anywhere on the earth, even in the shadow of her rainbow-seeking husband. No, *especially* in his shadow.

Even now she lived in a time and place that was changing, with the war for independence in the east. True, she lived in a frontier village that seemed so small and insignificant by comparison. Yet her village and others like it had been fought over by the French, the Indians, and the British. That spoke of great significance. And yet she had prayed so little in recent years.

She was sickened and angry that she had allowed her enemy to blind her with self-pity, not trusting that God, who saw and knew all, had a greater plan for her than her limited vision could recognize.

"Dear God—" She had let so many years be taken! Hope sank to her knees, tears running down her cheeks. "I am sorry, Lord. Your will—not mine," she cried out. "I am so sorry."

She felt better, even with such simple words, knowing that God had revealed to her the hidden depths of her heart. With renewed, humble resolve, she began to pray for her children and whatever else the Lord might trust her with.

---

QUIET FOX HAD disappeared.

Isabelle, Julian, and Samuel searched for the guide around the perimeter of the campsite, carefully moving brush and bush so as not to disturb any footprints, but they found nothing beyond their own prints, save the wolf's prints by the stream. Quiet Fox, or someone, had been careful to cover his tracks. Finally they decided they must go on without him.

Samuel kept them moving at a pace that made Isabelle's legs quiver in exhaustion, made sweat soak through the bodice of her dress and her tongue stick to the roof of her mouth.

Samuel didn't talk much, seemingly determined to keep some distance between them after the intense encounter of the night before. But Isabelle had caught him looking at her in a way that said he wasn't as disinterested as he wanted to appear. Why was he working so hard to ignore her? Had she frightened him off? It was all she could think about as they marched.

On the fourth day the trees gave way to the high grasses of blue-green prairies. Waving and rippling under the hot sun, buzzing with insects, tickling and itching, in places the grass reached to Isabelle's chin. She walked carefully at first, not knowing what might be slithering in the lush growth under her moccasined feet, but soon enough she didn't have the strength left to care. The wood had made walking difficult at times, but at least it had been shaded. Now the hazy heat of the sun beat down on their reddened faces, making them damp with sweat and causing the men to pull their hats low over their foreheads.

To make matters worse, the canteens were running low on water. Isabelle's hand shook with trepidation as the last warm, wet swallow disappeared down her scratchy throat. Lengthening her stride to catch up with Samuel, she grasped his arm.

He stopped, took off his hat, and wiped his brow with the sleeve of the arm Isabelle wasn't hanging onto. He then replaced the hat, not looking as hot or tired as she and her brother certainly did.

"Water," she croaked. "We need to find water."

Samuel looked into the distance ahead of them and squinted. He pulled his canteen out of its strap holder at his waist and handed it over as he talked. "Take mine. We might not reach another water source until the Kaskaskia River. It's why I am pushing us so hard. If we hurry, we should reach it by nightfall."

Isabelle took the offered canteen, looked back to judge how far Julian was behind them, then pulled the cork out. Looking into Samuel's eyes, she put her mouth on the lip of the canteen and tilted it back, taking a long swallow.

"Thank you," she said, holding out the water.

He took a quick drink, Isabelle unabashedly watching him, noticing the beginnings of a beard that had grown in the time since she'd met him. His eyes met hers with a tentative, afraid-of-what-she-might-do-next look in them. Taking pity on him, she only smiled and offered the cork.

He reached for it, his fingers touching hers for a moment. "Well, we should keep moving if you can. River should be a few hours ahead of us."

Suddenly there was a shout from Julian. He was gazing upward, his finger pointing to the sky.

Samuel and Isabelle looked up and went still. The sun was darkening at an alarming rate.

"What is it?" Isabelle breathed.

Samuel stood, braced. She could hear his quickening breath, knew that he was trying to assimilate the strange phenomenon above them.

Julian ran up to them, quoting Scripture. "'The sun will be turned to darkness and the moon to blood before the coming of the great and glorious day of the Lord.'"

Isabelle felt her heart pound at the words. Was that it? Was the world ending?

Suddenly Samuel pulled her toward him and pressed her head into his shoulder. His voice was low and intense as he commanded Julian, "Don't look at it. Look away."

Isabelle felt the muscles of Samuel's shoulder against her forehead, his hand against the back of her head. She breathed hard, wanting to look up but knowing that she could not move against the steady pressure of his hand.

"What is it?" she whispered.

"I don't know." His voice was against her ear. "But I know we shouldn't watch it."

"Is it evil?"

She could feel his whole body tense as he searched out the question. "Not evil," he said finally. "Just something we shouldn't look at."

"I don't understand," she wailed. "Let me go."

"Trust me."

He pulled her closer in an embrace that an hour ago she would have fought an army for, but now she felt trapped and small and weak.

"For goodness' sake. For once in your life, Isabelle, trust someone."

A few hours later they had exhausted every conceivable explanation of what had made the sun go dark and fell into silent marching. Now, with no river in sight, Isabelle began to feel a little desperate. The sun beat on the exposed back of her neck now, making it burn and sting when she turned her head. Her raging thirst was playing tricks on her, turning her thoughts to areas of her mind that she hadn't known existed until now—places of defeat, of hopelessness, of dark dread. Her legs continued to move of their own accord, pushing her forward in a sluggish line that wavered and weaved.

Julian moved alongside her and put his arm around her,

supporting some of her weight. "Are you okay, *ma soeur?*" he asked, using a name he hadn't called her since he was a boy.

Isabelle leaned into his shoulder, trying to put a smile into her voice. "Some water would be nice."

"Don't think about it so much."

"I cannot seem to think of anything else. I wonder if Samuel is right, that we'll reach the river by nightfall."

"Even if we don't, we will feel better after the sun goes down. We should walk faster if you can though. Samuel is getting farther and farther ahead of us."

This was different, Julian being the stronger of them. She touched his shoulder. "You are growing up, *mon frère.*"

He shook his head and looked down, embarrassed but with pleasure flooding his face.

She caught his dark blue eyes and smiled with compressed lips. "I am glad you are my brother."

She had never said that before, and he looked quickly away. "As if you had a choice."

"Well, there is that," she said, jabbing him in the shoulder and lightening the mood. Then she tilted her head and smiled at him. "It is true though. Don't forget it."

Julian just shook his head.

Turning brisk, Isabelle said loud enough for Samuel to hear, "I think we are lost." Then quieter, more serious. "What if he has given us false promises of his scouting and tracking abilities? We don't really know him."

"I thought you liked him," Julian teased.

"I did. Until he made fun of me. And then manhandled me."

"He did not."

"So quick to defend a stranger." She looked ahead to where Samuel walked several yards in front of them. "We don't really know anything about him," Isabelle stubbornly insisted as if to herself.

"We will be careful. But I think," Julian said in a faraway voice, "Samuel could be our friend. Don't lose faith in our scout just yet."

Isabelle lengthened her stride and nodded. "I hope you are right."

---

ON THE FIFTH day they traveled only a little way before seeing a dark smudge against the horizon. It felt like they had been adrift on a sea of grass for days and then, suddenly, up ahead was land. Salvation had come in the form of a dark tree line in the distance and the promise of the Kaskaskia River. Samuel didn't tell them how relieved he was to see it, how he had thought they might be lost and wandering straight into hostile territory. Instead, he spurred them on with renewed promises of water.

They walked faster now, saying little, conserving all their energy for the task of keeping one foot moving in front of the other in the tall grass. Samuel offered Isabelle his arm to lean on, but she spurned it saying, "I'm fine," and then proved it by walking ahead of all of them for the next fifteen minutes.

By noon they reached the farmhouse Samuel was sent on this mission to find, causing him internally to change hats from guide to spy, covertly studying the farmhouse as they approached it, as well as the surrounding land, its proximity to the river, and the availability of any boats and outlying buildings. It was just as the hunters had described.

It was perfect.

Isabelle ran toward the door, a raspy cry of relief escaping from her parched throat. Samuel started to stop her, then thought about it and regrouped. If the Renoirs cooperated, and he thought they would, this might prove a valuable front to explain his presence in the area. He watched as she banged on the door, saw a young woman open it, listening and nodding. He and Julian were now close enough to hear Isabelle say that they were traveling to Kaskaskia and had run out of water.

By the time Samuel and Julian got to the plank door, a man had joined the woman. He was quite a bit older than his wife but had bright, intelligent eyes and, after a thorough perusal of the three of them, held out his hand to Samuel.

"Henry Coffman."

Samuel grinned with friendly intent and nodded to Isabelle. "I hope my wife didn't startle you, sir. She's been mighty thirsty these last two days, and I didn't have the heart to stop her headlong rush to your door."

The couple smiled at the wide-eyed Isabelle as she stood by a barrel of water, drinking from a huge wooden ladle. Samuel gave her a look that said to go along with the story. She tilted her head at him and sauntered over, extending her hand to their hosts and passing the ladle to Julian.

"Do forgive me." She smiled and batted her eyelashes at Samuel, "My *husband* swore he knew the way." She pressed her lips together in mock innocence. "He always did have a tendency to get us lost. Why one time . . ."

Samuel stopped her, groaning internally, knowing that he had underestimated her yet again and that she was determined to make his life difficult at best. "This is Isabelle—"

"What is our last name, dear? I've forgotten." She dimpled at him, tilting her head again as Samuel silently cursed at himself.

"Holt." He smiled at the bewildered-looking hosts. "A sudden wedding. Recently."

Julian made a choking sound that Samuel tried to cover by pulling Julian to the forefront. "This is Julian Renoir."

"His brother-in-law," Isabelle said happily. "They knew each other first. Samuel wanted shooting lessons—can't hit the side of a barn with that fancy rifle of his to save his life, and wouldn't you know it, my brother is a sharpshooter." She shrugged. "I took one look at him, so big and strong and manly," she clung to his arm and looked up into his face with adoring eyes, "and I was smitten."

The young woman giggled. "Well, ain't that a story. Please come in and rest yourselves. I'm Missy and this," she went to a cradle and lifted out a tiny baby, "this is Benjamin. He's three weeks old today. Say howdy, Benjamin."

Isabelle smiled at the baby. "So precious. Why I was just telling Samuel the other day that I want a baby so bad I can hardly stand it."

Samuel nearly choked on the water he was drinking and thrust the ladle into Isabelle's chest. "Could you get me some more water, wife?"

"Why certainly, husband. You know I live and breathe to serve you." Another lingering, adoring smile, and she turned to do his bidding.

Maybe this wouldn't be so bad after all.

They all sat around the table, Missy heating up a stew they'd had for dinner, supplying plenty of water and making tea for them. Isabelle was holding the baby, looking a little uncomfortable as though she'd like to find a place to set him down, while Henry, who thankfully had turned out to be a fount of information about the area, sat and smoked from an old clay pipe and talked with Samuel and Julian.

Samuel learned that this was the only farm for miles this side of the Kaskaskia River and that the activity at the fort was normal for this time of year—Indians traveling in and out to trade and the British firmly, if absently, in control. It would take less than thirty minutes to hike to the fort from here. Henry owned two canoes and assured Samuel he would be happy to ferry them across in the morning so that they could continue on their mission of fetching the priest's books.

After dinner, feeling much better with a full stomach, Samuel rose and asked the location of the outhouse. He planned to get a better look at the layout of the farm.

"Oh, I'll come with you. You know how afraid of the dark I am," Isabelle said in a somewhat ominous tone. A vision of her killing the wolf flashed through Samuel's mind, and he almost laughed aloud but managed to duck his head instead and slap his hat down low on his head. "Come along then."

Once outside and safely out of earshot, Isabelle hissed in a whisper, "What was that all about? Your *wife*? Why didn't you tell them the truth? Who are you really, Samuel Holt?"

"Which question would you like answered first, sweetheart?"

"Sweetheart, is it? Why, I ought to shoot you for doing that to me without any warning."

"I knew you'd catch on quick enough. And anyway, you didn't let me lead. You tore off toward the front door before I had a chance to tell you my plan."

"I was *dying* of *thirst*, if you will remember. You certainly didn't know where to find water."

"I knew it was at the river; it just took us longer to get here than I thought it would."

"Don't get me sidetracked. Why would you need to lie? What is wrong with the truth?"

They had reached the outhouse door, a quaint moon and three stars cut out of the wood. Samuel leaned against it and sighed. "Can you keep a secret?"

Isabelle scowled. "What do you think?"

"I work for a large trading company. Out of New Orleans. I'm here scouting, fleshing out new areas of trade."

Isabelle stared hard at him, her head cocked to one side and her lips pressed together. "A trader. New Orleans? What is the company's name?"

Samuel searched his memory and blurted out the only one he knew of, the one the folks at Fort Boonesborough had been complaining about. "The Virginia Company. Do you doubt it?"

"Yes, I doubt it. What would a trader have to hide?"

Samuel gave a short laugh and his most condescending look. "Men are generally more honest if they don't know you are interested in their goods. Large quantities of goods."

Isabelle gave him a long considering look. "My father is a trader," she said, looking smug. "So be careful, Mr. Trader. I'm not ignorant about the ways of a *voyageur*."

Wonderful. He'd picked the one vocation she knew something about. Samuel reached over and touched her cheek, not being able to resist its creamy softness in the moonlight and knowing it would change the dynamic of their conversation. "Guard the door for me, love? I wouldn't want to be attacked by wild animals or anything while doing my business."

Sure enough, Isabelle's eyes grew dark and hot. "Too bad I don't have my gun," she said in a sultry voice. "I might just find something out here worth shooting, *husband*."

Samuel laughed and ducked into the dark outhouse, shaking his head. Could there be another woman on the face of this earth so different from his Sara?

THE STARS WERE filling up the sky as they walked slowly back to the house, lingering in the dark. They entered the cabin to find Julian playing Henry's guitar and singing a song—a sweet, heart-filled song about love lost that had Missy gazing at him with stars in her eyes. When the song ended, she clapped heartily and said to Isabelle on a long breath, "Your brother is so musical. My goodness, what talent."

Isabelle smiled at her, nodding, glancing at Samuel who seemed to be engrossed with Henry. Both were cleaning their guns. "Yes he is. My mother says when he cried as a baby it sounded more like a song than a complaint. He's been making up songs ever since."

Missy shook her head, leaning over her son. "I sure would like to see a talent like that in one of my children someday. What a joy." She glanced at her husband, and something sad flashed in her brown eyes. She quickly turned back to Isabelle and grinned, holding out her hand. "Come see the bed I made up for you and Mr. Holt."

Julian looked suddenly toward Isabelle, a frown furrowing his eyebrows. Samuel stopped cleaning the gun and looked at Isabelle with something like panic in his eyes. *He apparently hadn't thought this scheme through*, Isabelle thought with internal laughter. She grinned at him, saying to Missy, "Oh, you shouldn't have. But it'll be so nice to sleep on something other than the hard ground."

# 6

They climbed the rickety ladder to the loft, which smelled faintly of garlic and onions and lavender, much like her mother's cellar. Dried vegetables and herbs hung from the ceiling, and the sweet scent caused Isabelle her first pang of homesickness. A straw mattress lay in the middle of the floor, made up with two pillows and a couple of quilts. Isabelle found she wasn't tired now though. Her body was humming with anticipation, just waiting to see Samuel's head appear at the top of the ladder.

Missy said, "Julian can sleep in the baby's room, and we'll move little Benjamin's cradle into our bedroom. So, you see, there's plenty of room."

"Thank you, Missy, this is just perfect." Thinking of what two married women might say in private to each other, Isabelle lowered her voice. "You are so kind."

Missy blushed and held the baby tighter to her chest, looking a little wistful. "I—that is—" She started to tear up and turned her head away from Isabelle, blinking rapidly. "I'm glad for you," she managed, then quickly turned away and climbed back down the ladder.

Isabelle stared after her, wondering what was wrong. Hope had talked to Isabelle about what it would be like to be a wife, to share the marriage bed; and although there hadn't been many physical details, Isabelle was no stranger to forest and farm animals. She was certain she knew the fundamentals. But Missy seemed so sad and unhappy about something. Sighing, not knowing what to do to help, she turned her body and her mind to the bed and smiled a smug smile, reaching for the top button of her dress.

---

HENRY YAWNED FOR the third time, looked over to Samuel and nodded, his eyes watering. "Yes, well, dawn comes early."

Samuel grasped for some topic to keep the man from bed, to keep himself from having to climb those attic stairs.

Julian rose and stretched, giving Samuel a stern look. Then he took a couple of steps toward their host and stretched out his hand. "Thank you, sir. For the dinner and a bed for the night. I know I will sleep well not being in the open as we've been." He turned, gave Samuel one last long disapproving look, and made for the bedroom assigned to him.

Samuel heaved a sigh and stood. Maybe he should go to the outhouse and hang out there for a bit. Heaven knew after drinking so much tea he likely would be climbing up and down that rickety ladder all night. But no. Time to face the music of a lie that had sounded so sweet when he'd told it. He had no one to blame but himself and his own foolishness. He nodded goodnight toward Henry, then took hold of the ladder.

The loft was dark, which was good. He could just make out Isabelle's form under the blanket, the small rise and fall of her chest. Now, if he could just get into the bed without waking her. What had he been thinking to suggest they were married? It hadn't been one of his better ideas. He would be lucky to get any sleep at all this night, with her right next to him.

Calling on all of his training, he silently shrugged out of his jacket and moccasins. Next, he slipped out of his shirt but left the buckskin leggings on.

Slipping in between the blankets, he eased his body onto the mattress, careful not to touch her. She turned to her side with a quick jerk, facing him, but still breathing steadily in sleep. Samuel lay on his back and slowly, by careful degrees, relaxed his tired body and closed his eyes.

They just might make it through this unscathed.

He had no sooner thought this than her hand flopped down onto his belly. She huffed in her sleep and rolled closer, into his side, her hand curled against the bare skin of his stomach.

Every muscle in his body tensed. He felt the blood roar into his ears and barely breathed. He hadn't been with a woman since Sara died nearly two years ago. But Isabelle . . . her hand, her soft breast pressing against his arm, her leg looped over his. She made him want to run from the room or, worse, give in to his desire and gather her up in his arms. He imagined burying his face in her hair.

*Stop it! Think of something else and, for mercy's sake, get her to turn back over.*

Taking her hand by the wrist, he slowly lifted it and moved it to her side. She smiled then and plopped it back down and began caressing him, running her hand back and forth across his stomach.

"You've been awake this entire time, haven't you, you little minx?" Samuel growled. He turned abruptly, loudly, over onto his side, facing away from her, and hugged the edge of the mattress.

Next thing he knew, she was up, propped on an elbow and leaning over him, a dark curtain of her hair teasing his shoulder. "You have finally come to bed," she whispered. "I must have fallen asleep."

Looking back at her, over his shoulder, he commanded, "Go to sleep, Isabelle."

She smiled, and as his eyes adjusted to the light, he could now see the dark blue pools of her irises glowing at him, the creamy white of her shoulders revealing the lace of her undergarments.

"I'm not sleepy," she said softly.

Samuel bit off a curse and flopped unto his back, looking up at her. "Is that what you want? To *truly* pretend to be married?" He thought to scare her, to call her bluff. *Of all the brazen, wanton acts . . .*

She nodded and leaned toward him, her lips parted, anticipating a kiss.

He stopped her with the flat of his palm, a mistake as his hand grasped roundness instead of the throat he had been going for. "No. You don't know what you are asking for."

"How do you know what I know? Maybe I know exactly what I am asking for."

Samuel inhaled. "There have been others? You have done this before?"

Isabelle had the decency to flush and look away, uncertainty lighting her gaze.

Samuel breathed a sigh of relief. "Go to sleep, Isabelle."

She looked back at him, stricken, like a child whose toy had been snatched away. Samuel tried not to smile, seeing a glimpse of her as a little girl: round cheeks with dimples, dark eyes flashing with emotion, darker curls haloing a cherubic face. Had she always managed to get what she wanted?

Isabelle turned on her side, away from him, and Samuel

found his desire turning to compassion. Turning toward her, he pulled her into his chest and wrapped an arm around her middle, his chin in her hair, just as he'd imagined. Sighing into her hair, he closed his eyes, feeling her lithe body relax against his, the two of them curled together, fitting perfectly, feeling her breath go in and out, his nose buried in her sweet hair.

It felt like heaven.

It felt like home.

---

THE NEXT MORNING Julian was edgy and brooding in the kitchen as Isabelle followed Samuel down from the ladder. He was staring at the two of them, his lips a thin line as Isabelle blushed and stuttered, "G–Good morning." Hands on his hips, he glared at Samuel.

Samuel looked away to where Missy worked on a large pile of flapjacks. Then, deciding to meet the subject head on, he swung back around. "Let's go outside, take a look around." He looked Julian square in the eyes.

The younger man nodded briefly and reached for his hat.

Isabelle rose to go with them, but Samuel shook his head. "Stay here and help Missy with the breakfast, Isabelle."

She started to protest, her face a comical mix of outrage and shock and then, as she looked at Julian, as understanding dawned on her face, she nodded. "Oh, of course. Here, Missy, let me hold the baby and set the table while you work on those flapjacks. Mmm, that bacon smells heavenly."

Julian pulled his hat over his dark brown hair, his eyes grim. Samuel motioned him outside and shut the door behind them.

The sun was bright, promising a beautiful day. They walked to the calls of the morning birds, not saying anything until they had gone some distance away from the house, toward the river. At the bank Julian turned suddenly, facing Samuel. "What are your intentions toward my sister, sir?"

Samuel put a hand on his hip, shaking his head and looking down at the thick, green grass. "I don't really know. It was stupid of me to pretend we are married."

Julian did not respond.

"At the time, I thought it would look like less of a threat. . . . Folks are skittish as wild horses these days, with all the Indian attacks. But I didn't think through the sleeping arrangements."

A long, dead silence reigned.

Samuel knew the full force of his mistake in that silence.

"What if word gets out?" Julian finally said. "It usually does. Another man around these parts won't look at her, not for a wife anyway."

"Nothing happened." Samuel didn't mention that the sister Julian was trying to defend had made that most difficult for him.

Julian kicked at a dandelion, sending white fluff floating into the breeze. "It won't matter. Isabelle has always stirred up gossip. One time some men came upon her dancing in her chemise in the forest." He paused and took a deep breath. "It was lucky she had her rifle with her that day. One man lost an earlobe, and the one really going after her . . . well, let's just say he won't be fathering any children. Then there are the clothes she sometimes wears . . . *to church*." He pressed his lips together and stared at Samuel. "This will be the icing on the cake, lying the night through with a man."

"No one will know."

"Do you think the Coffmans won't talk about this in Kaskaskia? We're going to have to continue this story in town, or they will know it for the fabrication that it is, and Isabelle's reputation will be . . . My father will kill you for this." He stopped and looked sad. "And my mother. You've never met a better woman." He shook his head. "She will forgive you and pray for you, and believe me, that will feel worse than a good thrashing from my father. I should thrash you myself."

But they both knew he couldn't.

Samuel stared at Julian, weighing his next words carefully. "In a few days the citizens of Kaskaskia will have something much more pressing on their minds." His mouth turned up into a grim half smile. "And my deception will make more sense to everyone."

Julian stared, eyes squinting. "Who are you, really?"

"I have little reason to trust you with such knowledge. Beyond my gut instinct."

A thoughtful look entered Julian's eyes, and he said quietly, "You can trust me."

Samuel nodded, looked from Julian's intense face off into the distant sunrise, all yellow and orange and hopeful. With a short nod, he agreed. "I'm here with an army. An American army. We plan to take Kaskaskia in a few days."

"You are a spy?" Excitement laced Julian's youthful voice.

"A scout, yes."

Julian looked behind them, toward the east from where they had come. "They're behind us now?"

Samuel nodded. "A few days. I have to report back later today, after scouting the fort."

"Why do the Americans want Kaskaskia? It's such a little, out-of-the-way place. There are not even any British there to speak of."

Samuel's eyes locked with the young man's. "We are securing the land west of the Appalachians for the American government. We're all going to be Americans soon, Julian. No longer British citizens, or even French. We are becoming our own nation. You understand that, don't you?"

Julian looked excited, the familiar fire of independence heating his eyes. "Yes, but—"

"That's all I'm going to tell you, so don't ask any more questions. And don't tell Isabelle. I am trusting you with the lives of many men, with dreams of glory and freedom. Don't disappoint me."

---

HE SENT JULIAN inside and stared at the dark forms that were moving in the village across the river. He sincerely hoped he hadn't made a mistake, but he didn't think so. Julian was much the same as young men anywhere, straining for a cause to believe in, for something worthy to stand up and fight for. He thought of Isabelle and felt his blood go hot inside him.

Isabelle made every emotion he felt deepen in intensity. There were no grays with this woman, only color—the deep blues and greens of their rightness together, a deeper place of peace and connectedness; the oranges and reds of their passion, unrequited and pulsing; the purples, from lavender to deep violet, of her dance worship that left him breathless in awe. Most unsettling was the deep black he felt at moments, tiny snatches of time that stunned him with their intensity, leaving him grasping as to what his instincts were trying to tell him about him and her and their future together.

And they did have a future together. Since first laying eyes on her he had known. She had even said it aloud. They were meant to be together.

But what was that to look like in such a time and place as they found themselves? He was in the middle of a campaign, a war, and there was a good chance he would die in the fighting of it. The risk was easier to consider without anyone waiting for him to come back on the other side of it. He had no home, no place to rest his own head, much less a wife's.

He thought of the wife he had lost. Sara. It had been four years since her death, a death that had shocked him after only ten months of marriage. He tried to remember her face now and felt a gripping fear that it was fading. He looked up at the dawn sky, trying to call to mind the pale gray of her eyes, the sound of her voice, and hearing only the throaty trill of a mockingbird nearby.

"I can't see her face anymore," he whispered. When he closed his eyes, all he could see were Isabelle's gypsy features, so strong, so fierce in comparison to Sara's. Sara had been a faded beauty even at nineteen. He thought back to their wedding day, seeing only a pale visage, knowing that her hair had been blonde, her mouth small and bow-like, her eyes a dove's gray. On that day she had been full of a young woman's fear, reflecting the feelings in his heart, that they were being pushed into this thing by parents who wanted them joined for the land, for their dream of building an empire.

But he had loved her in a sudden, unmastered way. He'd thought her lovely, had anticipated the night to come with a young man's blood.

Their wedding night, though, had only bewildered him. He knew he had been clumsy and she, so still and stiff in his arms. He hadn't known what to do, falling asleep, feeling like a boy instead of a man. He remembered her in the sitting room with his mother and sisters the next day, bent over her sewing, smiling with them at some silly joke that had her turning pink and him feeling like an elephant in the room. She'd never, not once in the months to follow, crossed to the other side of the room to stand beside *him.* She hadn't understood him, his restless energy, his occasional attempts at teasing her that only led to a doe-eyed confusion. But how easily she had melded into that woman-life that ran its own course during the day.

She was a terrifying mystery causing him to feel that his wanting of her, his thinking of her during the day and wanting to reach for her every night, was some dark spot on her happiness. So he'd begun to make up excuses to be away, afraid of the overwhelming passion that was bursting inside him. Afraid he would somehow destroy her . . . and he had. He must have gotten her pregnant that first time. There had been little other opportunity.

Sara had been his family's choice of a wife, fitting so well in that life of Virginia plantation living, a place that left him feeling anchored, unchallenged, a square peg surrounded by round holes. And then she had died after a ghastly battle to birth his daughter. It was all a cloudy memory. But he would never forget her last words . . . her last word. *Isabelle.*

He thought she meant to name the child Isabelle. So he had done so, not knowing what to do with the squalling infant. The way she moved in his trembling hands, the way she turned her head toward the sound of his voice and opened dark eyes, the way she looked at him like she had come from a place with all of the answers. As he held the newborn at arm's length, his eyes blurred over, and he found himself shaking his head. His wife's lifeless body was just feet away! Why had they thrust this infant into his hands as if he would rejoice and find solace in this small bit of flesh? He turned, stricken and sick, to the midwife, knowing that if he held the child any longer he would drop her. The woman reached for the babe, but there was great unease in her eyes.

He couldn't bear it. Not the bed where his wife lay so still and pale. Not the infant, unknown flesh of his flesh. Not the midwife's eyes that said he should be more. So he left the infant in the woman's capable hands . . . and fled.

He walked away after the funeral service, turned his back on the grave site, his home, then finally, his entire inheritance. He joined the Virginia militia, rising quickly in the ranks with each bloody battle, becoming their finest sharpshooter and an unsurpassed tracker. It was here that he discovered a talent deep within that at first had terrified him. Something that left him leagues ahead of the other soldiers and, soon, commander of his own force. It was little but a sixth sense, a gut instinct for what was coming up ahead, around the next bend, through an open valley or wooded copse, some prophetic vision of things to come. He didn't know how or why he possessed this gift. But he learned how to use it, and it never failed him.

And now there was another Isabelle. A small part of him, that gut instinct, rose up to ask the question: Had Sara known something of the future? Had she known he would meet and love another woman? A woman called Isabelle?

# 7

Broad sunbeams filtered down through the smoke over the little village of Kaskaskia. Tents and smoldering campfires lined the bank of the Kaskaskia River where *coureurs de bois*, runners of the woods, stood talking to one another and gesturing toward two canoes filled with trade goods. A tall, grizzled man with a walking stick nodded to Samuel, curiosity sparking his hooded eyes, as the frontiersman passed by with Julian and Isabelle in tow. Samuel looked into his eyes briefly, felt a shock of the familiar as they nodded once to each other, and looked away. *This man would support their cause.* The feeling that it was true flowed through him. Samuel found it was like that sometimes with a stranger, as though they had known one another in some other place and time.

He studied the village with instincts long honed during years of gathering intelligence. While traders camped on the riverbanks, the citizens, in their French-style peasant dresses and pilfered Indian garb, traveled along the main road in their various pursuits, so domestic, so quiet, so not expecting the army that was coming.

Kaskaskia was inhabited by the French, with what appeared to be a small British regiment holding down the fort. Not much in the way of artillery was visible. The commandant, Philippe de Rocheblave, a French nobleman, held a British commission to rule. It was rumored that de Rocheblave enjoyed little support from either the British or the French. One of the hunters Clark captured off Corn Island had reported that the British had not sent men or supplies for months and that de Rocheblave was running the office out of his own pocket.

Clark had grinned at that and said to Samuel, "That can't be making him too happy."

"Nope." A disgruntled commander was all the easier to defeat.

The church, a humble log building with a belfry, was easy to spot in the center of the town. Samuel stopped and waited for Isabelle to catch up. "Father Gibault has the books?" he asked, seeing her hot face and handing over his canteen.

Isabelle took it, turned slightly away from him, and nodded. She drank, then wiped the sweat from her face with her sleeve. "Yes, we should hurry to the church. I want to be sure that they are truly, safely arrived."

"You're taking this mission pretty seriously," Samuel said with quiet teasing.

"I am proving myself." Isabelle looked up at him with something in her eyes that caused Samuel's heart to race.

Inside the one-room church their eyes took a moment to adjust. The meager light, provided by two small windows, revealed a simple wooden platform and altar and four wooden pews on either side of a narrow aisle.

Father Gibault turned from his place at a low desk in the corner of the church as they entered. Isabelle made her way toward him, her sturdy boots ringing on the wood floor.

"Father Gibault?"

The man stood and smiled, reaching out his hands toward her. "You must be Isabelle Renoir," he said with a proud grin and grasped her hands in welcome. Turning to Samuel and Julian, he repeated the action. "And you are Julian; I can see the family resemblance at once. But you, sir, do not look like the Indian described in the letter I received from Father Francis."

Samuel shook hands with the man. "No sir, I am Samuel Holt. I met the Renoirs en route to Kaskaskia. Quiet Fox was guiding them but disappeared the morning after I joined the party."

"Well, it was providential that you were there to help, was it not? We should thank the Father who watches out for all His children." He smiled again and motioned them over to a shelf. With a grand sweep of his hand he indicated about ten small, ancient-looking books. "Father Francis's books. I vow, I have been enjoying the use of them since they arrived and will miss them."

Isabelle nodded. "Such a fine library. Father Francis will be so pleased they have arrived safely. And I am certain he will lend you some when you come to Vincennes."

"Yes. I haven't been to Vincennes in some time, but I should go. I should go," he repeated, almost to himself. "Come though, you must all be tired, and hungry, eh?" He looked to Julian who was glaring expectantly at Samuel.

Father Gibault led them across the dirt street to a small but neat home. It was a typical bachelor's dwelling that lacked the warmth of rugs, window coverings, or knickknacks, save an old, ornate clock that ticked loudly like a welcoming pet. There was plenty of food though, and the priest soon busied himself roasting ham over an open flame and served it with thick slices of bread, apples, and some early garden peas.

Samuel said, "I noticed the gate was unmanned when we came into the village."

Father Gibault nodded. "We have little need for an active sentry."

"That's welcome news. I've just come up through Kentucky country where the Shawnee are attacking the settlers left and right. Have you had no problems with the Indians here?"

Father Gibault's eyes lit with interest on Samuel. "We are British held. The Indians of this area are aligned with the British and so do us no harm."

"But the citizens are French?"

"Yes, the British have mostly left us to ourselves. They've allowed us to keep our commander, de Rocheblave, a good man. But they've not given him much support. I daresay our little village is mostly forgotten by everyone save God."

Samuel nodded. The intelligence Clark had received appeared accurate. Wanting to see more of the town, Samuel finished his meal, drank down his mug of water, and stood. "I would like to see the village, make some inquires into a trading business."

"Are you a trader, then?" Father Gibault asked.

Samuel's glance took in Julian's stare. "Of a kind," he replied simply.

Isabelle looked up from her plate. "I should like to see the village. Can I join you?"

"Isabelle," Julian interrupted, "we have just arrived. Let Samuel go."

The flat line of her mouth and glare she shot her brother made clear to all her feelings of being so commanded.

Samuel grinned. "She can come. I'm just having a look around."

"Well, in that case, I should come too."

The priest laughed as Julian pushed back from the table, all noticing Isabelle's scowl.

---

CLARK MARCHED HIS men in a long, serpentine line through the tall grasses of an open field. Men who weeks ago couldn't command their legs to walk for more than a few hours at a time now had taken on the appearance of a shabby but semi-disciplined force—raw recruits on their way to becoming soldiers. Like wild-eyed pirates united in the quest for treasure—filthy, reeking, and, more often than not, cursing or, in the next phrase, giving praise to God—these men were determined to become everything that their leader said they could be.

The journey from the Falls of the Ohio to Kaskaskia had taken ten days thus far and had not been without certain struggles. At the outset, one hundred and seventy-eight men had smeared mud on their faces, checked their weapons, and boarded the canoes that lined the banks of Corn Island. They hunkered down into the belly of the vessels, feeling the light summer breeze and the warmth of the sun on their faces, belying the dangers ahead. They paddled, scanning the riverbanks for movement, their long rifles trained and ready as they slipped through the British-controlled country toward Kaskaskia.

Then a sudden shadow had appeared overhead, as if a great bird had flown over them and blocked the sun. Clark looked up at the sound of the men gasping. It took a moment to comprehend what he was seeing, then his heart sped up. The sun was darkening, slice by slice, becoming black. The light around them turned a silver color that bathed his army's stunned faces in an eerie glow.

"An eclipse," Clark said, as if to himself, staring rapt at the phenomenon. He had read of such a thing but had never thought to see it. Clark tore his gaze away from the sight and scanned his troops. Many sat with their jaws open, terror in their eyes. All paddling had ceased, which caused the canoes to bunch up on one another. Then the sound of rushing water brought Clark to his feet.

"Men! The falls! Man your canoes!"

The men bent to their paddles, straining to see the bubbling head of the rapids ahead of them. A strange stillness descended on them as they crested the peak of water. Then, as if falling from a hilltop, they dropped, boat by boat, tilting over the edge into a frothy stream that carried them, splashing, into a river head pool below.

Clark demanded they keep rowing, not giving their imagination time to dwell upon the superstitious implications of the darkening sun.

Once the small flotilla rested in calmer waters, they stopped paddling and gazed skyward, where the sun was reappearing by slow degrees. The murmurs of the men now reached Clark's ears.

"It's a curse of God. A sign. We should turn back," said a tall, lanky man.

"What if it's a blessing?" said another.

"We're cursed, I tell you. We'll never beat those redcoats now. We have to turn back."

"Perhaps the heavens stopped moving just to watch us," another opined.

Clark's gaze swept the men and saw that several were wide-eyed and fearful, others were agitated, and a few were looking for anyone to explain what they had never seen before.

He stood in his canoe as the waters around them calmed and waited until he held their attention. "It was merely an eclipse of the sun by the moon, my good men," Clark assured them. "But let us not look to the right or to the left or even above us. You men are the future of this nation, and nothing, not even signs from the heavens, will detract us from our mission."

There were a few cheers.

"We may see new things ahead, things that grip our hearts with fear. But mighty men see only their mission and their leader. Follow me. I will not lead you astray."

That night several men deserted despite Clark's assurances of faith and future victory. Clark remembered the Bible story of Gideon and how God commanded that Gideon's army be winnowed to a mere three hundred men. Clark didn't send a party out to find the deserters, though everything within insisted that he needed every man, every hand, every weapon. Instead, he decided that God had tested them, separating the mighty from those weak ones who might endanger their mission with unbelief.

---

AT FORT MASSAC the army abandoned their boats. Clark would have preferred to travel from the old fort by way of the Mississippi up the Kaskaskia River. That would only require seven miles of riverboat travel, but the risks were simply too great. The river was being watched by the British, the Indians, and maybe even the Spanish. This part of the country was valuable for its rivers, meaning trade and commerce. Clark doubted the inhabitants of small, quiet communities like Kaskaskia, Vincennes, and Cahokia understood the value of their presence here. But the British knew. That was why they had built forts and stationed an army to control the trade and the flow of the river all the way from Detroit and the headwaters of the Great Lakes down to the Gulf of Mexico.

So instead Clark pushed his remaining men overland to Kaskaskia, a hundred-mile journey north through fields and bogs with little rest. One night, after the men had bedded down in the deep grass, Clark walked a little ways from the camp and soon found himself on one knee, his buckskin pants growing wet and soggy in the damp earth. He turned his face heavenward, toward the diamond-inlaid velvet of the night sky, knowing that the One who called this dazzling firmament into existence had also made him, for this time, for this purpose.

"Dear God, one hundred and fifty men. To take a kingdom. I'll not do this alone!" he cried out, recognizing the utter hopelessness of his plan. "I can't do this alone." He bent his head over his raised knee, his breath coming in quick and short gasps, the night insects accompanying his prayer in song.

Now, after several days of marching, Clark surveyed his troops and couldn't help but grin. They looked like a pack of dogs, rising up and wagging their tails at him, ready for adventure.

Clark was holding it all together with the strength of his voice and the cadence of his conviction. He had convinced them that they could walk on water, if need be, by the Great God of heaven who was on their side. He led his men at the head, sloughing through the mire of stagnant water and weeds, bugs and snakes and nettles attacking them, marching through swamp and prairie. The days were marked by blazing sun with little water, the moonlit nights by too little sleep.

When they lagged in strength, Clark instinctively knew it and called out in a bellowing voice, "Who will follow me, boys? Who will match my steps?"

And as one they would respond. "We will, Colonel Clark. The Long Knives will follow you anywhere!" Then and every time they said it, a feeling that it was *true* would rise up in their hearts to keep their feet moving forward. Somehow they all knew that, together, they could do anything their redheaded leader would demand of them.

They were sore and tired. They were poor and wretched—but invincible.

On July 4 they came upon the farmhouse located just three miles from their first target, the small but important fort of Kaskaskia, the old French capital of the Illinois country. But Clark hesitated to proceed until he heard from Samuel Holt. Where was he? He was concerned that his scout had run into trouble; it wasn't like him to be anything less than efficient.

His men were crouched around him in the tall grass, listening to the crickets come out and watching the sun set on the horizon. Clark held his hand over his eyes, squinting as he scanned the area, weighing his decision whether to wait or proceed. The farmhouse was quiet, looked an easy target, but it would be far better to know the lay of the land. So they waited.

Then a flash of light caused Clark's face to break into a big grin. Samuel was running around the edge of the farm toward them, signaling with a mirror as he ran. The ragtag soldiers waited, quiet and intense, as Samuel tore across the flat field at an unbelievable gait. The sun was now low in the sky, the wind whipping about them, cooling their sweat-soaked faces and necks.

"I think they're at supper," Samuel said, panting, stopping in front of his commander and saluting with a big grin.

"So that's where you've been. Filling your stomach on enemy fare."

Samuel shrugged. "Mrs. Coffman's a fair hand in the kitchen. Shall we join them?"

Clark nodded, smiling, looking around at the excitement on the men's faces. "Do you think they'll have enough?"

"I think they may be able to scrounge something up for Lt. Colonel Clark and his army when they see your grand forces."

Clark laughed. "What have you learned?"

"They're a friendly sort. Kept me and a couple of new friends for the night last evening."

"New friends and nice meals . . . you *have* been on holiday out here, Samuel. Have you learned anything to help my army?"

Samuel grasped Clark's shoulder, his eyes suddenly intense. "Aye. We should meet little resistance in Kaskaskia. The fort is just as the hunters said, held by few militia and fewer weapons. The town is almost . . . sleepy."

"That *is* good news. And de Rocheblave?"

"Having dinner with the town's doctor when I left. He was very friendly toward me and gave me free reign to trade in Kaskaskia."

"So you were a trader this time, eh?"

"A trader with a wife and brother-in-law in tow." Samuel shook his head. "A story for another time."

Clark nodded, mischievous interest in his eyes, "A wife, eh? I won't forget to hear that tale." Turning toward his men he ordered them into marching lines. With a signal from his hand, they marched.

The farmhouse was large, with several outbuildings housing animals and grain. It had a large well, thank God, and a spring-house providing more water and a place to keep things cool. It was the perfect jumping-off point for the coming assault.

Clark had the men silently fan out and surround the place while he and Samuel strode to the front door. They knocked, then stood and waited, still and polite.

Henry Coffman opened the door, took in Samuel and his commander, and with terror mounting on his face, gazed over their shoulders to the army surrounding them. He backed up, his arms outstretched as if to ward them off. "What is this, Mr. Holt?" he sputtered in anger, confusion, and fear. "Please, don't kill us."

Clark and Samuel entered, guns resting easy and ready in hand for effect. Clark said, "We're not here to spill the blood of good citizens, sir. Only to commandeer this residence, temporarily, for my men."

The man had backed into the table where his wife sat unable to move, both looking to Samuel to explain. Clark removed his hat. Samuel followed suit. "We've need of water, some food if you have it, and a few hours' rest. We'll not molest your family if you cooperate."

The man glared at Samuel. "You were *spying* on us?"

Samuel nodded but kept his stern demeanor. "You'll come to no harm, Henry. This is Colonel Clark. We are of the Americans, Illinois Regiment of Virginia."

Missy gasped and put her hands to her face, a whispered phrase escaping her lips, "The Long Knives."

Henry looked frightened anew, sinking back into his bones, pointing to his yard and nodding. "Take anything you need, Colonel Clark, anything at all."

"My thanks." Clark nodded his head at the man and then his wife. To Samuel he murmured, "Secure any weapons and see that they stay inside."

Samuel nodded once and retrieved the rifle above the fireplace. As Clark stepped outside to take care of the army, Samuel silently gathered all the weapons in the house, then stood by the window, waiting for Clark's signal.

Missy rose and hurried to the stove to cook for them. "But Mr. Holt, where is your wife and her brother?"

Samuel glanced at the woman and grimaced. "She is not my wife, ma'am. I'm truly sorry for the deception, but . . . it seemed the best course at the time."

Missy was staring at him wide-eyed, most likely remembering putting them up together in the attic. "Oh." Her round cheeks were pink.

"I feel cheated." Henry glared at him. "Why did you lie?"

Samuel gave him a hard look. "I didn't know who lived here, where your alliances might lie, and I couldn't risk others hearing about what was to come. There are things going on here that you have little understanding of. You will just have to trust me."

"As if I have a choice," muttered Henry, looking at his hands.

Samuel just nodded at him and returned to watching the men as they settled into camp. Missy would feed and house the officers, but the others would cook on small fires hidden by the house and then lay low for a few hours while they awaited the cover of night.

---

IT WAS DARK now, almost dawn. The men were fed, rested, and ready.

Ready for their first battle of the campaign.

Suppressed excitement held their faces, their bodies straining to keep the slow, steady pace Clark demanded as he led them toward the fort, just three miles away.

After crossing the river, the company made its way up the banks of the river to the edge of town. Splitting the men into two groups, Clark, Samuel, and a few hand-picked men bore down upon the fort. They crept up to the unmanned gate, entering the enclosure without being challenged by so much as a sentry. Samuel hand signaled to Clark the location of the commander's house, dark and silent as the rest of the buildings lining the small, narrow street. A small armed contingency first surrounded the house and then quietly broke the latch on the front door.

Clark led his men inside. "Commander de Rocheblave," he said as the door slammed open against the wall, "your fort has been surrounded by the Americans, and we request your immediate surrender." Clark stated the fact almost politely.

The couple sat up in their bed, an abrupt movement of covers and clenched jaws. The wife clutched the covers to her chin, her cap askew. De Rocheblave's mouth opened and closed a moment before he snapped it shut and lifted his chin. "Who are you, sir? What is the meaning of this?"

Clark lifted the brim of his hat and grinned. "Colonel George Rogers Clark of the American army. Glad to make your acquaintance." He laughed, low and deep, seeming to enjoy the scene. "I am here to take over your fort. This is American country now."

The man looked ready to argue, then heaved a big breath and nodded. *"Personne ne sait qui le possède."*

At Clark's puzzled brow he interpreted. "I only said that no one knows who owns it. But for now, yes, it appears the Americans have it. What will you do with our town, George Rogers Clark?"

George's face lit up with the question. "Why, open up the territory for hardworking folk. Now, if you and the missus wouldn't mind getting dressed, we'll see to the business of it, shall we?"

It didn't take long for Clark to have the town under his control. A Frenchman in the company was assigned the task of raising the alarm to the townsfolk by shouting throughout the streets of Kaskaskia that it had been taken and ordering the good people of the village, on the pain of death, to remain indoors. Before the first rays of daylight, the people were disarmed and fearful of their fate.

---

"CITIZENS OF KASKASKIA," a French voice shouted in the street just feet from the window Isabelle was sleeping next to.

"Stay in your homes where it is safe. The Americans have taken the city."

Isabelle reared up, clutching the thin blanket at her waist, straining to hear anything else. The man repeated the phrase in various ways, but the message was clear: Do not raise arms against the Americans.

The Long Knives, as they were called, had taken the fort.

# 8

Isabelle pressed her ear against the bedroom door trying without success to hear what the soldiers were saying to Father Gibault. She eased the door open a crack, and, still standing in her nightgown, her toes curled into the wood floor, she peered out.

"The colonel would like to meet with all the leaders of the community," a tall, rough-clad officer was saying.

Father Gibault nodded, wrapping his sash about his priest's tunic. "Who has taken the city?" There was a quiver in his voice.

Isabelle strained to hear the answer.

"Colonel George Rogers Clark and the Americans, sir."

Father Gibault's head jerked up to look at the man, and Isabelle gasped.

The Long Knives.

She had heard stories of their brutality, a bribe mothers used to coerce obedience from their children. "You'd better get yourself inside or the Long Knives will get ya." Or, "Best eat all that dinner afore the Long Knives come to eat it up and you with it." Her own mother had never stooped to such levels, but Isabelle had heard the stories.

She watched as the priest followed the soldier out, then shut the bedroom door and gathered her clothing. Julian was still asleep on the floor, so she slipped quietly into her dress, knowing that if she woke him he would try to keep her from following Father Gibault. Taking up her rifle, which had been hidden under the covers with her during the night, she looked one last time at Julian and left the room.

The first rays of sun were brightening the sky. The air was sweet, with a breeze that blew her long, unbound hair into her face. Isabelle thought she should have taken time to stuff it under a bonnet, but little matter now. Skirting the edges of the buildings that made up the main street, she made her way to the center of town where a crowd of men had gathered. They were mumbling quietly, eyes darting here and there, feet shuffling, clothing in disarray from the hurry and panic of this meeting. Isabelle spotted Father Gibault near the front. He was turned away from her and talking to several men, gesturing with sweeping motions of his hands and an intense look in his eyes.

A tall, redheaded man came out of the trading post with three other men flanking him. He wore buckskins from head to toe, the color of honey with fringe swaying as he walked. He was quite tall, but there was something in his carriage that made him seem enormous. A rare authority sat upon his shoulders, lending him the air of a king. King of the Long Knives.

Isabelle's breathing caught in awe as the colonel towered over the men from the porch of the trading post.

One man cried out in a loud voice, "Don't kill us! Let us be your slaves, lord."

Isabelle bit down on her bottom lip, straining to hear but unable to make out more than the sounds of the citizenry begging for mercy. Crouching down, she crept to a tall water barrel and hunkered behind it. Another sideways dodge and she was barely hidden behind the doctor's front-porch pillar and a wooden rocking chair. Peeking between the slats in the chair she could now see and hear.

"Citizens of Kaskaskia," the colonel began in the pained voice of one offended, "I am mortified to learn of your low opinion of the Americans. We do not come to enslave, but to set free. You have heard tales that are false. Let me tell you the truth of the Americans."

Isabelle listened in growing astonishment as Clark declared that the Americans were taking the fort from the British. They intended to stop the bloodshed by the Indians of the Illinois country and Kentucky, and they hoped to break the alliance between the British and the Indians. He explained that the Americans—yes, the Long Knives—were here to free the people of Kaskaskia from British tyranny to live the life of their hearts in this new land where anything was possible.

Isabelle strained to see the faces of the French citizens. They had been shocked into silence. Rising before she had time to really consider what she was doing, she moved closer, dashing toward a watering trough right next to Clark.

His gaze swung to her, piercing blue, full of fire and ice, outrage, and weighing judgment. Isabelle froze, still crouched, grasping her weapon in her right hand with a terrorized grip. All eyes turned toward her. Suddenly a man materialized from Clark's side and she lifted her gaze into the point of a rifle, her rifle being torn from her grasp.

"Isabelle?"

Isabelle looked up from the rifle into the eyes of Samuel Holt. Exhaling with relief, she gave him a tight smile. "I'm . . . sorry?"

Samuel hauled her to her feet and marched her over to Clark, where she stood with her hair blowing around her shoulders and into her face like a great black veil. With her right hand she held her hair back from her face and lifted her eyes to Clark's.

"What do we have here, Sam? This wouldn't be your *wife*, would it?"

He said it low, and Isabelle thought that possibly no one else had heard him, but it so infuriated her that she kicked out at Samuel's shins and hissed at the colonel, "I'm no wife of his, sir."

"Then why aren't you with the other obedient citizens who are waiting *patiently* in their houses?" Clark demanded.

Isabelle took a breath, started to speak, then changed her mind and admitted with a resigned tone, "I've always had somewhat of a problem with obedience, sir."

Clark looked shocked for a moment, then threw back his head and laughed. "Take her to my headquarters, Samuel. I think we can come up with some practice lessons for her, don't you?"

Samuel nodded, scowling at her for the kick. With a tight grip on her upper arm and her rifle gripped in the other, he pulled her along to the doctor's house where Clark had set up his office. Once inside Isabelle turned on him, hackles raised and fluttering.

"You're with *them*? You are one of the *Americans*."

Samuel gave her a quick nod, staring hard at her.

"Why didn't you tell me?"

"I couldn't. It was a scouting mission, Isabelle."

"So you used us, Julian and me, as a front." She stopped suddenly, eyes widening. "That's why you told those people we were married!"

Samuel had the decency to flush and shrug one shoulder. "It seemed a good idea at the time."

"How convenient for you."

"I'm sorry."

Isabelle stared out the window at the men still listening to Clark. "You got what you wanted, didn't you?"

"I guess you could say that."

"So what are you going to do now? Or is that a secret too?"

"Isabelle . . ." Samuel sighed. "I am sorry."

Isabelle turned away from the sight of this tall and handsome scout. She didn't want to soften. She was confused by the events and didn't know what to think of them. "Will they let Julian and me go? We were planning to head back to Vincennes today."

Samuel stepped closer, standing just behind her shoulders, leaning toward her head a little. "I don't know. I'll speak with Clark about it."

She turned, looking up into his eyes, studying his face for truth. "He doesn't really plan to keep me here and teach me a lesson, does he?"

Samuel grinned, looking at her mouth. "I won't let him torture you."

"Hmph. That's not likely, in any case."

"Do you fear nothing?" he asked in a soft whisper.

"I heard what he said. He wants peace. And . . . and freedom." She smiled at him, her voice lowering. "There is only one thing I fear."

"What is that?"

She debated, staring into his eyes, wanting him to read the answer inside hers, to see her hopes and fears where he was concerned.

She was saved from having to answer by Clark walking in the door and chuckling. "Am I interrupting something, Samuel?"

Samuel turned and gave his colonel a slow smile. "Would that you were." Bringing Isabelle forward, her waist in his grasp, he introduced her. "This is Isabelle Renoir. From Vincennes."

Interest lit Clark's eyes. "And what is the lovely lady doing in Kaskaskia?"

Isabelle swallowed past the lump in her throat and chose to answer for herself. "I'm on an errand of books, sir. My priest sent me and my brother to fetch them from Father Gibault."

"Hmm. A good man, Father Gibault, I think." He looked thoughtful as if no longer in the room with them. Then his gaze suddenly locked with Isabelle's. "How is it, miss, that you remained armed when my men checked the houses for weapons?"

Isabelle shrugged, unable to help the smile that curved her lips. "I doubt they checked the priest's house." She paused, looking to Samuel. "Besides, I sleep with my rifle. They wouldn't check a lone woman's bed, would they?"

Clark laughed, and Samuel scowled. "A worthy quality in a wife, I'd say. I think you might consider making it permanent."

Samuel ignored the comment. "She and her brother plan to leave with the books for Vincennes tomorrow. I'm thinking of accompanying them."

Clark nodded, thoughtful. "A worthy ruse."

Isabelle took a step forward. "You'll not use my brother and me again for spying. Do you intend to go after Vincennes next?"

Samuel put his hand on his hip. "Have no fear. We will not travel as a married couple this time. I will merely be your guide."

"We can take care of ourselves."

Clark smiled. "Perhaps." He nodded, looking out the far window of the house, looking lost in sudden, intense thought. Then he turned his gaze back to her, so blue and reading every nuance of her response. "But can you be trusted with such knowledge? Do you understand what we are about here, Miss Renoir?" Clark's face was suddenly grave and intense.

"I will not be detained, sir. I am on a mission of old and musty books, nothing else. I will speak of nothing else." She paused, looking into these two faces, bold and daring, sure and strong . . . and something else—something that told her this was important, that something vast and beyond her understanding was happening. She gripped her skirt by both sides, imbuing her words with passion. "But no, to answer your question, I don't really know what the Long Knives want with our little towns."

Clark walked over, poured her a drink of water from a pitcher, and bade her sit down. "Mayhap I can enlighten you."

That he was taking the time and effort to explain it to her, a woman, and not even a citizen of this place, had her sinking into a chair, grasping the water glass in a tight fist, looking up into the colonel's taut face as he told her about the Americans and their fight for freedom. As he explained it in his eloquent way, she found herself engulfed, overcome with emotions that she had not known she'd suppressed. This man, George Rogers Clark, spoke of a new land where any cost for this vision of freedom was small and light. He spoke of it like a deliverance, from monarch on foreign soil, from attack by enemies seen and unseen, to a place like . . . heaven.

Isabelle found it hard to breathe as she listened, everything else forgotten as he spoke into the room, his words resounding. They bounced about her, ideas unformed, but some internal knowing rising up to say that he was right. She found herself nodding and agreeing, willing to put to use any skill she might have for his cause. What if he was right? What if this land was meant for something greater than these European countries were scrabbling at? What if, as Americans, they were meant for more?

She found her heart shouting a resounding "yes!". She found, within this man's impassioned speech, a new purpose.

# 9

Julian and Isabelle, along with the whole town, had bowed on one knee and sworn allegiance to the Americans and the ideals of American freedom. Then it was decided that Samuel would guide brother and sister back to Vincennes.

It was early afternoon on the second day of the return journey, with sun rays pervading the shade of the leaves overhead, lighting their path through the woods and making it dappled with shade and light, that the three of them happened upon a cabin in a little clearing. Twin, giant oak trees stood sentry on either side. A swing hung from each tree's sturdiest branch, swaying, empty in the summer breeze.

"Look, they have a well," Julian pointed out, relief in his voice. "Maybe they will be kind enough to feed us too."

Samuel nodded, scanning the area and committing the lay of the land to memory. It was a small cabin, typical in its lonely simplicity. A rough-hewn door hung on leather hinges and fitted in the hole none too well. Two windows were cut, rough and ragged, on each side of the door that, in the middle of summer, was open and without their winter paper to seal out the cold. At night the family might hang mosquito netting over the windows to keep out the insects. Then again, maybe not. Netting could be hard to come by and a luxury not afforded these folks.

Samuel thought of his home in Virginia, where his family owned a tobacco plantation. Their house was a white stone mansion that sparkled in the sun and could be seen from a mile away amid its setting of lush poplars. His sisters were the beauties of the county, and his mother reigned as social queen in nearby Williamsburg. Theirs was the life of the English gentry, an imitation of worldly prosperity. But Samuel had been bored and restless with it all and, after signing on with General Washington, had few occasions of looking back. It hadn't taken long for the life of a soldier, then a frontiersman, to latch onto him, body and soul, stirring him to life abundant.

As they approached this home on the outskirts of nowhere, Samuel acknowledged to himself that he would be happier here in this meager cabin in the woods, with its smoke-spitting stove and paper windows, than back in the tight-noosed whirl of Virginian society.

A little boy of about six suddenly ran out the door, shrieking with laughter. Two other boys, each looking two years older than the last, barreled out behind him, yelling and chasing each other with whittled wooden rifles. When they saw Samuel and then Isabelle and Julian, the boys came to a collective stop and shyly stood and stared.

A woman's voice called out from within the cabin. Then she appeared in the open doorway, a tall, thin woman with dark-blonde hair.

"Thomas, Eli—" she called, then stopped, suddenly seeing the strangers. Her hand went to her hair, trying to catch up wisps that had fallen out of the loose bun she wore. Her face was pretty but looking older than it should. She stepped out into the light with a wary but friendly smile. "Good day to you."

Samuel nodded his head, quickly closing the gap, respect in every step he took across the cool, green grass. He knew this kind of woman, had seen her type a hundred times, and still it brought a response from deep within him. He swept his hat from his head and clutched it to his chest as he said, "Good day, ma'am. We're traveling to Vincennes and wondered if you might spare some water. The name's Samuel Holt." Samuel held out his hand to the woman, who smiled very prettily at him and shook it. "Naomi Lynn, sir."

Isabelle stepped forward. "Hello, I'm Isabelle Renoir, and this is my brother, Julian."

The woman nodded politely to them, her gaze returning to Samuel. "My husband's just come in for the noon meal. Please, join us." She turned back to the house, waving for them to follow her. "We have a watering trough for your horse at the barn." She must have noticed the surprisingly good horseflesh Father Gibault had loaned them to carry the books. "Boys, water Mr. Holt's horse, then go and fetch more wood from the woodpile," she said to the wide-eyed threesome. "And don't dally. Dinner is nearly ready."

A tall, lean man, wearing a faded calico shirt that matched his wife's skirt, introduced himself as Jake Lynn. Inside were two daughters—Rose, a cherubic three-year-old with chubby cheeks and round, brown ringlets, and Millie, tall and solemn like her father, the eldest, who looked up from her chore of setting the table and stared at the visitors.

Samuel learned that Jake was an American sympathizer and began a scout's discussion as to the state of the fort and the Indians in the area. The family had not yet heard of the capture of Kaskaskia nor of George Rogers Clark.

"The British have been taking great pains to stir up the French against the Americans for some time. But I reckon the French pay little heed to them. As long as they can trade and live the way they want, they don't much care who is running the forts."

Samuel nodded. "And the Indians. Have they been peaceable here?"

Jake lowered his voice and leaned in a little. "You never can tell what they're up to; that's the only certainty with them. No trouble lately, but we live close to our rifles."

"Yes." Samuel grinned at the little girl, Rose, who was staring at him with big, round eyes from across the table. His own daughter's infant face flashed across his mind, then he quickly moved beyond it. "You've a nice family, Mr. Lynn. The farming good here?"

"Corn's as tall as Millie." Jake leaned back in his chair, grasped the waist of his daughter, and pulled her close. "We've been here three summers now. The first year was lean, but this year should be the best yet, eh, Naomi?"

His wife smiled and sat down, her hand finding his across the table. "We pray every day it will be so." Her face was tired, but she wore a contented smile.

Samuel's gaze sought Isabelle as she sat silently across from him. He wondered, for a moment, what it would be like to be married again, imagining what it would be like to live with a woman like Isabelle, to have children with her. And, for only a moment, he let himself imagine that this was his cabin, his life.

Something must have shown on his face, because Isabelle suddenly grinned at him, full of devilment and knowing, and sassed him by announcing, "I don't imagine growing corn is so exciting." Then quickly to her hosts, "Noble, I am sure, but I crave a life more adventurous than fields to hoe."

Naomi laughed, ladling steaming stew into bowls. "No, miss, growing corn doesn't hold much excitement," then she reached for Rose and pulled gently on a ringlet, "but feeding growing youngsters can be pretty satisfying, all the same."

"I suppose so, ma'am, but . . ." Isabelle sighed, seeming in genuine resignation of her own nature. "I want something . . . more . . ."

They all laughed, but Samuel felt a pang in his chest. He might be a man like this Jake Lynn, but Isabelle was no Naomi and never would be. It would be good to remember that.

Naomi rose from the table. "Speaking of youngsters, those boys should be back from the woodpile by now." With a frown she walked to the door. Then a thin, boyish scream rent the air. Then another. Naomi jerked the door open, her face void of color.

---

SUDDENLY, THE WORLD was chaos.

Indians charged into the cabin, tomahawks swinging. Naomi, being just inside the door, was the first target. A tall savage, heavily painted, with his head shaved save a tuft at the crown, grasped a handful of her hair and lifted it high above her head. Naomi screamed, wild-eyed, as he swung his lean, muscled arm, scalping her with one sure swing.

Samuel registered the blood dripping from the weapon as he snapped back to conscious thought and action. Naomi fell to the floor in a crumpled heap as Samuel dove for his weapon, seeing everything, assessing the enemy's strength. War whoops and a flurry of swinging weapons surrounded them, making it difficult to hear and see what was going on.

Samuel grasped his long rifle that had been lying on the floor beside his chair. He looked to Jake in time to see the blade of a knife being shoved into the farmer's chest, hearing the gasp of bubbling air that followed. Then Samuel locked eyes with Jake's killer who now turned toward Samuel, advancing, intending to kill the men first.

Samuel raised his rifle and shot his attacker through the heart. He then scooped up Jake's gun, took quick aim and fired again, killing the one he thought to be the leader, judging from his face paint and the ring of ornate feathers woven into his black hair.

With no time to reload, Samuel dropped the rifle to the floor and grasped the familiar handles of his tomahawk and knife.

Now would come the hard part.

Glancing across the room, he saw that Julian had been cornered and was without defense. Isabelle was in the other corner, rifle in hand, God love her. Samuel found he couldn't think clearly. Which way to go? Julian or Isabelle? Julian had no chance without his help. Isabelle was armed, but could he turn his back on her? For a moment he stood, motionless, wavering. He could not save them both.

The choice was taken from him as a warrior advanced. On instinct alone he fought off the Indian in his face, a giant of a man with a war club. Reaching out he grasped the club, feeling the man's strength pushing against him. Samuel allowed his foe to push the club up near his throat, a trick he had learned from Simon Kenton that misled the opponent to believe his enemy was weak. Just as the club touched his throat, Samuel put the full force of his muscle behind it, turning it neatly with practiced ease and smashing the man's head with his own weapon. Instinct had him moving toward Isabelle. Had she fired the rifle?

Out of the corner of his eye, he saw that Millie was hiding behind the door, unnoticed. He thought he had seen Rose hit but was reasonably sure she had crawled under the table, alive. He heard a gun go off, saw a warrior fall at Isabelle's feet, but another nearby was reaching for her hair.

Fighting off what looked to be little more than a boy, Samuel quickly knocked him to the ground with the blunt side of his tomahawk, ducking under the swing of yet another war club, moving deftly to drive his knife between the man's shoulder blades. Samuel was almost to Isabelle.

He heard her then. A sound coming from her throat, a screaming, enraged whooping as savage as that of any Indian in the room. He felt more than saw her stab her attacker with the long knife Clark had given her. The blade effortlessly penetrated his throat, immediately silencing the warrior, and he crumbled to the floor. With a quick jerk she pulled the weapon from his neck and looked up into Samuel's eyes, legs spread in a fighting stance, her black hair wild about her face, eyes flashing fire. "Julian," she breathed, knowing his thoughts and telling him she could take care of herself. Where had she learned to fight like that?

Samuel turned from her, pulled his smaller knife from his thigh, found a vulnerable spot between the upper ribs of the Indian to his right and buried the knife in his heart, thus clearing the path to Julian.

Only four enemy warriors remained standing. One, tall and hairless, with a lone feather hanging down his back, his face painted half black and half white, had backed Julian into a corner. Samuel saw that Julian had a knife raised, something that must have been hidden on his person. The warrior easily knocked it from his hand and advanced with a panther-like grace that bespoke his skill. This man was no mere brute; he knew hand-to-hand combat as a dance. Samuel had seen it before and knew that if he didn't get to Julian immediately, he was a dead man. And it wouldn't be a quick death either. This man would torture him.

The warrior in front of Samuel fell to the floor with a sinking thud. Samuel couldn't even remember how he'd killed him—he was fighting from his subconscious now, moving on instinct more than anything. He reached Julian, thinking the young man should have been dead long ago; it seemed to Samuel that hours had passed since the first Indian had appeared in the doorway. Something shifted inside him, and he realized: Something other than a cold-blooded massacre was intended here.

Samuel let out a guttural yell as the Indian swung his war club into Julian's body, dropping him to the floor like a rag doll. The savage turned then, sudden and aware, toward Samuel. There was a light in his wide-eyed challenge—a light of certain victory.

Samuel faltered as recognition bloomed inside him like an explosion.

It was Quiet Fox.

His wild, painted face and savage grace bore no resemblance to the sulking guide he had met on the trail . . . *but it was him.*

Samuel didn't have time to assimilate fully the implications of Quiet Fox's presence in this room. To his left, Isabelle had managed with light-footed swiftness to move closer to Samuel. In mere seconds she had picked up another rifle, loaded it, swung around in a semi-crouch, aimed, and fired, killing another assailant. The sound reverberated through the room as Samuel's heart swelled with pride. She was amazing.

Suddenly there came a horrendous cry from outside the cabin, and Samuel could now smell smoke. *God help us.*

Isabelle screamed then, drawing Samuel's attention away from the door. The man they had known as Quiet Fox had grasped Isabelle by the hair and turned her toward him. Time stood still as he swung back his mighty arm, and there he held his war club poised in midair. He turned his shaven head and stared, victorious and deep, into Samuel's eyes while Isabelle kicked and clawed at him. Then, with abrupt movements, the savage leaned his face into Isabelle's, his black eyes wide and demented, looking as though he had no soul.

Isabelle's face changed, from that of warrior to slave, her gaze now terrified. Samuel heard her gasp of recognition.

He dove for Quiet Fox's arm, wrenching it behind his back. He heard a crack as the man's shoulder gave way, then a grunt from the Indian. Shock and rage lit the Indian's features as he looked back at Samuel. Then, using his other hand, he grasped his war club and broadsided Isabelle across the head.

Samuel watched with a wave of sick dread as Isabelle's head snapped from the impact. Her eyes rolled back into her head. Her body dropped to the floor.

With a cry that came from such a deep place inside him he didn't recognize it as his own, Samuel launched himself onto the man, stabbing at him with his knife. But this Indian had unnatural strength. His arm, the one Samuel was sure he had broken, appeared suddenly sound. With a shrill scream the man turned, rolled his head back and forth on his shoulders, then brought down his war club.

The last thing Samuel saw was those eyes—those black, unearthly eyes.

Then *everything* went black.

# 10

A bright light was beckoning Isabelle. She looked up at it, blinking against the sharp intensity. She noticed how the light poured down through the translucent cloud of swirling waters where she simply free-floated. She looked down at her body, at the strange garment she wore, at the way she floated, up and up, through the clear blueness, her hair all around her, her body moving with preternatural grace. She could see her hands moving through the watery substance, helping to propel her along in an invisible arc toward the surface and the light. It was as if she was coming out of a deep sleep into another state of awareness where intense, flooding peace reigned supreme.

Now she saw an open door, and something leapt inside her, spreading pure joy throughout her being. *Yes. Yes!* The closer she moved toward the light, the more she strained with anticipation of an intense connection with it.

Then she heard the first faint strains of music. Soft at first, but slowly, achingly slow, it grew, rising and so beautiful she gasped. She detected the haunting echo of a bagpipe, joined soon by the yearning of a pan flute, instruments she had never heard nor known the name of before now. The music beckoned her spirit, reaching down and touching guarded chords inside her, opening her whole being, like a key to some place she hadn't known was locked. She was powerless to resist—couldn't imagine how she ever had. Stringed lutes and violins joined in, filling empty spaces in her body. Then the gentle hum of harp strings joined with angelic voices. They sang in a language she had never heard and yet was familiar, as if she could understand if she only listened long enough. The voices rose in crescendo with an aching sweetness, until her chest began to heave with pent-up sobs of joy.

Full of wonder. Full of love.

Yes, so full of love.

Swimming faster she hurried onward, wanting more, wanting the light to consume her. The music grew until it surrounded her, filling her and embracing her, touching her in a thousand different places at once. She let out another sob, feeling an enormous release. And then another as the music penetrated to her very core. Any hardness, any barriers she had erected, the doubts and worries and confusion of life—all melted away.

She was engulfed in complete love. It was something she had never felt before but recognized in a flash of insight that it was something she had hungered after and searched for her whole life. It was the missing piece.

Isabelle swam faster now, in a panic to reach it. Nothing mattered beyond throwing herself into that light, becoming one with it. Her arms pumped, her longing for the light rising until she felt she would burst with pure joy.

Her desperation increased as she suddenly realized something was holding her in the water. Something had a firm grip around her ankles, keeping her from rising any higher. She fought it, kicked at it, but to no avail. Its grasp held firm, as if it had rights. Angry, and with a frantic sadness that went so deep she could hardly breathe, she looked down to see who or what it was that held her firm between life and death.

The water below her was all darkness and movement. Then she was suddenly outside herself, watching herself panic as she searched the murkiness beneath her feet. Then the water changed somehow. It shifted.

She took a shuddering breath as she saw it . . . and screamed.

---

ISABELLE WOKE TO the sound of cries—her own—coming from what seemed a great distance. Awful, spine-chilling sounds. The sounds of the lost. Now a nightmarish dirge drummed through her body, pooling at her throbbing head.

She opened her eyes, saw the ceiling of the cabin, then images flashing overly bright, then snapping away, recent memories of angels and Indians, of light and terror battling to rise to her notice. She struggled to sit up, bracing one hand on the floor and slowly rising. Her head felt thick and sticky. Her eyes saw red all over her. The air itself seemed endued with blood—*my own?*—and a haze blurred her vision. She blinked several times, trying to clear it.

Her hand, she saw as she lifted it to locate the source of the agonizing pain in her head, was covered with the vital fluid, making her stomach spasm with dread. She found a long gash extending from her right temple up and into her hair and probed it with her fingers, trying to remember how it came to be there. Turning from the wall, she scanned the floor of the cabin, panic and sickness rushing over her. Bodies of several Indians lay at her feet. Further up, the body of a white man—Jake, wasn't it?—lay face down, arms raised above his head, hands spread wide in a death plea. Visual memories rushed over her, touching her skin, making it crawl for a hole to hide in. But her thoughts were so disjointed that she still couldn't understand what her eyes were seeing.

A faint movement from under the table made her suck in her breath and hold it, hold her whole body as still as the wall she lay against. She strained to see the small form, making out only a hazy shadow. Was it one of the girls? There had been two, hadn't there?

Then she saw Naomi lying by the door. Was her chest moving? Struggling to stand, Isabelle slowly picked her way over to the woman's side. Squatting beside her, Isabelle grasped her shoulder and shook her, trying not to look at the bloody, hairless top of her scalp. "Naomi . . . Naomi, can you hear me?"

The woman groaned and turned her head on the floor. She was alive. Isabelle shook harder. "Wake up." Turning to the form under the table, Isabelle motioned with her hand, thinking a daughter's voice would rouse a mother. "Rose, is that you? Come here, Rose. We must wake your mother."

A sobbing sound came from the shadow. Isabelle shakily stood, stepping over forms that she averted her eyes from, and coaxed the child from her hiding place. Taking the child's hand she helped her out, hugging her as she came into Isabelle's arms, the small body quaking. "Come, Rose."

Isabelle walked her back to Naomi, fighting the dizziness that threatened her head and clinched her stomach. "Rose, your mother has been wounded. But don't look at the wound, Rose. Just look at her face and shake her and call to her. Do you understand?" Isabelle looked hard at the little girl, who seemed incapable of answering, staring back in a glassy-eyed gaze.

"I'll do it," a voice said from behind the door. And then the face of Millie, sheet white but cognizant, peered at them from around it.

"Oh, Millie. Thank the Lord. Come and wake your mother." Isabelle motioned her over, marveling that the two girls were completely unhurt. Then remembering the boys, she looked up at the door and straightened, knowing she was going to have to go outside and look for them.

Her movements now growing quicker and surer, she picked up two rifles and found some ammunition, felt the core knot of determination that was so much a part of her. The long column of her back stretched to its full height, little by little, bone by bone, taking over the fear. This was the familiar. This was known.

Stepping over dead bodies and pools of blood, she made it to the open door. With a last look at the girls and Naomi still on the floor, she assured them, "I will return." Then she quickly loaded the rifles, stepping outside, staying close to the walls of the cabin, then the nearby springhouse, picking her way across the clearing.

Smoke billowed from the area of the woodpile. A few more steps into the open, and there, by the woodpile, were the farmer's sons. All dead, their bodies lying like blackened dolls on top of the blazing woodpile.

"No . . . no!" she cried out, now running toward the horrific scene. She fell on her knees a few feet away, knowing there was nothing she could do, rocking back and forth, sobs wringing from her throat. She was unable to tear herself away from the vision of a small arm dangling over a log, smeared black with smoke.

"Oh God, help us!" Her ragged cry rent the air as she covered her face in her hands. Just . . . trying . . . to . . . breathe.

She saw it then. In her mind's eye, the half-black, half-white painted face of the Indian that had struck her down. She remembered him . . . remembered his name. Quiet Fox.

Tremors of fear and anger and something else that she had no idea how to identify now overtook her, coursing through her body. She stood and ran about the area, ignoring the blood coursing down her cheek, the excruciating pain from the gash, searching for any sign of the man responsible for this tragedy. Searching for any outlet for a woman's anguished rage.

Finding no one, she finally stopped, breathing heavily, remembering the girls and how frightened they were, how long she'd been gone.

She rushed, stumbling in a shocked state at the entrance, seeing again and smelling anew the carnage of the cabin—once a haven from the elements for a frontier family, now a bloody grave won by the devil.

She took a long, deep breath. "I can do this," she said to no one and anyone. "I *will* do this."

Naomi was sitting up with a red-soaked rag held to her torn head. She was dazed and bleeding badly but alive, the scalping short of its mark. Isabelle looked around the room, at each body, carefully and thoroughly.

Where were Julian and Samuel?

*"Mon frère, mon ami d'enfance,"* she cried aloud.

---

A GROAN FROM Naomi had Isabelle rushing to her side. "Can you talk? Can you get up?" She had to get them all out of this hellish place.

Naomi looked at her girls, turned her mangled head toward Isabelle and nodded. "I can get up."

Isabelle held out her hand, helping her stand. They took a few breaths, waiting to see if Naomi would be overcome and faint. When she didn't, they turned toward the door.

Naomi said, "Go outside girls, it's safe now."

Isabelle nodded at their questioning looks as Naomi stopped and turned back, staring at the lifeless form of her husband.

His face was clear, no injury to mar its handsomeness. Naomi took a long look, then turned, hard-eyed, and staggered out the door. To Isabelle she said, "I see that you are not in much better shape than I am, but if you could get some food, a water bucket, and some rags out of the cupboard, I would appreciate it."

Isabelle nodded.

Isabelle managed to gather the supplies and carry the heavy burden over to a tree where mother and daughters now sat. She unwrapped some salve she'd found, not knowing if it could help with such a massive wound, trying not to look but unable to ignore the sight of Naomi's scalp. Isabelle helped Naomi press a fresh rag against the wound until the bleeding subsided.

The Indian who had tried to scalp her had missed his mark—a rare occurrence, Isabelle knew. Only the very top of Naomi's scalp was gone, and while she would never have hair on the top of her head again, she might live if the dreaded infection didn't set in.

"Naomi, we have to get you and the girls to Kaskaskia. Do you own a wagon, a horse, something to carry you?"

Naomi's voice was surprisingly strong. "In the barn, if the savages haven't stolen them, there is a wagon and two horses. They . . . they were Jake's pride and joy." She covered her trembling mouth with her hand, looking deep and dark into Isabelle's eyes.

There was such anguish in her eyes as she spoke her husband's name that Isabelle wanted to turn away, but she did not. They stared at each other, each communicating hereto unknown depths of pain. And something else, something they both felt core deep—the need for revenge.

Isabelle gripped Naomi's hand, looking hard at this woman whom she had only just met but who now, in this moment, was closer than a sister. "We can do this. Just lie back and rest while I ready the wagon." Her gaze switched to the daughters, her voice commanding. "You girls, stay with your mother. If the bleeding starts up again, come and get me. I will be in the barn." They looked so frightened, so in shock, that she didn't know if they had even heard her.

Naomi grasped Isabelle's skirt, stopping her. "My sons. Tell me what has happened to my sons."

Tears sprung to Isabelle's eyes. She could only stare at Naomi for a long moment, then whispered, "I found them on the woodpile."

Naomi turned her head away, her face ashen.

Before Isabelle had taken two steps, Naomi was calling at her again, asking, "And your brother? And Mr. Holt? I did not see them in the cabin."

Isabelle turned back toward Naomi. "They are not here. Which means they may have been captured. I have to track them if I have any hope of ever getting my brother back . . . and I must leave soon. Millie can drive you to Kaskaskia."

"You would go after them? Alone? You should go with us. Tell the American army what has happened and let them find your brother."

Isabelle shook her head. "I can't wait. The Indians may mean to torture them, and Julian could never withstand it. Tell the Americans that I will leave them signs to follow, gashes in the trees. And then we'll see . . ."

"See?"

"See what the Americans *really* mean by freedom." Isabelle turned to walk away, but Naomi stopped her in her tracks with a whispered plea. "Who are you, really?"

She slowly turned her head back to the woman with whom she now shared so much, her blood-soaked hair sticking to her shoulder, her gaze shattered. "I am only a woman like you Naomi. A woman desperate for the justice of God."

# 11

As the wagon carrying Naomi and the girls faded into the long summer sun, Isabelle fell to her knees. She closed her eyes, a beggar's wail rising to the sky.

"Father! *Mon Dieu!*"

She stopped, her throat too tight to go on. A sob burst from her throat, but she stopped the next one. She breathed deep and long and paused, not knowing how to begin her plea. Words from the Psalms, words her mother had read aloud to her from the Bible rang through her mind. Her voice started out small. Started out unsure.

"You live above the circle of the earth," she whispered, thick and heavy. "God of the sun and the stars, the mountains and the sea and all this glorious creation." She paused, remembering the light in her death dream, remembering the love. She tilted her head toward heaven, felt her long hair fall back to pool in the grass, felt her throat exposed.

With growing faith she shouted to the heavens, "Turn your eyes toward me. See my desperation, my great need. Julian, my brother, is gone. Samuel, my friend, is missing.

From all appearances, evil has won this day. But you, O Lord, are mighty!" She began to cry, to break. "You, O God, are powerful."

She thought more than said aloud the rest in quick staccato. "I need the wisdom of Solomon to track them. I need the strength of Samson to fight to regain them. I need the courage of David to approach the giant in this land. Clothe me with your power and might." She leaned forward, her long hair a curtain around her grief. Then she whispered, "Let us win this day. Let . . . me win."

Tears poured down her cheeks as she lifted her face toward the heavens. She sat still, in God's presence, basking in His love, knowing His power.

A warm wind rose and blew gently in her face, drying her tears. She stood, her knees strengthened, as though someone were holding her upright. Energy filled her. She turned toward the woods, mounting the borrowed horse that still carried the priest's old books. She didn't know which way to go, and yet she did. Somehow she knew.

---

SAMUEL WOKE TO the jostling of a horse. He was tied, his hands behind his back, his feet bound together, draped face down over the back of the animal, like a recent kill being taken to camp. His stomach heaved beneath him, making him think he might vomit or, worse, fall off. His head pounded where he had been struck down, but he saw no blood. He looked up to see that Quiet Fox rode just ahead, leading the horse Samuel lay on. He strained to take stock of the rest of the party, but there was no one else. Only the two of them.

Quiet Fox turned now, seeing that Samuel had regained consciousness. Black eyes, full of fury and satisfaction, locked on to Samuel's.

"Quiet Fox is a lie," Samuel bit out.

"Yes," the Indian smiled in agreement. "My name is Sunukkuhkau . . . *he who crushes*." He said it as if he thought this to himself many times a day.

"Why were you with Isabelle and Julian Renoir?" Samuel demanded, mustering up as much dignity as he could from his position.

Sunukkuhkau shrugged. "I am often paid as a scout."

"Then why did you desert them?"

The Indian said nothing, only dug his heels into the brown speckled pony he was riding. Samuel's head fell back against the jolting of the horse's belly while he contemplated his situation.

A shouting string of incomprehensible words rang out from behind them, causing Sunukkuhkau to slow and then stop. Samuel turned his head to see another Indian coming up behind them leading yet another horse. While the two Shawnee spoke, Samuel craned his neck to see Julian tied down to the fourth horse, much like he. He appeared to be unconscious, and blood dripped from a wound in his side onto the horse's spotted hide.

Samuel tried to retrace what had happened.

Julian had gone down first, then Isabelle, at the hands of this guide-turned-warrior. He could still see the Indian's crazed eyes watching him fall. He remembered the pain as it seared through his skull. The blow had been more forceful than someone of his size looked capable of, and Quiet Fox had fought them off easily. Samuel was amazed he was still alive.

Come to think of it, *why was* he alive? The raiding party had killed everyone else, hadn't they? Why take Julian and him captive? Was Isabelle dead too, lying in a bloody heap on the floor of the cabin? A deep wretchedness overwhelmed him at the thought. His mind replayed the blow to her head, her sliding, slow drop to the floor, her face becoming white and still. A fury filled him anew. He had to somehow break free and get back to her. What if she was alive and needed him? Samuel searched his feelings, the intuition that always stayed him in any circumstance, but felt only blankness, a void. Yet he chose to believe she was alive. Until he held Isabelle's body in his arms, he would believe nothing else.

Sunukkuhkau was watching him, allowing his horse to slow so that he could engage Samuel. When Samuel looked into his eyes, he wished he hadn't. The triumphant stare, filled with a sightless, single-minded malevolence, swept through Samuel's weakened body, making him shake inside. This was not like looking into the face of death; this was looking into the face of hell. And it was more terrifying than anything Samuel had yet experienced.

"Where is Isabelle?" he demanded, his voice weak and rasping. "Where is the woman?"

Sunukkuhkau looked troubled, kicking his horse into a faster gait. "Dead," he said simply, and Samuel got the distinct impression that the final blow hadn't been meant to kill her, that they had wanted her too. He let his head fall back against the horse's flank, watching the blur of woodland grass and trying to breathe, trying to still the tremors within.

They rode like this for another hour, Samuel fading in and out of consciousness but careful not to look back up, careful to focus his scattered thoughts on things solid, such as the horse's hide against his cheek, a stone or leaf passing by on the ground below, pretending he was somewhere else and that his sanity was not on the verge of forsaking him.

Finally the jostling stopped. Samuel saw they had arrived at a Shawnee camp. The encampment was small, with wigwams in neat rows, campfires burning with the smells of cooking meat, and dogs roaming the dirt path.

Men, women, and children emerged from the shelters and walked toward them, cautiously at first. Then Sunukkuhkau flung Samuel from the back of his horse, and their audience broke out in laughter as he landed, face first, in the dirt. His lips and face were covered with a fine film of dust, his head throbbing. Samuel took a couple of deep breaths, spitting out the dirt and turning his head toward the growing crowd. He watched as Julian was similarly thrown from his horse, landing on his back with a deep groan, slowly becoming conscious.

The Indians drew closer as Julian kicked out in a panic, crying out, "What is this?"

Samuel watched in utter rage as his captor kicked Julian in the side, saying something in their language that Samuel didn't understand but which brought a cheer from the spectators.

Julian had begun to sob.

Samuel shouted over to him, hoping to turn the crowd's malevolent attention toward him. "I'm here, Julian."

Julian's head jerked toward Samuel, his face marked with terror and relief and tears.

The ploy worked. Samuel's captor grasped him by the shoulders and heaved him up, like a prize won at the fair. He was pushed toward the crowd, Sunukkuhkau saying in a loud voice, "Long Knife! Behold the Glorious One of the Long Knives!"

Samuel recognized the name he had been given by the tribal chiefs.

The spectators grew more excited, talking at once, raising their arms with shrill yelps, celebration on their faces.

Samuel was shoved forward, falling in the dirt again, while another, younger brave was directed to untie his feet. Samuel waited, telling himself to be patient and not provoke them. There would be a chance of escape—he had nothing else but to believe it with all his heart.

He was hauled up again, seeing that Julian's feet were also now untied. They were pushed together as the Indian's placed leashes about their throats and led them in a triumphal parade through the camp, the people falling in behind them, shouting and whooping in victory.

Then Samuel felt a sharp pain as a walnut-sized rock hit him in the chest, heard laughter as he jerked in reaction, then saw others, mostly women and children, stooping in glee to pick up rocks. He and Julian held their bound arms up to cover their faces and heads as best they could as rocks of all sizes pelted them. A large one caught Samuel on the cheek, and he felt a fresh trickle of blood down the side of his face. Yelling over to Julian, who looked ready to collapse, he shouted, "Get behind me!"

Julian scrambled to obey.

This didn't please the crowd, but they seemed to tire of the sport and soon threw down their rocks. They grew silent and stared as one at the pair. Almost tangible malice carried across the air and wrapped Julian and Samuel in a suffocating blanket.

"Stand strong, Julian. They despise weakness. Stand strong."

Julian quaked at his back but nodded and adjusted his stance, trying to put on a brave face.

With little but strength of will, they held their terror at bay.

Samuel's captor began speaking again. Samuel knew many native tongues, but Shawnee was foreign to him, so he listened instead to the pitch and cadence of Sunukkuhkau's words, hoping to find some clue as to his intent. The Indian seemed to be reciting something, some chant or story, as they often did. Like a play, the speaker built the anticipation of his audience to a hot fever. As he reached the climax, his words took on more strength, growing louder and more boastful. Hardened warriors, hard-eyed women, and gleeful children all chanted back to him, then whooped again in victory, the sound sending fresh tremors through the young man at Samuel's back.

"What are they saying?" Julian whispered.

"I don't know. But they think they have a prize. They've won something this day."

"Why would they want *us*? Why didn't they just leave us to die?"

"I don't know. I've been asking myself the same. We will have to wait for events to unfold. Brace yourself with everything you've got, Julian. It will not be easy."

Next he knew, Samuel was bludgeoned again with a war club. Then he felt nothing. Then he saw nothing.

# 12

The woods were fast growing dark. Isabelle reined in the borrowed horse, a fine specimen that responded to her gentle guidance with the ease of long association. She dismounted, leading the horse to the sounds of water trickling over rocks. It was small, this stream she'd found, but it would suffice. Letting the horse look after its own sustenance, she kneeled by the water, scooping up handfuls to her face, first to drink and then to cool and cleanse her dusty skin. She scrubbed at the dried blood on her cheek, then carefully probed the gash, cleaning it the best she could. If she were in town, she would get stitched up by the doctor; but as that was not an option, she could only pray for a miraculous closing and healing of the wound. She had been talking with God constantly since departing the battle-razed clearing.

And her prayers thus far had been answered. She'd quickly found the prints of four horses leading away from the massacre. The riders had made no attempt to cover their tracks, which made Isabelle suspicious and cautious of a trap; but after two hours of solid riding, the woods growing deeper and darker, her progress had been uncontested. Yet the trail remained clear—broken twigs, roughened bark, and best of all, hoof prints in the soft soil of the forest floor, where moss and grass grew only in patches as sunlight found its way through the dense foliage to give them life.

Now she had to consider whether to stop and camp for the night. It was too dark to see anything, and she was loath to make a torch that would draw the attention of who knew what. She appraised her condition and the cover provided by her current location. She wasn't tired. She wasn't hungry. And now that her thirst had been slaked, she wanted nothing more than to go on.

"What think you, Samoa?" She had named the horse, temporarily at least, because she hadn't the heart to call it Horse. Samoa looked at her with intelligent eyes, as if considering the question. Smiling, Isabelle moved to a stand of trees just up from the creek and sat back against a tree trunk, picking burrs and nettles from her skirt. She leaned her head back against the trunk and closed her eyes. It would only waste time to try and track them in the dark. She would wait for first light.

As she drifted into a light sleep, images flashed through Isabelle's mind. A watery grave. Someone pulling at her feet. Then she saw a man, the sharp angular lines of his face changing into something bright on one side and dark on the other. He fought with a spirit that reminded her of herself when she danced in worship, only he moved with malevolent violence. She dreamed that the two of them floated above the ground, fighting as if underwater, eye to eye, hand to hand, neither giving the other a chance for a death strike, equally matched forces. He leaned into her face, eyes wild, so close she could feel his breath across her skin, like that of a dog panting. Then his face changed into that of the wolf she had killed by the river. She wavered only a moment. Then the wolf snarled and leapt at her throat.

Isabelle gasped awake, fear rushing over the surface of her

skin, raising gooseflesh, her breath rasping in her chest. Who was this fiend? Why did he want to kill her so badly?

A hissing rattle sounded immediately behind her.

She leapt to her feet, fear pounding in her like a battering ram, and ran from the tree toward the clearing and the water. "What was that?"

The moon had risen. She crouched, shivering in its pale, cold light. She backed up to a small ledge that overlooked the stream, legs braced, expecting an attack, trying to see through the darkness. A sudden breeze tossed her long, tangled hair back from her face. "What is it? Show me what it is."

Isabelle threw back her head and threw her arms out wide. "I want to kill him. I know it's wrong and . . . forgive me, but I want his life. Give me his life."

She heard nothing but the gentle wind blowing through the trees.

Clicking to the horse, she mounted. It no longer mattered that it was dark. Something beyond her eyes and ears was guiding her. She decided to trust it, determined that nothing would cause her to let it go. Speaking softly to Samoa, she headed back into the woods.

The horse, too, seemed to sense some kind of supernatural guidance. She easily sidestepped fallen branches and thick patches of stinging nettle. She turned, and Isabelle had a shaft of doubt, wondering if they shouldn't go around a grouping of bushes the other way. As she stopped, searching her feelings, an owl hooted off to the left. She grinned, turning Samoa toward the bird, then seeing in the faint moonlight the recently broken branches of a tree going that way. It was as if evil was all around them but could not touch them. She rode in the moonlight like water sliding through the grooves of a streambed—such was their path, laid out before them.

---

SAMUEL CAME TO with a strangled gasp as a strong, stinging smell engulfed him. He struggled to breathe, realizing as he rose to consciousness that a wet rag was being pressed over his nose and mouth. The sucked-in air stung as it made its way down into his lungs, causing them to spasm, giving him a moment's panic as he wondered if he was to rise to consciousness only to die now.

Then, behind closed eyes, he saw a vision of Isabelle's face. Saw her on a brown horse. Saw her coming to them.

She was alive.

Turning his head, he fought, kicking, rising up, jabbing with his shoulder. He heard a grunt of pain as his shoulder struck something solid, the rag suddenly gone. Taking great gulps of fresh air, Samuel's eyes opened and blazed with anger at his captor. A stout Indian woman glared back at him as she backed away. She threw the rag into the fire, where it quickly caught, turning bright blue with a sudden blaze, soon engulfed by the whole.

Samuel spit the evil taste from his mouth.

"Water," he demanded, looking hard at the woman.

She considered him for a moment, then acquiesced. She turned away, coming back with a hollowed-out gourd.

His hands were still tied behind his back, so the woman set the edge of the gourd on his lower lip and tilted it up. Water trickled down his chin. Samuel gulped down as much as he could before she took it away. The woman smiled, showing a gap-toothed grin, as if his earlier attack had pleased instead of riled her.

Samuel struggled to adjust his sitting position, swinging his legs toward the edge of the sleeping pallet. He rolled his neck and shoulders, trying to lessen the ache in his muscles.

"Your name?" he said to the woman.

The woman shook her head, not understanding.

Samuel gestured to himself with his chin. "Samuel." Then he jutted his chin toward her. "You?"

The woman's face broke into a smile, pleased she understood. "Chinkachook."

Samuel nodded gravely, relishing this small success. If he could keep any kind of upper hand with the enemy, he could win. He tilted his head to the side and swung his hands out from behind his back as far as he could, gesturing. "Untie?"

The woman comprehended immediately, shook her head no and scowled as if to say, *Do you think me a fool?* Samuel couldn't help but acknowledge that it was a ridiculous request. Sighing, he settled for another. "Food? Eat?" He imitated chewing with his mouth, thinking that he had to keep her focused on sustenance, something women everywhere knew womb-deep.

The woman nodded and brought out a bowl of what looked like corn mush. Samuel made himself swallow as fast as she ladled it into his mouth, knowing any food would bolster his strength.

Sunukkuhkau stepped into the wigwam midway through the bowl, causing the woman to shrink back and avert her eyes. "Get up," he demanded in thick English.

Samuel glared at him from under scowling brows. But he obeyed, scooting to the edge of the pallet, shifting his weight to his feet, then struggling to gain his balance.

"Why didn't you kill us when you had the chance?"

The Indian smiled, spreading his lips over straight teeth. "I want the honor of your death, Glorious One of the Long Knives."

Samuel scoffed. "Let Julian go. He is only a traveler on an errand. He is nothing to you."

Sunukkuhkau reached for Samuel's arm and jerked him toward the door. "I wanted the woman. I will settle for the brother."

# 13

Isabelle startled awake to a shaft of pain, feeling like someone had thrust a knife through her skull. She righted herself in the saddle, blinking rapidly into the morning sun, realizing that she had fallen asleep on her horse and was about to fall off. She touched her temple where it throbbed, hoping these tortuous episodes would soon pass.

She licked her dry lips, realizing that she must stop, get her bearings, and locate traces of the captive party. Water, too, was a telling need hovering at the edges of her mind. Food and water. Her stomach was gnawing with hunger despite the pain-induced nausea.

A sound, shrill and heart-faint familiar, pierced the dawn. She felt her flesh crawl, started to panic with recent memories, hauling on the reins to stop and listen. She knew that sound well now.

The scream died off, giving way to the cheers of a crowd. Isabelle nudged Samoa's flanks in sudden urgency. As the woods gave way to a well-traveled path, she leaned low over the horse's neck whispering words of encouragement.

*"Venez la rapidité le jour, mi, mon doux."*

The sounds grew louder as she approached. It had to be the Shawnee camp. She reined Samoa in behind a large stand of trees, then leaned over and petted the horse's silky withers. "Make no sound," she admonished.

She hefted the rifles and ammunition, checking the powder, ascertaining that the guns were loaded and ready. She then carefully guided Samoa through moss and brush, deeper into the tall trees, hoping the uproarious shouting coming from the village would cover any sounds the horse made. As they gained ground, she nudged Samoa to the edge of the trees, then stopped, took a deep breath, and pushed a large, leafy branch out of her way.

Then she saw them.

---

SAMUEL WAS PUSHED and prodded like a recalcitrant mule into the bright morning sun, the wind whipping through his gilded hair. Much of it had torn loose from the twine he used to secure his ponytail and now hung in his face. He allowed his head to fall back for a moment, soaking in the illusion of freedom, his gaze sweeping the tops of the tall poplars and white ash surrounding the campsite. The wind sounded like the rush of waters over stones in a creek bed. His arms ached, his shoulders ached, and the wound on his head throbbed red and pulsating like an angry hive of bees . . . swarming . . . needling . . . constant in its demand for attention.

In the center of the village stood two lines of Shawnee. Whole families stood strangely excited with clubs and sticks in their hands, their faces wearing varying degrees of paint.

And Julian. Julian stood at the head of the gauntlet,

trembling and blindfolded, unaware of what was about to happen to him.

Samuel yanked free of Sunukkuhkau's grasp, and looked up into his captor's dark eyes, so unreadable, so deadened.

"No," he heard himself appeal. "Take me instead. I'll do it."

The Indian gave him the same smile as before, that look of certain death and the preeminent relish of it. "Have no fear. You are first."

He shoved Samuel to the beginning of the gauntlet, pushing him into Julian, who fell to the ground, his face a fear-mask around the scarlet cloth of his blindfold.

One of the Shawnee bent to untie Samuel's hands, ignoring Julian.

"Samuel? Is that you?"

"It's me," Samuel replied grimly over the yelps and excited chatter of the Indians, the feeling rushing back into his arms in waves of prickles and heat. He reached to help Julian up.

"What are they doing? What . . . what's happening?" The young man's voice trembled, reminding Samuel of himself as a small boy, afraid of noises under the bed, in the wardrobe, in the dark.

"We're to run the gauntlet. Looks like I get to go first."

"The gauntlet?" Julian's knees buckled.

Samuel reached out to steady him. "I see you are acquainted with the tales of such a test," Samuel said with forced levity, trying to cheer him. "It's nothing but sticks in the hands of children. Brace yourself, man."

Julian nodded, his hair sweat-pasted against his forehead, his lips trembling and compressed in a white line. He was too young for this. Too frail. Everything in Samuel wanted to protect him from it, but there was nothing he could do.

Samuel turned to the parallel lines to study his tormentors, saw their faces change from celebratory to malevolent, saw where the strongest braves stood, noting with rising concern that Sunukkuhkau held a tomahawk.

He meant to kill him.

Their voices rose in a cacophony of frenzied, fatal intent. Samuel braced his legs, ready to run like he hoped he could, thankful for the coaxed gruel of the morning, wishing he wasn't so stiff from yesterday's battle and that his shoulders didn't ache so from being bound all night. He leaned into a starting position as he had when racing his friends as a boy. With shallow, rapid breaths, he waited for the signal.

The Shawnee, seeing a man determined and showing no fear, grew more animated, ready for their chance. Even the children glared with murderous eyes, waving sticks above their heads in his direction. Samuel took a deep breath and blocked them from his mind. With extreme focus, as if he were looking down the sights of his long rifle, he directed his full intent onto the grassy space at end of the line, his landing place in this trial of pain.

Without warning, a brave shoved him suddenly forward, causing him to falter at the beginning, almost falling beneath the sticks of the children before even reaching the real test. He righted himself, feeling the hits against his legs and chest. The yelps around him intensified as he plunged forward, blows now raining down on his head and shoulders, back and thighs. Long shafts of pain radiated through his body. But he ignored everything, blotted out all feeling except the motion of his feet, the solidness of the earth beneath his moccasins. He took mighty strides, his whole body straining for that patch of grass that would mean he had passed their test.

---

ISABELLE LET OUT her held breath as Samuel collapsed to his knees at the end of the line, not realizing that she held her rifle trained through the leaves on the man who had shoved Samuel into the line of torture. She had heard of such tests but had never seen them, and she didn't know what to do. What did it mean that he had completed the gauntlet? Would they make him run it again until he succumbed to their blows?

She dashed tears away, but her arms remained strong and steady. Her heart might be galloping, but her thighs kept the horse still beneath her. She felt her determination grow into something rock hard, and she knew she had to stand and watch this horror. To wait for an opportune moment.

---

THE INDIANS SEEMED glad of Samuel's accomplishment, cheering for him now and regarding him with respect. Samuel, lying on the grassy patch of hope, could only pray that meant he was safe, for now anyway.

He was heaved up, bloody and torn, his flesh open in areas, his head light and fuzzy but mostly in one piece. They stood him at the end of the line so that he could have a clear view as they took up the next victim. The atmosphere turned from one of admiration to sneering hatred, their voices renewed with whoops of victory.

Samuel watched as they removed Julian's blindfold, his eyes sweeping the crowd with their clubs and sticks waving at him, not comprehending what was about to happen. Samuel could see his knees begin to shake. Fear coated his gaze as it finally settled on Samuel.

"Keep your eyes on me," Samuel shouted. "Julian, do you hear me? Don't fall. And run, Julian. Run as fast as you can."

Julian nodded that he had heard, but his whole body was visibly shuddering now.

A long, singsong scream pierced the air, causing the Indians to quiet and raise their weapons in anticipation. Another cry was raised, and Julian was shoved forward. He nearly fell right away.

"Run, Julian, run!"

Julian darted forward, sinking toward the ground as a club came down on his shoulder. He tottered but, with a giant step, caught himself and continued running, arms covering his head, a feeble shield of flesh and bone.

Samuel watched in dismay as the blows rained on the young man, slowing him to a crouching, staggered sideways motion. Samuel ignored his own screaming flesh, legs that wanted to collapse, and instead cupped his hands to his mouth and yelled encouragement, wanting badly to be able to explain that if Julian failed this test, the Indians would likely burn him at the stake. He wanted to shout that the Indians understood only strength and courage and that he must make it to the other side. There would be no second chances. No mercy.

Julian was bleeding profusely now from his face, his shoulders, arms and legs. Samuel cried aloud as he saw him falter again, almost stopping in the middle of the line. "God, help him! Help him!" he heard himself beseech. "Look at me, Julian!" he shouted with all his might above the yelping of the tribe. Julian stumbled, one knee nearly touching the grass, but he looked up, and Samuel lifted his arms, his muscles quivering with the effort, wanting to infuse some of his strength into Julian. Julian rose up, stood against the war club that slammed into his back, and sprinted a few more feet forward.

Samuel's throat was raw. "Run! Run! Run!"

Sunukkuhkau stood near the end of the line. He turned and stared into Samuel's eyes. The Indian's chin jutted up and forward and, without even looking to see where Julian was, he swung his tomahawk around in a slow arc toward Julian's head.

Samuel heard screams. He didn't know if they were his or Julian's, but he saw the sudden red stream, watched as the young man faltered and folded, the culmination of an easy victory. *Oh God, have mercy!,* Samuel silently screamed, head thrown back, eyes clenched and then open again.

Then, in all the confusion, he heard another kind of scream.

"Nooooo!"

It rose and fell like a lilting eulogy song from the trees in the distance. His head jerked toward the woods. He knew that voice, knew it deep in the core of his being.

Isabelle had come.

# 14

As Isabelle watched Julian run the bloody line of torture, and as each blow landed, odd flashes away from this time and place played across her consciousness. She saw him as a little brother, as he'd been in her mother's house, peaceful natured, sweet, the very opposite of her own fierce-eyed bravado. She remembered how afraid of the woods he had been, eyes wide and shaking his head at her, how she'd had to goad and tease him to follow her into its dark recesses. She remembered his resistance at trying anything new and outside his range of comfort, the bow and arrows their father had brought home for him ending up *her* first weapon, so little he'd touched it, and finally, how he had held the bow out to her with that look. Julian couldn't bear to take a life, not even to fill an empty stomach.

The guitar had become his favorite pastime. And as they grew together, they learned how to depend on one another's strengths and cover for the other's weaknesses. They would support or deny, concealing and protecting, depending on the circumstances. She may have been braver, but when her foolhardy ways got her into trouble, he had been her lightning rod, grounding her to the solidness of the earth, and giving her the perspective of an unchangeable nature.

Now her brother lay in a heap on the dusty ground, as if his bones had dissolved and left only a small mound of flesh, his ghost hovering over him.

She watched, heartsick, horror filling her as they dragged him to his feet, shook him awake, then shoved him toward the front of the line again. One of his legs collapsed beneath his weight, broken and twisted away from his body. He fell with a weak cry. Isabelle's stomach turned over as tears raced down her dirty cheeks. They couldn't make him run it again! He couldn't do it.

The Indians must have thought otherwise as they raised him up and carried his limp frame to the front of the line. Samuel was straining against the two captors who held him, trying to get to Julian. Isabelle could hear his cry ring across the camp. "Let me! I will run it for him!"

They ignored him, tightening their hold on his struggling body.

She couldn't help what happened next, her protective spirit rising and compelling her forward. She heard the scream leave her throat, felt her heels kick Samoa into action as involuntary as breath. She charged to her beloved brother's rescue, abandoning her hidden place among the trees.

Just as they shoved Julian forward once more, the sticks of the weaker women and children at the head of the line beginning to rain down on his battered body, Isabelle shot out of the woods, a banshee war cry ripping from her throat, a shot ringing from the rifle in her arms.

---

THE INDIANS STOPPED, frozen by the chilling scream, and turned as one toward the vision from Hades that was charging at them from the woods. Leaning low over the horse's neck, Isabelle rode as the wind, her long, black hair whipping like a living, black flag behind her, her eyes blazing with the certain promise of death.

One of their braves, the one next to Sunukkuhkau, crumpled to the ground. They could barely comprehend that he had been felled by the rifle, such was the distance between them. This dark rider could not be human. As one they backed away from the oncoming she-devil, fear in their eyes, shrieks like even they had never heard coming from her throat.

All were terrified but for Sunukkuhkau and Samuel, both of whom were smiling. But it wasn't the same smile, not the same smile at all. Sunukkuhkau said aloud in English, "She was dead. She has risen from the dead!" He let out a war whoop and shouted again in his native tongue.

---

SAMUEL TRIED TO take advantage of the enemy's momentary distraction. Thrusting his full weight into one of the warriors at his side, he knocked him to the ground, then quickly spun toward another one, deftly taking the knife that dangled from the man's side and using the blunt side of it to cudgel the brave to the ground. It would only take moments of heart-pounding, breath-rasping running to escape, and this might have been the wiser choice, but he couldn't. He couldn't leave Isabelle and Julian at their mercy. Instead, he raced around the perimeter of the gauntlet toward her, watching as she pulled rein before them, the other loaded rifle leveled on the chief, clearly identifiable by his age and ceremonial dress.

Samuel took his stand beside her horse, facing their enemy together.

Isabelle's hair settled around her like a great, dark cape, her eyes flashing fire. "Release my brother, Julian Renoir, or your chief will die." She had the rifle trained on his chest, and they had seen what she could do with a rifle.

Sunukkuhkau whooped, a warlike cry, drawing some attention away from her, then translated. Samuel reached up and grasped the horse's reins, ready to mount and flee with Isabelle should the need arise. Isabelle didn't even glance at him, her focus steady and menacing on Sunukkuhkau, daring him to make her a fool.

The Indians' voices rose in a cacophony of confused sound. They wanted to know who she was.

Sunukkuhkau walked over to Julian, lifted his lifeless body by the hair, and stared straight into Isabelle's soul while saying in English and then in Shawnee. "She is nothing but his sister."

Samuel recognized that this wasn't exactly the best argument Sunukkuhkau could have made as the Shawnee, like most tribes, understood the deep rivers of family loyalty. He knew this was why he had been captured instead of killed outright at the cabin—he'd taken more than one of their brothers over the years; and his scalp was highly prized, his torture well planned. Just because he'd run the gauntlet successfully didn't mean that they loved him now. No, their plans for him had only begun. Julian, though, appeared already dead, but Isabelle was clearly bent on saving him and wasn't letting that thought enter her head.

My, but she was beautiful up there on her steed, a woman warrior. She was like something from history—Joan of Arc or Mary Queen of Scots going to her beheading. So regal and utterly righteous.

The chief stepped forward, his slow, arthritic joints making stiff progress of the walk to Isabelle. But his eyes bespoke long authority and the willingness to see justice done.

Sunukkuhkau dragged Julian's body over to Isabelle, standing beside his chief as the tribe looked on in shock, wondering how this turn of events could have happened, still wondering what power this woman could possibly hold. For she must be an evil spirit, a charmer of some sort to have their honored men walk up to *her.*

Isabelle looked down into their faces with metered hatred, glancing only briefly at her brother's face.

The chief began speaking. Sunukkuhkau translated. "Your brother lies in our hands this day, given to us by the gods to assuage our grief for the many brothers we have lost to the Glorious One. Many braves have died under his blade." He gestured toward Samuel.

Samuel only stared back, eyes blank of anything save confidence. He had done only what he'd had to do to survive and help the frontier settlers survive. He wouldn't regret it.

Isabelle flashed him a look, comprehension dawning across her face. In a loud voice she said, "My brother has nothing to do with your fallen brothers. We hardly know this man you call the Glorious One. Let me have him." She kicked out at Samuel, rejecting him in front of the assembled tribe.

Sunukkuhkau smiled his feral smile, then translated, but the others looked upon her in confusion. Were these white ones not united?

The chief shook his head. "The Glorious One has passed the test in the manner of his name. He will be adopted into the tribe." He glanced down at the unconscious Julian, and scorn filled the loose, tan folds of his flesh. "We will burn this man for our fallen ones." He looked consideringly at Isabelle. "And you will become wife to Sunukkuhkau, and your offspring will live to burn the white man from our land. We will be stronger with you and Sunukkuhkau together, strong together."

There was a great shout of victory from the Shawnee. Up it went, like the smoke from their fires, like the beating of their drums, declaring victory over their oppressors.

Isabelle pointed the rifle once more at the old man. "I only want one man here. My brother. I will not leave without him."

The chief did not look afraid. His eyes turned cold and not a little admiring. "All the stars here will fade," he predicted quietly, the people straining to hear, "but yours will live on. Yes, I can see it." He closed his eyes, a smile playing across his thin, wrinkled lips. Then abruptly he opened his eyes and stared hard at her. "Put away your gun, child. You will not kill this day."

Clapping his hands once, he gathered everyone's attention. "I would keep this woman among our people so that we will live forever. Julian, the weak one, will burn."

The Indians rose and cheered, their fists to the sky.

Isabelle held tightly to her gun and looked into Samuel's face for the first time.

"What have you done?" she whispered.

# 15

The sun was going down. Aquamarine streaked the western sky between swaths of red and orange, a fiery sunset that lit the edges of the hills and the creeping darkness of leafy forest shadows.

Shawnee warriors took hold of Julian, rousing him to consciousness. Wild-eyed with fear, he was dragged toward a spot where wood was being heaped upon a fire. Julian was quickly lashed to a stake and raised up among the rising flames.

Isabelle lifted her rifle, aiming at the chief's back.

She was jerked from her horse by Samuel and held tight to his chest, her gun, now wrested from her, in his hands.

"Let me have it!" she screeched, wildly trying to disengage herself from his hold.

"You'll only assure all our deaths by killing the chief."

Sunukkuhkau pulled Isabelle from Samuel's arms, and Samuel quickly backed away, the rifle ready in his hands.

Isabelle looked back at him with horror, with hatred, as they laid their hands on her and dragged her toward the scene. Her eyes told him she would never forgive him for this betrayal.

The spark and crackle of the fire brought her head around as she turned toward the scene and gazed, shock and fear, shock and despair, shock and sick dread rising to her throat at the sight. The fire was catching, rising, hungry for food. Julian's eyes were open, searching for her.

She held his gaze as they hauled her to the front of the intent throng, barely aware that ropes were being twined around her wrists, binding her hands behind her back, binding her in a slower death than Julian's.

All she could feel, all she could see, was her brother's terror-filled gaze.

A chant grew among them, their throated grunts rising up and up into the fading light. Isabelle's head fell back, her throat exposed, working in a silent scream. She opened her eyes, her head dropping to one side, her dark, heavy hair swaying and pulling. Screams, her brother's and her own, filled the air. But his eyes stayed wide on hers.

Isabelle would not look away and deprive him her meager comfort. She would look upon his horror, feeling that life had ended, that she had been consigned to a hellish place where people did this to other people.

"Julian," her voice croaked. "Julian!" A bereft soloist sounding loud against their cheering gong, she wailed, panting, flinging herself away from her captor's grasp and onto her knees as the flames caught his shirt, covering his face in a red, merciless blaze. Wild hate and fear now penetrated her every fiber. She collapsed, her captors on either side of her hauling her up by the elbows like the arms of a cross.

Then a shot rang out, exploding against the noise, its verdict loud and final. Julian now lay limp upon the stake, a trickle of life oozing from the middle of his forehead.

Isabelle's head jerked back, saw Samuel standing a short

distance away with her smoking rifle, saw him throw it to the ground and hang his head.

She fell to the ground.

---

THE WOMEN OF the tribe took her then. Their thirst for vengeance unquenched, enraged that Samuel had stolen their victory, they came at her, a mob of hate, women her age and younger and older, their tanned faces totem masks of fury, tearing at her clothes, scratching and hitting and kicking.

She fell to the dusty earth. Felt its grains in her mouth and eyes, felt the blood flow where their aim was true, felt her clothes being torn from her, heard the ripping and knew the exposure, sudden wind against a cold sweat.

Naked, her torso bathed in blood, she lay beneath them as they spent their anger, until finally they drew back, panting from their efforts. But their eyes promised something more to come.

Isabelle pushed herself up with her bound arms to sit among them, her long black hair a dusty curtain around her, a veil against the nakedness. She looked up and saw Sunukkuhkau approach. His eyes took her in, all of her, even those parts covered by her thick hair, showing satisfaction that she sat in the dirt, wearing a film of it, that she cowered before them.

At that, Isabelle, her hands still bound, gracefully rose upon strong muscular legs. She stood tall and proud, her legs braced apart. She shook her hair back, not caring that she relinquished her covering. She stood strong and tall and glared back at him. Only blood would cover her body. Her blood. Their sin on her. Nothing else. She glared in challenge at him.

The warrior broke into a smile, looking her up and down, admiration in his eyes. "You will be mine," he said with a broad smile.

It was a stupid man's smile.

Isabelle tilted her head, her hair hanging to her hips at one side and narrowed her eyes. "If you think so, then you shall prove yourself a fool."

At her words there was a scuffle to her right, and she turned toward the sound. It was Samuel, bound now and straining against it. He was pushed toward her, knocking him into her. He sought her gaze. "I am sorry."

"Wake me up," she breathed. "I can't wake up." Tears sprang to her eyes, the blindness a blessing.

Samuel closed his eyes. Then he took a deep breath and leaned close to Isabelle's face as they dragged him away. "Stay alive. Do what you must to stay alive." He heaved the words through the air between them. "Have faith."

Isabelle blinked out the blur, her shattered gaze roaming his face and then his bindings, pointing out the obvious without saying it. She turned away and looked down at her trembling thighs.

A sob tore from her throat as she fell forward. Her brother. Her childhood friend. Gone. And for what? Her throat, raw from wailing, worked in silence, the tears dried with the blood on her face, empty of more.

*Where is my Savior? Where is my Savior now?*

# 16

They hauled her up, two women, one stocky and regal, wearing a dark-yellow deerskin dress decorated with turquoise beads, the other tall and slender, wearing a lighter dress of skin, almost white, with a beautiful broad face and straight, white teeth. As they dragged her away, Isabelle craned her neck to catch a last glimpse of Samuel's receding back, thinking this was the end for both of them. She screamed to go to him, her bound arms reaching toward his body, but they hauled her up and toward the river.

They stumbled, the three of them, in their haste through the forest bramble toward the sound of water. It was a sound Isabelle had always cherished, the music to her dance, but she was sure that this time they meant to hold her under that sound until the life was gone from her. So she fought them, they being women and she being unusually strong.

She got away briefly, ran at full strength, though out of balance because of her bound arms. She stumbled, fell. And they were on her, hushing her with words she didn't understand. Guttural sounds, nothing like the flowing French she adored from her father's lips. Nothing still compared to the clipped English of her mother's tongue.

These sounds came from the throat and sounded much like the strangulation of the water she imagined was her grave. She swatted at them with her shoulders and knees, her strikes as innocent as a fly's she realized, dazed. *Please God, if they would only untie my hands, I could do so much more!*

Arriving at the narrow bank, they shoved her into the cold water. Deeper and deeper the three moved, like a small school of fish connected by unseen forces of moonlight. When her breasts were covered they stopped, taking up a rag and some soap that seemed to come from nowhere. They dunked her, and she shook her head back and forth under the water, feeling clumps of hair floating around her, wondering how long the pressure of their palms would remain on the top of her head. Suddenly she was up again, being soaped from head to toe. They carefully worked the lather through her hair against the last of the sun.

Then her face. The rag was gentle as it washed away the blood from her eyebrows, cheeks and jaw line, her lips, the crevices of her ears and down the long column of her neck. Isabelle just breathed. Like a stallion in the thrall of the corral for the first time, her nostrils flared in rebellion. It was a raspy breath, out of her nose, then her mouth, through her teeth, making a defiant noise that rasped with anger and hate and fear at not knowing what to expect next.

Finished with head and hair, the women pulled her up the bank to wash her body, the soft squishy mud registering for the first time on the outer consciousness of Isabelle's mind. Were there snakes in this water? She had never willingly taken a bath in the river. Hot kettle water and an iron tub was the only bathing she had known, and she hadn't taken them very often, a fact her mother despaired of. But these women seemed determined to scrub her completely clean. What was it they wished to wash away?

She drifted in and out of shock and semiconsciousness.

Without comment they led her, dripping, naked, and clean beyond anything she'd ever known, back to the shore. There they cut her bindings and dried her, clucking now, like mothers, the two of them sharing some precious daughter. They patted her with soft blankets, careful to dry every pore, rubbing every strand of hair till the life was flowing back into it.

Then they held out a beautiful dress, made of deerskin like theirs, but covered with multicolored beads in sparkling, sweeping patterns of delight against a pale blue-dyed background. They slipped it over her head, helping her place her arms through the long, fringed sleeves, then standing back and admiring her, cooing over her dignified beauty. They put moccasins on her feet, matching the dress in color and adornment.

Then they brought out a comb. It must have been a European comb, for it was of finest ivory and had perfectly set teeth. Directing her to sit, they slowly, carefully combed out her dark glory, exclaiming over it, their smiling faces hovering like benevolent gods saying, "It is good." As it dried, her hair became a silken curtain draping her to the waist in a tumult of dark waves.

Isabelle sat mute under these astonishing ministrations, no longer knowing what to think, what to feel. Her brother was dead, and they, these sudden mothers, were making an Indian maiden out of her. It no longer registered with her that her ropes had been cut, that her hands hung free, that she might fight and run. She could only sit silent as the stone on which they had placed her.

The women led her back to the village, displaying her like a conquering princess, as if they had bathed away the English, the French, the American even. As if she were one of them, their daughter, and a prized one at that.

Isabelle found herself holding her chin high, wondering in some small part of her mind where they had taken Julian's body.

Would there be a grave to visit? Would they allow her the freedom of gathering woodland flowers to adorn his grave? Would she really be alive long enough to do such things?

They gently pushed her into a wigwam filled with women and children, where the smoke tried in vain to escape through the small hole at the pinnacle of the structure. Would that she could become a vapor of smoke and lift up and away into the freedom of the night sky, turning into a wisp . . . and then nothing at all. She turned her head away, her only rebellion left this day, then collapsed on the appointed pallet. And blessed sleep rushed over her.

---

SAMUEL STOOD WATCHING her being led away, seeing the flash of her bare thighs in the pale, lingering light, seeing her hair sway back and forth, black as the panther and as ready to strike. His heart sank.

Never in all his days had such regret filled him. What had he done that they had come to such unimaginable fate? How had he not saved them?

His Isabelle.

Now more than ever, he knew it to be so. She had been taken from him, but she was his. And he would fight, regain her in some way. Whether the next days proved it or not, she belonged to him, no matter the past and his previous commitments.

The warriors led him to a longhouse and gave him food in a wooden bowl which he wolfed down, knowing better than to turn up his nose at it. He was then directed to a pallet. He lay down, turning away from them on a soft fur, looking up through the smoke hole and seeing a single star shining a cold and unreachable light, like himself unable to sleep.

THE NEXT MORNING Samuel awakened suddenly and rolled, unbound and with a freedom of sorts—an adopted son's freedom—from his sleepless night, and stood straight and tall, braced for whatever was to happen next.

They took him out into the center of the village where he saw Isabelle being similarly led from a different lodge. She was dressed in a long, light-blue dress, the hem mid calf, showing an expanse of skin between the hem and the top of her moccasins, looking like an Indian maiden. He inhaled as their eyes met, willing her strength for what was to come.

They were placed together, sitting side by side, in an ever-growing circle of Indians waiting in silence. Samuel could hear Isabelle's shallow breath, but she would not meet his eyes.

A sudden, loud careening cry split the dawn, as if a bereft spirit had left the owner's throat, fleeing across the distance to the place where they sat.

Isabelle tensed, nearly panting.

Another woman's voice added to it, raising and then dropping in apparent agony. Then there were others, moaning and wailing, falling to their knees, shrill and crying. One old woman dropped directly in front of Samuel and Isabelle, her tanned, wrinkled throat straining to cry out. She moaned, her head thrown back, the thin skin of her arms wrinkled and upraised. She was joined by her sisters, throwing themselves onto the ground beside her, joining her cry, so close Samuel could see the tears track down their cheeks.

"What?" Isabelle gasped to him, looking at him full in the face for the first time. "What are they doing?"

Samuel leaned toward her, his shoulder touching hers. "They are mourning."

Isabelle's face, that beautiful, fierce face, turned toward him and demanded, "Mourning for what? Not my brother?"

Samuel stared at her, wanting more than anything to pull her into his arms. "No." He shook his head slowly back and forth, not breaking the contact of their eyes as their captors' cry grew deafening. "They are mourning the loss of a loved one. One of their own."

"But why? Are we not the ones who should be mourning?" Her eyes were slashes of raw pain. "Should *I* not be the one mourning this day?"

"Yes." Samuel looked down into his lap, wishing, wanting more than anything, that he could have spared her this. He looked again into those deep blue eyes, the eyes of a stormy day. "Yes."

Isabelle then rose to her feet, suddenly against them. She stood tall, her chest thrown back, her head falling back, her hands balling into fists at her side. He watched her take a deep breath, knowing what was to come, knowing that she didn't understand that this was their adoption ceremony.

Isabelle's exhale became a cry. Like theirs . . . but not. Deeper, then rising to a scream. Stronger . . . more guttural than even these could manage. She stood to her full height, threw back her shoulders, and wailed her anguish, her arms slowly rising until they lifted full toward the morning sky. She inhaled once more. The cry that followed was so great, so piercing, that the authors of her death cry drew back in silent horror, staring in awe at her brilliance.

She reached up and tore at her hair, shaking the waves of blackness around her, a mourning cloak. Her cry grew, loud and then whimpering, full and then still, shrill but softer, shaking her hair about her, eyes and fists tightly clenched, railing toward the sky, toward God.

And then she turned on them.

The Shawnee were a passionate people. They knew the

depths of expressing their grief, but this . . . this frightened even them. Her eyes opened, and Isabelle leaned at the waist toward them, sweeping from one end of the crowd to the other, impaling them with her gaze and her outstretched arms.

Samuel saw their astonishment of her.

A captive was taking over their ceremony.

She glared her hatred at them. Her arms swooped from one side of the gathered Indians to the other as she spoke in a quiet, harsh voice, looking each of them in the eye as her gazed passed by—the women, the braves, the children, even the chief. She feared nothing and no one.

"You killed my brother."

She confronted them, first in English, then in French. Then again in English.

Samuel wanted to reach up and grab her, even found himself on his feet beside her. He wanted to tell her that this wasn't the way, that they must play their part for a time, pretending to be a newly adopted son and daughter while plotting their escape. He wanted to tell her to trust him, that he would find a way. That he knew these Indians, knew their customs and their ways, knew how to work them to his advantage. But all he could do was stare and feel her grief, fighting a clog of emotion in his throat. He knew there was nothing he could do. She would have this moment of blame, even if it meant the end of both their lives.

Then he realized, biting back the words to stop her, that he was willing to give whatever price for her. She deserved this moment.

---

AS HER WAILING quieted into rapid, short breaths, Isabelle collapsed back to the hard earth, taking fistfuls of dust from the ground and pouring them over her bent head. The sobbing subsided, and a deep, hate-filled silence enveloped her. When she finally looked back up, she once again glared her hate.

Samuel sat back down beside her. "This is an adoption ceremony. They grieve their lost ones, then adopt us into the families that need replacements."

She turned toward him, her chiseled, dirt-streaked face so disbelieving that it made him wonder how he'd ever accepted it.

"And whom will I adopt?" she whispered in a hiss. "Who will assuage the loss of *my* brother?"

She turned, half-mad, toward an Indian boy and pointed at him, causing the lad to lean toward his mother. "Him? Will *he* be my Julian?" She pointed at another, older man. "Or him? Will he magically become my best friend?" She threw back her head and laugh-cried, a sound that sent chills down Samuel's spine, then abruptly stopped and stared back at Samuel. "Only a fool would replace a brother with a dog." Her eyes were slits of scorn. "Only desperate, stupid hearts could so easily replace a loved one."

"It is their way. Isabelle, we must go along with this, or we will be lost."

She tilted her head and stared at him, through him, scorn and sadness filling her eyes. "Can you not see? They cannot do anything more to harm me." She smiled, and it was not lovely. "I am already lost."

She rose, turning away from him, then walked calmly away from them all, her back strong and straight, toward the charred remains of the fire that had taken her brother.

Samuel and the whole tribe turned and watched her kneel at the site. She reached toward the ashes, like a mother gathering her family to her, and slowly, methodically, rubbed ashes into the deerskin they'd adorned her with, turning the dress from a lovely sky-blue to the gray of her grief.

# 17

They had continued with the adoption ceremony. Samuel was renamed Patamon, meaning "tempest." Isabelle, too, was renamed. They called her Cocheta—"That You Cannot Imagine"—and Samuel had to agree that it fit. He noted that they seemed afraid even to look upon her still form sitting at Julian's grave site. Such a thing must never have happened to them before, a captive turning their mourning against them, mocking it to their face. No one knew what to make of her. She had practically dared them to burn her, but they clearly feared her. Even the chief looked uncertain.

After the ceremony, a quiet affair now, they led Samuel to his new family. A tall, thin man, about his age had lost both a father and a son. Samuel understood that he was being greatly honored by replacing both. Apparently he was worth two family members. He was led to their lodge, given new clothes—a breechcloth, a deerskin shirt and breeches for cooler days, and a pair of moccasins. The woman, his new "mother," fawned over him, carefully preparing his dinner of cornmeal and pumpkin. She brought him the food, waiting patiently beside him to see if he liked it, but he could hardly force it down, wondering what Isabelle was doing. Where was she? Was she fighting them? Would she force them to kill her? It seemed to be what she wanted.

As soon as seemed permissible, he said in his stilted Shawnee that he needed to go outside. The woman nodded and opened the hide flap for him.

Isabelle was still there, prostrate now, covered from head to toe in ash and dust, looking like she was trying to bury herself. He turned away, knowing that he couldn't help her yet. He would let this scene play out, watch for any opportunity to rescue her.

---

THEY FINALLY URGED her up, and she seemed spent and willing. She was led to a different lodge from the one she'd slept in the night before. Two women, the two who had given her the bath, offered her a skin of water. Her mouth was full of the grit of the earth, and she found herself willing to drink the water, feeling it cool and sweet as it slid down her dry throat. They clucked over her ruined dress, pulling it from her slack body. She had little strength left to resist them.

Naked, she stood before them, seeing out of glassy eyes as they sponged away the dirt, dressing her in another dress of softest deerskin, brown this time, plain but clean.

The world had rounded strangely on her, facing her, asking her what she would do next, her face burning from hours in the sun.

"Rest, Cocheta," one of the women said.

She was led to a pallet of furs where she obediently collapsed. Nearly asleep at once, she suddenly roused, rising up on an elbow. "What did you call me?"

"Cocheta. Shawnee name," the tall, stately woman said kindly, as if Isabelle had been given a mysterious gift.

Isabelle slowly blinked at her. "My name is Isabelle Renoir." She lay down again, cradling her head in her curled arms. "Isabelle . . . my name is Isabelle Renoir," she said in a whisper before succumbing to exhaustion.

---

THEY WOKE HER the next morning, these two benevolent women. She didn't care who they were or why they thought she should be made to be like them. She didn't want to know which family had "adopted" her. What job they would give, what food she would eat, what man had "won" her as wife. She turned away from their attempts at conversation, ignoring their efforts to embrace her. The older of the two directed her to sit while she slowly and patiently brushed out Isabelle's long, dark hair. Isabelle sat mute as her wild dust tangles were fashioned into braids.

Sitting under their ministrations, she remembered her mother. Dear God, it seemed so long since she'd seen her face, and Isabelle knew, deep within her being, that if she ever saw her mother again, everything would be different. She was no longer a girl. Or a daughter even. But she clung to the image of her mother's face, her eyes so pretty against her dark-blonde, swept-up hair, her countenance so kind despite the hardships of life. Isabelle envisioned that sweet, beloved face, holding it close, while they tightly braided her hair.

Isabelle had never let her mother touch her hair, at least, not for as long as she could remember. She'd always rejected the customs and fashions of her day, instead twining brightly colored ribbons brought back from her father's trips, tied to her crown and twirling throughout the long, wavy mass. Her mother had soon given up. She recognized Isabelle's spirit for what it was, calling her "little gypsy" and accepting her despite the girl's habit of flinging a hand in the face of society. Her father, too, had approved. And so she'd always roamed her own way, sticking close to her heart's song.

Now she waited as they bound her hair, patient as a cat lounging upon the wrinkled bark of a tree limb, eyes slanting, seemingly convalescent. As soon as they were done, as soon as they stood back to admire their handiwork, Isabelle slowly rose to a regal stance and turned toward them. Looking the two women in the eyes and smiling her cat-confident smile, she reached for the first braid. A tiny laugh escaped her throat as she untied the cord at the bottom of the braid. Her gaze turned condescending as she quickly, surely unwound their intricate work.

They stared at her in uncertainty as she unbound the other braid. She shook out her hair, running her fingers through its glorious length, her chin up.

Then she called to them, making her declaration, "I am Isabelle Renoir. My parents are Joseph and Hope Renoir of Vincennes. I am an American and a supporter of George Rogers Clark and the Long Knives." She paused, growing still and strong, finishing with a narrow-eyed hiss, "*And we will win this day.*"

She smiled at them then, a little crazed, throwing back her head and laughing out loud. Her laugh resounded about the room like a trumpet's blare. Then she turned her gaze on them, daring them to gainsay her.

They stared back in shock, not understanding her.

So she shouted at the top of her voice into their faces, "I will always be Isabelle Renoir!" She took a menacing step toward them, threw out her arm, and pointed toward the exit. "Leave me!"

The two women scrambled to get out, Isabelle's mad cackle chasing them like a haunting spirit.

They didn't approach her the rest of that day. She was left alone, without food or water, sitting in the lodge, feeding the fire with sticks she found piled in a corner.

She fed the fire, not because she was cold, for she was too cold to feel cold. No, she fed it because she wanted to see the hunger of it, consuming each stick, watching it turn into ash and vapors of smoke as it rose toward the opening of this paltry stick hut. She fed it like she fed her hate. If only they would come and burn her too. . . .

It was all she wanted.

---

AT DUSK, IN their desperation, the women sent Samuel in to talk to her. He brought her a small bowl of deer broth, which she ignored, looking at him wild-eyed with hate.

"What do you want?"

"Isabelle," he said simply, his hand reaching in aching need toward the air around her. "They think you are a witch."

She saw his chiseled, distressed face, and a laugh escaped her throat. A victorious smile curved her lips. "Good."

"No. This is not good. Do you know what they do to witches?"

She turned from him, sinking down onto her pallet. She rubbed the supple fur, feeling its softness, gathering it to her throat, then looked up at him. "I don't care."

"You should." Samuel moved to her, knelt down beside her cot, and set the steaming bowl on the ground.

His chest was bare, and he looked like a white man playing dress-up. Isabelle imagined him as a boy who'd lost some game with his friends and had to play the part of "the Indian." She chuckled aloud. Her first impression of him, in armor, as a knight of old, fitted him so much better. In his Shawnee garb he looked . . . displaced . . . dishonored . . . and deeply concerned for her.

He reached for her hand, and her gaze traveled up his strong, tanned arm.

"They will try to cut it from you," he said. "Little slices from your flesh that they will poke pine needles into to flush out the evil."

One of her dark, elegant brows rose in derision. "If evil dwells in me, they'll not find it in my skin. Tell them to cut into the soul, Samuel." She flung his hand away and lay back on the bed, looking at the ceiling. "Others have tried to take it from me. See if *they* can find the root of it."

"You don't know what you're saying." He squatted beside her, his hands loosely clasped together. She stared at his fingers, seeing them intertwined, wanting that closeness with him, even here, even now.

"I am not afraid of pain." Her voice was as the dead.

"You know not what you speak!" Samuel reached for her hand and raised it to his cheek. "Even if you could bear it, I could not."

She slanted him a look. "What care do you have of me, Samuel Holt? Tell me the truth."

He looked momentarily befuddled, adrift, then stared at her. "I only want you safe."

She laughed, leaned in to kiss him full on the mouth.

"Fool." She said it compassionately, as if she spoke to a child. Her head tilted, and a long curtain of dark hair cascaded to one side, pooling on the cot. "Nothing will ever be safe again," she whispered. Then she smiled, leaning back into her fur nest, giving him a heated look. "Maybe I am a witch."

He exhaled. "No."

She tilted her head at him, smiling her cat's smile again. "Are you certain? You don't really know me."

He pulled her from the bed, made her stand, drawing her close to his chest. "You are devastated by what has happened, and rightly so." He looked down briefly, pressing his lips together. He took a deep breath and looked back up at her.

She saw his face in that moment of pause. *The Glorious One*, they'd called him, and she could see it. His hair, so blond, like a child's, his face chiseled male authority. Strength rode high on his cheekbones, his hooded eyes seeing more than what his vision perceived. Isabelle saw his whiskers, darker blond, covering his lower face, but still sparse. And his lips. He had wonderful lips.

His next words shook her from her spell.

"You are a coward. I never thought it of you. You are giving up."

Isabelle stared into his amber-colored eyes, the color of molten honey, and didn't like what she saw. A challenge. And so much compassion. Her breathing increased as she allowed it in, turning her head away, hiding the sudden tears.

"They burned him. In front of me."

"Yes."

"I can't bear it."

"Yes, you can."

"I can't. I'd rather die than bear it."

"Look at me."

She looked at him.

His eyes filled and spilled forth. His face was warm, radiating heat toward her, real and alive.

She reached up to touch his cheek. She exhaled, breaking.

"I can't breathe if I don't hate them."

He pulled her close, burying his face in her neck, clasping her to him. His breath moved over her neck, up to her ear, where he rasped, "You might want to die, hope to die, pray to die to bear the pain of it. But you . . . will . . . not . . . die."

His lips grazed her jawline, caressing her other cheek with his thumb. His mouth found hers.

"You can't leave me," he said.

His lips moved over hers, taking her breath and giving his, infusing his strength into her.

She felt his lips moving over hers. Felt the heat and the life, resisting at first by the immobility to his words . . . and then giving in, grasping his shoulders, feeling the muscle, the life of him. Her hands moved over his chest, then up to his shoulders, wrapping around his neck and hanging on, hanging by the last sane thread to this man, this moment, this lifeline in a wild sea, never wanting to let go of something so solid and real.

"I am yours," she breathed into his mouth, wanting nothing more than to be his.

He only kissed her more deeply. He pulled her flush with his body until there was nothing between them. "Then live." His hand clasped the back of her head, his fingers splayed through her hair, holding her in the palm of his hand. He kissed her deeper.

Isabelle lost herself, giving over to this falling, flailing feeling. It was a feeling of pleasure, so opposite of the pain she'd been diligently building a wall against. Maybe she did want to live. Live with this man. No matter the cost of bearing up against such horror every day. Maybe it would be worth the sacrifice.

She pulled back suddenly, breathing heavily. "We have to escape."

"Yes," Samuel breathed, holding her to him.

"No." Isabelle stopped his advance. "Now. This moment. Before they can come and take this away from us. Sunukkuhkau will make me his wife."

He looked dazed, coming out of their passion dance. "How?" he whispered, understanding her meaning. "How can we escape now?"

"I don't know." She grasped his hands. "But we have to try. In the next minute, in the next day, they will change us. I can feel how hungry they are for us. If we give in, it will destroy everything we are meant to be."

Samuel stared at her, looked down at the foreign soil of the lodge house, then back at her, and nodded.

He looked into her eyes. "I will get word to you when I think the time is right. One day very soon. It should be after midnight. Two hours after you are certain they are asleep, then we will leave."

Isabelle nodded, grasping his face, staring into his eyes.

"Meet me in the trees, where you first watched the gauntlet. I will wait for you, and if I'm not there, you will wait for me."

"Weapons," she said. "We'll need them."

Samuel nodded, smiling a little and shaking his head as he said, "You know, I should have been the one saying that to you."

Isabelle drew back, her lips a bud of provocative nectar. "Do you think so?" She laughed in pleasure. "You don't know me well enough then. But you will. You will."

She reached for him and took a deep breath. Taking his hands firmly into hers, she said, "You don't need the strength of weapons to endear me to you, though you are renowned for such strength. Let me tell you what I feel for you." She took a deep breath and leaned in. "I, Isabelle Renoir, will relinquish my *revelation* of myself to you. No matter what occurs, I will only, ever willingly be *yours*." She leaned upon his chest, her face buried in his warm skin, as if she'd just given him all of her.

Samuel lowered his head, breathing in her scent, her hair, grasping a handful of the dark silken waterfall. He looked close to tears. Overwhelmed. Undone. "You will always be yourself," he whispered.

"*Non.*" She looked up at him, feeling sad and happy at the same time, a death and a birth in the same day. "Together . . . together we will be more than I could ever hope to be."

They stared at each other, both ravished, both fierce, not knowing how to reconcile such a thing. These Indians would not recognize this covenant they had made. The Shawnee had their own plans for their prized captives.

---

THE ONLY THING Samuel knew for certain was, it would never be a light thing, his being the one to whom Isabelle Renoir gave her heart.

# 18

Sunukkuhkau approached her in seeming deference. A princess holding court over an iron pot, she watched him with her peripheral vision, eyes appropriately downcast, trying to fool them and play along now that she'd given her word to Samuel, but still she tensed.

She had expected Sunukkuhkau to drag her off and rape her or force her to a heathen altar, but neither had happened. She'd seen little of him these past days beyond sudden, brief nods and looks—looks that held her terrorized as to their meaning.

He would show up at odd times, never allowing her to be fully prepared for the battle of wills to come. This time she was bending over a cooking pot, watching the meat turn from pink to brown, taking in its acrid odor, giving cause to her lean frame.

"You cook again. That is good."

She smiled, rising, remembering her moment of rebellion earlier that morning when she had spit in it as she'd stirred. "Will you taste it for me?" she asked in feigned innocence.

He nodded eagerly, not having learned from their past skirmishes.

She held out a steaming spoonful, benign lips curved upward, eyes slanted. He took it to his broad lips, inhaling the steam as he shoved it into his mouth. Immediately he spat it out, cursing in his native tongue and turning on her.

"You poison me!"

She shrugged. "I never said I could cook," she said in his Indian tongue. It was the only phrase she'd thus far bothered to learn. Then she laughed, quickly ducking her head in mock humility.

At her laughter his face changed from anger to something else—something heated that brought true concern to her belly.

"You speak truth," he said simply, nodding once, considering. "Come." He held out a long, tanned, muscular arm.

Isabelle studied the hand. It was as human as hers, and he might take her away from her womanly chores. Nodding once, she took it.

The moment she did, had it firmly clasped in hers, she glanced up and saw him, saw Samuel for the first time in days, their vows of escape echoing between them across the expanse of the camp. He was staring hard at her and this Indian. She jerked her hand free, heat filling her face.

She wanted to run to him, her body straining to do just that. Her insides burst into life. Exuberance. Anger. Longing. Just to hold his face between her palms. Just to have that chance. It was what gave her the courage for this place.

Sunukkuhkau followed her gaze, then looked quickly back at her, making her realize her mistake. They couldn't know—these savages could never know her feelings for Samuel. It might mean his death.

Taking sudden grasp of Sunukkuhkau's hand, her eyes

slanted toward him in a way that no one had ever taught her but that she knew would work, she said a bit breathlessly, "Show me."

He stared hard at her, uncertain at this shift, then caved in, as they all did, and nodded, leading Isabelle away from the camp and toward his longhouse on the outskirts of the camp.

Once inside the small dwelling, he proceeded to take up many weapons, holding some, putting others aside. Finally, he handed Isabelle a delicately carved bow. He leaned into a corner, bringing out a deerskin quiver of white suede, full of arrows, their ends adorned with brown dappled feathers. It was like nothing she'd ever seen, and she gasped in delight. She reached for it.

He walked slowly toward her and murmured something in his tongue, but she could only shake her head, looking longingly at the prize.

"*C'était à ton épouse?*" Isabelle looked up into his eyes, reaching tentatively toward the offered gift. "It was your wife's?"

He nodded, placing it firmly into her hands.

"What happened to her?"

"Smallpox. A slow death."

Isabelle looked down at the prize, then back up at the warrior. "I am sorry for your loss." She nodded at the gift. "*Merci.*" She grasped it tightly.

He smiled then—a big, toothful smile that softened the harsh planes of his cheekbones. "She did not shoot it," he said in stilted English.

"Not a huntress?" Isabelle asked in French, switching to something more comfortable for him.

"*Non.*" He was still smiling. "She cooked . . . good." He patted his bare, taut belly.

Isabelle couldn't help but laugh, looking up into his dark brown eyes, caught for a shared moment.

"It was meant for you." Sunukkuhkau smiled, turning serious and intent.

Isabelle shook her head. "How can that be? You didn't know I would come here."

Sunukkuhkau leaned in toward her, then looked up and around at the ceiling of the tent, motioning with his muscled arm, a dance-like movement that held her to the floor, the familiarity of it so strong. "The spirits knew."

Isabelle caught herself looking up as if some being lived in the stretched animal skin of the roof. "Did they?"

Sunukkuhkau nodded. "Our grandmother knows all things." Then he took her gently by the shoulder, leading her outside and toward the edge of the woods.

---

THEY TRAVELED QUICK FOOTED and well matched through the forest. Isabelle found to her disquiet and a small thrill that she could match him step for silent step, that she knew instinctively where they were going and even somehow seemed to lead at times.

Deeper and deeper into the forest they roamed, taking long drinks from the same hide filled with cool, clear water. Never talking. Only stalking . . . looking for the prize.

About midday they saw their quarry. Its silken fur blended with the forest bramble, revealing itself to their eyes only when the animal twitched an ear. Isabelle raised her weapon. The bow was tight, never broken in, and took more strength to draw back the arrow than she thought it would. Her chest heaved with the effort, but within moments she had the measure of the bow, knew instinctively the draw length and cast of the weapon. She looked down the sight, feeling Sunukkuhkau's presence beside her—so still, so confident in her, so . . . proud. She found she wanted more than anything to show him she could do it.

The deer looked up, some sixth sense alerting it to danger. Isabelle let the arrow fly. For a moment she thought she had missed, and then a red mark appeared in the deer's neck. It bucked, kicking up its hind legs in a shock-dance before bolting. Sunukkuhkau quickly pulled back his arrow and let it fly. It lodged just above Isabelle's, causing the deer to fall, lashing out in the leaves. In the moments it took Isabelle and Sunukkuhkau to reach her, she had stilled.

Sunukkuhkau put the beast out of its misery with a knife to the heart region, then stood back to smile broadly at Isabelle. But as she gazed at his lips, she saw the feral edge, knew him in the moment in the cabin where he'd fought her in his war dance, remembered her brother, falling and now fallen. She relived it all in seconds—the battle of the cabin, the blaze of Julian's pyre, the women beating her. She turned her back to the warrior.

How was it possible that she felt so torn into two persons? Half of her exhilarated in the kill and his exultation, while the other half was filled with hate and dread toward this man who had helped to murder her brother. Then came the waves of guilt, overwhelming her, incredible guilt that she could look this murderer directly in the eyes, that she had even once touched his hand.

Quickly she turned, fleeing him, running through the forest, her moccasins quiet and soft and comfortable and suddenly hated, tripping over exposed tree roots, desperate to outrun her panic.

She heard soft steps behind her gaining ground, making her run faster, her legs stretching out against the hide of her skirt. Silent tears coursed down her cheeks as she panted with the effort of escape.

He caught her then, his long, lean fingers wrapping around her pumping arm, stilling her feet as they twisted toward him in the dry earth. Like a colt roped, she bucked against his grip, pulling away, her hair wild and in her eyes.

"Let me go," she snarled.

He just stood there, staring at her with those chiseled features, the dark eyes that nonetheless were readable—patient, cold, sure, waiting for her to comprehend her defeat.

"No." She shook her head slowly back and forth answering his unasked question. "Never."

"Let Samuel go. He will be a great warrior."

And there it was. They had thought they were so secret.

"It is not Samuel I won't let go of." She pulled away from him, and this time he turned her loose, causing her to stumble back. But she didn't fall. She would not fall.

Instead she took a few steps away, then stopped, her moccasins turning in the dust. She turned her head to stare back at him and smiled the smile that only she had. Isabelle. Isabelle! She let it fill her face, she felt it catch . . . glow, her voice a radiant hum. "My name is Isabelle Renoir."

She breathed as if she had just run a race. And she had. She was running to keep herself. Quieter, but with strength, chest heaving, her head down but her eyes locked with his, she said it again. "My name is Isabelle—'consecrated to God.'" She dared him to deny it, her head tilting in the fading light as it gave way to forest shadows. "Say it, Sunukkuhkau, say my real name."

"You would be Cocheta—That You Cannot Imagine. What more glory could you seek?"

She exhaled in a laugh-cry. "Why would I want to be something you cannot imagine . . . when I can be set apart to God, my Creator? I could never desire more."

She took a step toward him, her brows together, her words an entreaty. "Don't you see? There is nothing you can give me that I don't already have."

His lips pursed together as he inhaled, deep and long. He stood straight, his chest expanding. "You reject a great honor."

She laughed at him. She couldn't help it. A crazy joy rose from her throat and expanded throughout her body until she threw back her head and laughed with the joy of it. "Yes!" She shouted to him and to the treetops and the forest and to the spinning circle of life around them. "I reject what you have to offer me." Her laughter died down, and then she just stared at him. "I don't *need* you."

He watched her as if she possessed some magic, looking afraid for what must be the first time in his thirty-some years.

It was clear to both that she was as sure in her faith as he was in his.

"I will kill him if you will not come into our way."

Everything in Isabelle grew still. The laughter suddenly stopped. The sure faith wavered. She wavered. "Whom will you kill?"

"The Glorious One will die beneath my blade."

"Samuel," she whispered, not wanting to give anything away. She knew. She wasn't stupid. She knew that the next few moments could mean life or death to the only man she would ever love.

She had gambled her own life with threats of her identity in her Creator, but she hadn't known this brave would see the truth of her heart so quickly, so completely. She decided to try for bravado and ignorance.

"Samuel doesn't want your greatness."

"You know not what you say."

"Then enlighten me." She raised her brows at him. "Why should we forsake our Father, our God, for yours?" The question hung, long and penetrating into the shadows, challenging him.

Sunukkuhkau looked momentarily at a loss, as if all people should know this. "He would be honored, in life and death—a legend that our people's children's children would tell of."

Isabelle laughed. "He is already a legend, and a reluctant one at that. *My* hero was burned at your stake. And I will see that my children will remember *him* forever."

She leaned a little toward him and smiled even—it was a fierce victory smile where there was no victory at hand. "You won't have us," she hissed on a breath. She let her head fall back, saw the tops of the swaying branches of richly green leaves and laughed, the sound building and building until it rang out in the forest.

"God in heaven, hear me," she shouted. "They won't have us!" Then, quieter, almost as if to herself, "You will be my Savior."

She looked back at Sunukkuhkau, leaning toward him and breathing into his face. "My God will save us. And even if He does not, I will still love Him."

Sunukkuhkau stared hard at her, taking hold of her arm again. "What god can save you from my strong grasp? If my god blesses our union, none other will destroy that."

A passage from the book of Isaiah sprang to her lips. It was one of many of her mother's lessons in memorization of Scripture. Isabelle quoted it often, internalizing it for this time and this place. "Be strong, fear not: behold, your God will come with vengeance, even God with a recompense; He will come and save you."

"My god is strong," he said but looked uncertain.

She smiled, as if to a child. "Your god is a grandmother." She gently pried Sunukkuhkau's fingers from her upper arm. "My God is the great I AM. The beginning and the end. The Alpha and Omega. Test Him, if you've the courage."

Sunukkuhkau seemed to consider her offer, then nodded. "We will test the gods."

Isabelle felt a tiny tremor of doubt, of fear. Had she stepped out of the boat onto the waves of a mad sea? Would God, Yahweh, really show up? But she stuck out her chin and nodded. "What shall it be?"

Sunukkuhkau slanted her a look. "We will wait. To see what the fates provide us." He motioned with his arm toward the camp. "Let us go back."

She realized at that moment that he carried the deer with him, that he had run after her, nearly silent, for nearly a half-mile, with a two-hundred-pound dead animal on his square shoulders.

It was something she would not have been able to do.

She looked down . . . and saw the waves.

# 19

Samuel breathed a sigh of relief as he watched Isabelle pick her way across the village toward him. He didn't know what had happened between her and Sunukkuhkau that long afternoon. But upon returning she had given him a nod and an intense look. A signal.

Something had happened. They needed to make their escape.

Tonight.

Now he watched as she clung to shadows, crouching when he would have, walking like a delicate deer, the fringe of her dress swaying in the moonlight.

It had been easier than he'd thought, getting her the message that tonight was the night, then sneaking out of the lodge. His "family" had fallen into a deep slumber over an hour ago, but he'd waited, wanting to be sure and to give Isabelle more time.

Then he'd turned abruptly, as if in sleep, while grasping up a tomahawk that Miakoda, his new brother, had stowed under his cot. There was a rifle on the other side of the lodge, but Samuel had only gazed at it in longing, taking the more prudent path to the door.

Once outside the rustle of the fur a mere whisper as he'd moved beyond the door, he paused, looking around and forcing himself to breath evenly.

All was quiet outside. Even the village dogs seemed tuckered out past curiosity. Had he been planning an escape with anyone else, he would have made for their lodge to help.

But this was Isabelle.

If anyone could escape with as much stealth as he, or Simon Kenton or even George Rogers Clark, it would be her. He found he had complete faith in her abilities.

Now he smiled, watching her move with the shadows, knowing that if they could put a mile between them and the Shawnee before the hue and cry was raised, they might just make it.

She reached the tree and threw herself silently into his arms, kissing him square on the mouth. Just as his breathing was turning deep, she reared back and whispered, "Shall we take horses? It would be ever so much faster."

Samuel shook his head. "Too much noise." He noticed how heavily armed she was and grinned. "I see that you took your own advice."

She glanced down at the tomahawk in her leather sash, the rifle grasped in her left hand, then nodded, smiling. "And look," she raised the hem of her dress to reveal two, long, wicked-looking knives, "one for each of us."

Samuel resisted the urge to laugh. "You were more successful than I. I have only this." He raised the tomahawk in the air, feathers fluttering.

Isabelle gasped. "Your new brother's tomahawk? You didn't!"

Samuel chuckled and nodded. "Stole it right out from under him."

"It's a good thing you will have me nearby when he comes after it," Isabelle teased as she handed him one of the knives. "You will need help."

Samuel reached over and kissed her temple. "Ye of little faith," he chuckled into her ear. "Come, let us move."

They started back the way Isabelle had come, she remembering the way better than Samuel as he had been semiconscious for most of the trip to the village.

They didn't talk now, just ran-crept through the moonlit marsh, swooping under branches, leaning and dodging and jumping over bush and bramble. The night air was crisp, invigorating them, giving strength to their legs. Samuel was surprised at how fast she could run and for how long. But he chided himself, knowing he shouldn't have been surprised at all. This woman could do anything he could. But more than that, it was her spirit—it rooted him somehow, gave him some grounded purpose that he hadn't known he lacked.

They had been at a dead run for over an hour when Samuel heard the first sounds of pursuit. Horses. He paused, leaning and breathing deep for a moment as Isabelle stopped and turned back toward him.

"What is it?" she panted. "Are they coming?"

Samuel nodded, scanning the area, looking for opportunities. They could run, or they could hide. Those were the only options.

Isabelle must have been thinking the same. "We have to go on. They will find us if we try to hide here. There is nothing but skinny trees for cover."

He didn't have time to debate with her, and anyway, if she could keep pace, they might be able to reach better hiding. "Do you hear water?"

Isabelle nodded and was off toward it before he could say another word.

They tore through the woods as one, breathing ragged, side by side, breaking trail for each other when the way became too narrow.

The pursuit remained at a distance but was gaining. The Indian ponies were quiet—no noisy harnesses, no clattering metal shoes, and as trained in the dark as their owners. But still, they made enough noise for Samuel to know that they were gaining on them. It wouldn't be long now.

---

ISABELLE REACHED THE river first, Samuel at her heels. The water rushed and glistened like a world of its own. They plunged into its glittering darkness, legs kicking under the water, weapons and Isabelle's skirt dragging them down. Isabelle shrugged off the rifle and threw it aside just as a noise behind them broke from the trees.

Isabelle didn't know how much further she could go. Her lungs felt ready to burst. The horrible, blinding headaches that had receded in the past days came back with a bludgeoning effect. She found herself sinking below the surface, darkness enveloping her.

A hard kick of her legs pushed her back to the surface. She gasped for air as her head broke free, her wet hair a heavy weight around her face. She was soon pulled down again, felt the water lap against her cheeks and then her eyebrows and then the top of her head. Her dream in the aftermath of the cabin massacre rushed over her, something she hadn't allowed herself to remember.

So, it had been prophetic then.

This was how she would die. A watery grave.

She sank deeper, unable to make her legs move fast enough to carry her up. She opened her eyes under the water, wanting to see her last, dim, watery moments. The water was dark, but as she turned her head back and forth, seeing only the little bubbles of her last breath, a shallow shaft of moonlight penetrated the depths and reached toward her.

She felt a hand on her upper arm dragging her up and clung to the arm just as she felt the water seep into her nostrils.

Samuel and Isabelle broke the surface together to shouts and shrill sounds coming from the bank of the river, and somewhere in the back of her mind she knew they had been found, but she couldn't seem to care. She just clung to Samuel's suede-covered arm and choked and coughed and gasped for air.

But Samuel dragged her along. Swimming fast away from the pelting of bullets making little splashes in the water all around them, he struggled with her dead weight, the current fighting them, her lack of energy fighting them, and then he said something that changed everything.

"I love you, Isabelle Renoir."

He dragged her farther, swimming with strokes that seemed impossibly strong and enlivened.

Then she began to swim too.

Energy poured through her, reaching into every limb and fiber of her being. So much so that she laughed aloud.

She pulled free of Samuel's arm and began to swim on her own. Together they closed in on the opposite bank.

They were looking into each other's eyes as their feet hit solid river bottom. They were sharing their triumph when they heard another sound, this time in front of them.

They turned as one, and the blood drained from their faces.

Three mounted Shawnee stood waiting for them.

# 20

Samuel pulled the tomahawk from his belt as he waded up the bank. Isabelle, close behind, had a knife in one hand, a tomahawk in the other. They watched as the Indians dismounted, pulling forth their weapons.

"Keep to my back," Samuel instructed her.

"If I can," she answered, catching her breath.

They took a fighting stance, back to back, as the three Indians approached. A wicked gleam off a scythe caught the water and added to its glitter. Sunukkuhkau approached Samuel, the gleam of his weapon matching the promise in his eyes.

Another, smaller warrior whom Isabelle did not recognize approached her, condescension radiating from him. Isabelle nodded at him, smiling. Let him be overconfident; it was always easier that way.

Then she remembered how tired she was after the miles of running, the swimming against a strong current, the near drowning. She now stood cold, her clothes hanging like a dead, water-logged animal around her shoulders. She could still swing the tomahawk, but she knew, as surely as she stood there, that she only had a few good swings in her. That they had to count.

She felt Samuel move away from her as the swinging scythe arced toward his shoulder. He dodged it, then righted himself and swung the tomahawk. High to the left, quickly back, then low to the right. He caught Sunukkahkau's ribs a mighty blow, but the warrior barely flinched. The scythe was swinging for Samuel's neck.

---

SAMUEL QUICKLY DUCKED, then turned, knowing a presence behind him. But no one was there. Breathing heavily, his hair swinging free from its leather thong, he turned back, seeing Sunukkuhkau bearing down on him. But it had given him a second to assess. Isabelle was holding her own against the small one, but where was the third? And then he saw him in the shadows, kneeling in the dirt and doing something with an open bundle that made the blood congeal in Samuel's veins.

They weren't just fighting men in this battle.

The Shawnee had brought a shaman.

"Pray!" Samuel shouted to Isabelle. "Call on the name of the Lord."

---

ISABELLE SAW THE Indian, not knowing what he was doing but understanding that something was happening that was darker than this physical battle.

She faltered, fear seizing her, seeing in that brief moment the crazed, dilated eyes of the one who watched them. Then he rattled something at her, and her whole body spasmed. *God in heaven, help us*, she silently cried out, not having any other words. She found she couldn't lift her tomahawk. Her arms refused to move.

"Samuel?" she whimpered as the warrior grew close and grasped her by the hair. The tomahawk dropped from her hand, thudding to the ground.

Samuel jerked and then groaned. Isabelle turned her head as far as she could, pain radiating from her scalp, and watched Samuel fall to the ground, a knife in Sunukkahkau's hand, ready to slit his throat.

"Noooo!" she screamed at the warrior. "I will be Cocheta. Don't kill him. I will do it."

Sunukkuhkau stared at her, eyebrows raised, nostrils flared and puffing, ready to kill, judging the truth of her words.

Isabelle met his stare, breathing hard. The wind around them had suddenly died out, as if it, too, were listening for the warrior's response.

Suddenly Sunukkuhkau reared back and sheathed his knife. He heaved Samuel up, tied his wrists with the leather thong from his long black hair, then he pushed Samuel toward his horse.

A rope was found, thrown over Samuel's head, and tightened about his neck. After several barked orders from Sunukkuhkau, Isabelle was pushed past Samuel and heaved up onto Sunukkuhkau's horse. She grasped hold of the horse's mane with tight fists, realizing with a sinking feeling that, while she would ride back, Samuel would be dragged behind them.

Sunukkuhkau mounted up behind her. She felt his arm grasp her around the waist, felt the smile in his voice, a whisper in her ear. "My Cocheta."

A deep shiver ran through her body.

Sunukkuhkau pulled Isabelle into his chest and said, "If you fight, he dies."

Isabelle nodded, glancing back at Samuel, seeing his narrowed eyes, then back to the man who would have her at any cost.

---

CLARK SAT IN his office staring out the window, turning over in his mind the message he had just received: Cahokia had been peacefully taken by his second in command, Captain Bowman, and a handful of French. He had just received word of their compliance while sitting in his easily won accommodations in Kaskaskia. And while he sat and waited, he wrote letters to his superiors in Virginia, reporting on the unexpected turn of events.

This sitting and waiting—the other side of war—made his men edgy and had them looking for trouble, hoping for trouble. These men didn't travel nine hundred miles just to waltz into a fort and take up sentry posts. They hankered for a bloody thatch of hair, Indian-style, to hang on their belts, to prove their mettle in battle.

To the surprise of the entire company, their conquest of Kaskaskia and Cahokia had been so easy. Too easy.

Clark rose to pace.

He should be thankful. He should, even now, be on his knees giving thanks to God. But for some reason he was restless. He growled, his neck flushing, as someone knocked with a hesitant-sounding scrape on the door. "Enter," he barked.

A woman stepped around the door, and Clark paused. Her head was wrapped in a huge cloth, making her look like the black serving women of his childhood plantation home. His brow knitted as he waved her in.

"Sir, I am sorry to disturb you, but I've come with news of one of your men. Samuel Holt."

Clark immediately bade her to sit in the only other chair in the room and shut the door. This didn't bode well.

"You have seen Samuel?"

"Yes, sir." She began to shake visibly. "My name is Naomi Lynn. Mr. Holt and his friends stopped off at our cabin for provisions on their way to Vincennes. I had just set the noon meal on the table for us when we were attacked by the Shawnee." She looked up at him, her eyes hard and pain racked. "They killed my husband, Jake, and my boys." Her voice wavered, but she rallied with visible determination. "Best we could tell, they took Mr. Holt and Isabelle's brother, Julian Renoir, captive. Me and my girls survived, thanks to Isabelle. Then she went after them."

"Alone?" Clark gaped at her.

Naomi nodded. "She said the trail was fresh. Helped me and my two girls hitch up our wagon and then rode off into the woods. She was injured pretty bad. A head wound. I tried to convince her to come here, but she was determined to rescue her brother from the savages."

Clark turned away, rubbing his chin as he stared hard out the window at the peaceful Kaskaskia street. What kind of woman was this Isabelle Renoir? Turning back toward her, he asked, "How many were there?"

Naomi shook her head. "At least eight, but I couldn't be sure."

"Shawnee are usually raiding Kentucky, not this far north. Why? Do you know why they attacked you?"

Naomi again shook her head. "We've never had any real trouble from the Indians before, but," she shrugged, looking tired beyond her years, "they have been raiding up and down the rivers for months, or so I've heard tell. I was hoping you might know."

Clark sighed. There could be any number of reasons to rile them, but he feared that they had heard of the capture of

Kaskaskia and were striking back. The Shawnee were no friend to the Americans. The other surrounding tribes were a battle of another kind that he was determined to win. But the Shawnee? He had little hope of convincing them to his side.

"When did this happen?"

"Thirteen days ago. In the afternoon. I would have come right away, but it took me and the girls longer to get here than I imagined it would. I kept losing consciousness," she gestured to her wrapped head, "the blood loss, I would think, and the girls had to drive the wagon. Then, when we arrived in Kaskaskia, I wasn't able to walk steady, and I didn't leave my bed at Mrs. Fontaine's store where me and my girls are staying until now. I do hope I'm not too late."

Clark looked at the woman, comprehension dawning that the cloth covered a scalping, and he was filled with compassion. "Of course not. I am sorry for your loss, ma'am. Thank you for coming when you could." He sat at his desk and poised his quill, then bent to writing. Looking up, he asked, "Where is your home, Mrs. Lynn?"

"About thirty miles west of here. Two days on foot, one with fast horses. I could show you."

Clark shook his head. "I will not have you traveling. We will find it."

The woman nodded, looking relieved.

"I'll send a detachment to the farm. We will find them, Mrs. Lynn. Thank you."

Naomi rose from her chair and stretched out a surprisingly young-looking hand, a glimpse of a beforehand life of promise and hope. Clark saw so much in that hand—hope for a land of their own and the fruit of their labors to comfort them in the years to come. All ruined now. In a single day, all in ruins.

But this woman who stood before him with pain and determination in her pale blue eyes *thanked* him.

"Thank you, Colonel Clark. I know of you. My husband was a supporter of the Americans and all you Long Knives do to keep us safe. I will go back to my farm." Tears filled her eyes, and she looked down self-consciously, then back up at him, held herself upright, and finished. "We will not let them win, sir. Me and my girls will finish what my husband and I began here."

Clark's chest filled with admiration. "Samuel is one of my best, ma'am. If he couldn't keep your family from harm, God only knows what could have. Thank you for coming to me, and for your courage. People like you will be the making of this country."

She gave him a slow nod of assent, then turned toward the door.

Clark turned back to the window as she left, closing the door behind her. He sighed again, deep in concentration.

He would have to get Samuel and his friends back, no matter the cost.

And the Indians . . .

He had planned to wait until Vincennes was firmly in his grasp before trying to win them over, but now he felt he must act. Now was the time to make a stand and to bluff like he'd never bluffed and blustered before. He would send the tribes the white wampum of peace and red wampum of war, with the message of a golden opportunity: an alliance with the American government—a government that was not yet in full existence. Pray God, they choose the white. He didn't have the men for the red blood of war with the Illinois alliance.

And Vincennes waited.

With Samuel captured, he would have to send someone else. He took a deep breath, seeing the word *Vincennes* on his paper in front of him, the ink yet to dry, shining black on the page. For some reason he felt it was the crown jewel of this country. If he could take it—and hold it—from the clutches of the British and Henry the Hairbuyer, then, by the grace of God, he would.

"Let it be so, Lord," he said aloud in his empty office, looking up and out the window at the village street. This tiny outpost looked like nothing important, but he knew it meant everything at this moment in history.

"Yes. Let it be so."

---

HOPE TURNED HER head sharply at the opening of the front door, hope rising in her breast at the sound, thinking of her children.

"On your knees, again, I see." Joseph's greeting was laced with disdain.

Hope rose and smoothed down her long, dusky-blue skirt as a second-nature gesture, while judging the waver of his steps and his mood. "Yes," she said simply, chin rising. "You're home."

He nodded. "And with a canoe still full of trade goods. Where is Julian? I'll need him to help me unload and sort through it all."

He took a step toward her. She took a step back.

His lip curled. "It never matters how long I'm gone, does it?"

Hope ignored the observation. "There is something I must tell you."

"News?"

Hope hedged, not knowing where to begin. "Sit down, Joseph. Do you need something to drink? Some coffee?"

Joseph pulled a flask from the pocket of his long coat and grinned at her. "I've got what I need. What is it?"

"It's the children. They have gone on a journey, an errand for Father Francis." She rushed the next. "They should have been back by now. I'm getting worried."

Joseph sank into a chair at their kitchen table, the flask resting on the top, loosely held, his dusty clothes clinging to his sweat. "What errand could Father Francis have?"

She waved a hand in the air. "Some books. The ones he has always mourned not having with him. He received a letter that they arrived in Kaskaskia. He couldn't go himself, you know how frail he is getting, so he asked Isabelle and Julian to fetch them."

"You allowed them to go to Kaskaskia? Why would you agree to a fool thing like that?"

Hope had been wondering that exact thing herself but tried to explain. "You know how Isabelle is. . . . She's so restless. I thought," she looked helplessly at him, then in a stronger voice said, "I hoped it might give her some purpose. For a time anyway. I did hire a guide. A well-renowned Indian guide."

Joseph frowned, took a long pull on the flask, setting it down with a thump. "I could have gotten the books on my next trip. Might even have taken Isabelle with me this time. Who did you hire?"

Hope knew this was a lie. Isabelle had been begging to go with her father on these supply trips for years, and he'd always told her no, saying that she was a girl and girls didn't run around with a bunch of men. It was an excuse, Hope knew. Joseph little cared that Isabelle had many skills and interests more common to men—hunting, shooting, sleuth-searching, and woodland forages. No, Joseph simply didn't want his daughter to know what he really did on these trips. The drinking. The gambling. The women.

"Quiet Fox. I have it from a reliable source that he is a trusted guide."

"Never heard of him. Who told you he was so trusted?"

They stared at each other for a long moment, then Hope flushed and turned away. "Just the word around town."

"When did they go?" Joseph demanded while pulling off a boot and wiggling his toes to stretch them.

"Weeks ago. I should have heard from them by now." Hope took another chair at the table and leaned toward him. "I feel something has happened. Something bad."

Joseph scowled at her. "You should have waited until I returned to make this decision."

"How could I?" She looked up at him, pleading. "You are never here."

"That's my work."

Hope shook her head. "It's your heart. It is never here." She looked toward the ceiling, wondering if God heard her weak, sorrowful tone. "You are always off somewhere, looking for something that I can't give you."

Joseph scowled at her. "You know not what you say."

Hope turned brisk, walking away from him, staring out the window at the town that was Vincennes. "I gave up everything to follow you here; you give up nothing for me and the children."

Joseph stood, went to her, and grasped her hand and brought it to his lips. Gently, he kissed each knuckle. "I still love you, my Hope."

She leaned her head to one side, tears springing up. He hadn't called her that in so long. But she resisted. "I need more than the words this time."

"What can I give you?" He looked around the room. "I have given you a home. I have provided for this family and abided your moods when I wanted more children and you refused me night after night, while you weep and wail in some kind of prayer. Some men think I allow you too much freedom."

She wanted to rise up and rail at him but instead smiled a kind but sorrowful smile. "Those are good things, and I am thankful. But Joseph, you have pulled away from my heart. We two no longer seem to be one. And I don't know how to regain that."

"I will give you anything I can."

"You want to give me something? Find our children."

Joseph laughed, and it was a bitter sound. "Isabelle has likely convinced Julian to extend their little adventure, staying in Kaskaskia. She is the most misbegotten hellion I have ever seen."

Hope screamed internally in frustration. Joseph never wanted to face anything, always believed whatever was most convenient for him. She watched in despair as he turned, scratching his head through his still-thick, dark hair and turned away from her, heading for their bedroom, likely to sleep until evening.

"If you will not go after them, then I must." She stared into his dark-brown eyes, seeing the crinkles around them that didn't used to be there, the lashes gone slack and white, seeing years that had passed by.

Joseph turned with a short laugh. "You do that."

She pleaded, "They should have been back weeks ago. Anything could have happened."

He sighed, rubbing his rosy face with one hand. "If they have not returned within another week, I will go."

It was the best she was going to get.

# 21

Samuel saw her from the other side of the camp, nearly a week after their recapture, and hardly recognized her. Isabelle's hair, that wild, living thing that became her like a best cloak, lay in tight braids on either side of her shoulders. Her head hung down, showing the tanned expanse of her forehead. She seemed to be looking for something lost on the ground. Two bright circles of red paint rode high on her cheekbones.

Her whole being appeared lost.

He shouted her name across the expanse of the camp, despite the attention it might draw. After a long moment, she looked up. He gasped at the shattered gaze, so unlike anything he'd ever seen, even on this ravished frontier. She didn't shout back or even look in his direction. She appeared . . . afraid. What were they doing to her?

He knew she had been going along with anything they demanded since that night at the river, and he had been doing much the same, outwardly at least, making them believe in his acquiescence—all the while hatching new plans of escape. He hadn't fooled them, he knew, but it was enough to keep his scalp intact. The tribe maintained hope of his full assimilation in time. He prayed time would become his answer—the second their guard was down—he would make good their escape. All he needed was time, and time was all they had.

But he would never leave here without her.

Until the opportune moment presented itself, he had no choice but to abide—abide their laughing ridicule as he pretended weakness where there was none, as he feigned admiration where he abhorred their methods and their means. It wasn't that he had never learned anything from Indian ways. Oh yes, he'd learned them well. Back in Dunmore's War, when he was still green, a runaway lad, he had seen firsthand the advantages of the natives' ways over traditional English fighting techniques. Up against a tribal war party, the lines of red-coated soldiers, marching bravely in straight-backed formation, became a left-to-right death dance, convincing Samuel and others, George Rogers Clark among them, that there was much they could learn from the Indians in matters of warfare.

Honor came to a brave after death, not marching toward it. And so he had become one of them then, as much as he ever would. He and Clark had learned how to become hidden forest warriors, with cunning and skill. Lessons beyond the ken of hardened, disciplined British soldiers had come easy to the independent-natured colonists. After living in this land alongside the Indians for decades, the American frontiersmen had risen to the challenge, becoming death hunters with the eyes of the woodland on their side. They'd learned how to strike fear into the enemy's heart with shrill battle cries, immobilizing them before they had a chance to lift their better weapons.

The Americans latched onto this unfamiliar warfare like puppies to a teat, knowing, somehow, in their desperation for this land, its sure sustenance. They were a new breed, these Americans. Able to take the best from each culture and make it their own.

Able to rise up and fight with all that they embodied—Irish rebellion and independence, English endurance and confidence, German economy and warrior spirit, French artistry, African nobility, the joy of the Scots—and brought it all together in a melting pot of strength.

Samuel had seen it in their eyes when commanding a troop, the women's eyes when waving their men off with tears and pride, and yes, even in the children's eyes. The young boys would stand with pitchforks and field scythes waving above their heads, over their hard-won fields, determined to do a man's work while their fathers left to protect it. These people hadn't traveled a sea and left a country and their forebears for nothing. They would have a field of their own crop to defend, by the great Almighty!

It was a lesson ingrained in him, giving him an edge as a leader. He felt their passion, their pains to make it real. He knew, like he'd never known anything, that he was meant for more than life in his father's straight-laced household. This was something he could help make happen.

This was his destiny.

Sometimes Samuel awoke suddenly from strange dreams of a time where people lived in huge cities of stone, their buildings crowded, reaching into the clouds, where the green and forest and woodland had given way to a hard, gray, people-packed civilization. But he didn't feel sad when he dreamed it. He would awake with an indrawn breath of exultation. "What is it, Lord?" he would wonder aloud amid his tangled covers. "What do You have planned for this land?"

But the morning always dawned on the edges of a forest yet to be hewn, of green as far as the eye could see, of promise and sacrifice for that promise, of work and sweat beyond measure with an early death almost certain, of vision, a vision so strong that they didn't really know where it came from, yet it lived like a fire in each of their hearts so that they were willing, eager even, to give up everything to possess it. This America. These Americans.

That was his daylight. But now, for the first time, Samuel wanted something more than acres of belly-filling dirt and a hand-hewn cabin to call his own.

He wanted a woman.

This woman with the wild hair that wrapped her when she danced.

And he would wait. Wait until he could snatch her back from the enemy haunting them both. He *would* ride off with this stolen prize. If he accomplished nothing else in his whole life, he would conquer this thing.

---

"*JE M'APPELLE* ISABELLE," she whispered to the hide she was scraping, "so nice to make your acquaintance." She curtseyed to the brown fur, hiding her smile at the absurdity and yet knowing that she must continue to do this. Something inside told her not to forget. She had promised to go by "Cocheta" now, and she was, gaining small ground of trust with the tribe, convincing them that they had finally conquered some small part of her. But secretly she rebelled. Since seeing Samuel across the camp, since hearing her name being called, she'd been shocked out of her slow slide into their ways. It had ignited a spark back to life inside her, like a lightning bolt. She would remember who she was. She would say it out loud at every opportunity.

---

HOPE ROSE EARLY, quietly packing, though something in her knew Joseph would wake up and see.

"What are you doing?" His voice was groggy with sleep, confused.

Hope turned, looking at him from over her shoulder. She was still a beautiful woman, her blonde hair darker now, pulled back in a messy knot at her nape, strands escaping in her early-morning haste, her eyes still sleepy but determined. "I'm going to Kaskaskia," she said quietly, belying the fear within.

"I told you I would go in a week or two if they don't return." Joseph pulled on his breeches as he spoke. Going to the bedroom door, he leaned against the edge. "Come back to bed."

Hope shook her head. "You have never listened to me before. I can't expect that you will now." She walked off toward the kitchen, intending to pack any means necessary to vital sustenance on a journey of this sort. What would she need most? She pondered her cupboards, hearing Joseph follow her into the kitchen.

"Just give it some time, for heaven's sake," he was mumbling as he pulled his shirt over his head.

Hope turned from her packing. She looked at him, felt the familiar attraction, and fought it. He was still a fine-looking man. A little gray in his hair, but that added an air of distinction. A broad, unlined, and rosy face. Eyes that twinkled when he was happy, snapped when he was impatient or angry or worse, frustrated by lack of understanding what was going on around him. She'd seen that face often in the rearing of their children. Joseph understood Joseph and little else. He was never one to be able to walk in another's shoes. No, it was almost as if he expected that everyone else should wear *his* shoes. And if they didn't, *they* were the ignorant ones.

Hope took a long breath and faced him. "I'm going. There is nothing you can do. Something is wrong, I know it. I have to go."

Joseph looked off into the distance and scratched his head. "Can't you wait a week? I have one more run, and then I will have some time. You can't go after them alone."

Hope shook her head sadly. "There is always 'one more run.'" She paused, knowing the impact. "I am not going alone."

His face reddened. He puffed out his cheeks like a bull ready to charge. "Who is it?"

Hope turned away, not able to face what was in his eyes. "You needn't worry," she said. "I will be safe."

"Who is it?" he demanded. But they both knew.

Hope bundled some bread into her pack, followed by dried cherries, dates, persimmons, and jarred honey. "I ran into Adam while you were gone. He offered to help." She dared not look at him in the ensuing silence.

Finally he said, "You would harlot yourself then? For the children, I am sure."

She whirled on him. She had never been so angry. "Adam Harrison would never ask anything of me, and you know it. Shame on you for thinking such a thing!"

He nodded and smiled. It was the smile she dreaded, said everything she never was or could hope to be.

"The man is just biding his time, Hope. Waiting for the time I don't make it back, some Indian's arrow in my chest. Don't be a fool."

"Not every man is like you," Hope said with quiet conviction. "He respects me."

"Oh yes," Joseph agreed. "He *respects* you all right. He will hold you on a pedestal until you succumb to it. That grand respect." He turned, his hand flinging out toward her. "Go on with you then. Save your children. But don't expect a home when you get back."

Hope watched him trudge off to the bedroom, wondering how sure his threat was. There was fear inside her, a fear of losing him, though that had happened long ago. Fear of not finding a solid roof over her head when she returned. She reminded herself, as she turned to place the essentials of fire and bed in her pack, that her God was the God of the Israelites, a people that in their most abject sin had clothes that never wore out and food, the food of angels, that appeared with each morning dawn. She battled internally as she packed, not knowing the future, yet knowing, like only a mother does, that her children needed her and that, whatever the cost, she would go.

# 22

Isabelle stood with the women of her lodge house. Today was the day of the Green Corn Festival, a day of dancing and feasting to celebrate the emergence of the season's first shoots of corn. The women of the tribe had been cooking all day to prepare for the great feast, assigning Isabelle the simplest of tasks. But before the feasting began, she had learned by the stilted speech and pantomime of her new mother, that there would be a ball game.

The tribe of over two hundred had divided themselves, men against women, on either side of an open field. They waited as the old chief slowly made his way to the center of the grass. He held a ball in his hands and a gleeful smile on his weathered face. Suddenly, with more energy than he seemed capable of, he threw the ball high into the air. Everyone yelped and cheered, rushing forward toward the ball as the old chief hurried off to the side to watch.

Isabelle found herself running, not knowing the rules, not knowing what she would do should she happen to get hold of it. A young brave reached the ball first and kicked it toward a goal of two stakes on the women's side of the field. One of the younger women quickly scooped it into her arms and began to run toward the other goal. Isabelle laughed, a little shocked, as one of the braves stepped into the girl's path, wrapped his arms around her and shook her with such force that the tightly clasped ball fell from her arms. Isabelle was surprised when the brave didn't scoop it up; instead he kicked it back into a large group of women and men.

Isabelle caught sight of Samuel's blond hair gleaming in the late-afternoon sun. She ran toward him, dodging the running feet and flailing arms of her teammates. Reaching his side, she ran with him, and asked, laughing, "What are the rules?"

Samuel grinned back at her and yelled, "Get the ball through your goal. I think the women can carry it and throw it, but the men can only kick it." He laughed. "All I know for sure is that they warned me not to touch it with my hands or . . ." He made a slicing motion across his throat.

Isabelle gave a quick nod. "I guess that makes us enemies."

Samuel laughed, running toward the ball, "For this hour only, my sweet."

Isabelle watched as Samuel tried to muscle his way through the throng of people toward the tan skin ball. She quickly sized up her opportunities and decided on a different tack, making her way toward their goal and into the open. She laughed as she ran, feeling light and happy, her hide skirts keeping her from breaking into a full stride.

There was so much laughing and shrill yelping going on that Isabelle had to call out at the top of her lungs when she saw that Sinchi, a young woman who had only shyly smiled at Isabelle these past weeks, had actually managed to grasp the ball. The woman was surprisingly quick footed, darting in and out of the groups of men following her. One of them grasped hold of her skirt as he went down, dragging her to a stop. Before he could rise to his feet and shake her, Isabelle yelled, "Sinchi! Here!" Isabelle raised her hands high, hoping the woman would understand. There was a smile, and then the woman reared back to throw it. All eyes watched in some amazement as the ball sailed through the air, straight into Isabelle's outreached arms.

"Whooo!" Isabelle yelled, her moccasins turning in the grass, her legs straining against the blasted dress. She ran toward the goal with all her might.

Suddenly she felt strong hands grasp hold of her shoulders, felt panting breath on her bare neck. Thinking it was Samuel, by the excited rise in her chest at his touch, she half-turned toward him, pulling away from the grasp as hard as she could, with a huge grin on her face. But it wasn't Samuel. It was Sunukkuhkau.

And he looked like he wanted to win something bigger than a ball game.

Isabelle's grin faded. Her eyes slanted in determination. He would not get this ball. He would not.

She'd kept moving forward through the exchange, just within the reach of hands, but he didn't have a firm grip on her yet. Jagging quickly to the right, she was able to dislodge one of his hands from her shoulder. Now she twisted suddenly, elbow out and sharp, and was able to drive it into his ribs, catching him off guard. The moment his hands lost their contact, she drove her feet the other direction, running as fast as she could toward the goal.

Sunukkuhkau had recovered quickly though, and now there were about twenty more braves at her heels. She'd lost precious time, and there was no one closer to the goal to throw the ball to. She had two choices: throw it toward the goal, which was still a good distance away, or keep running.

The choice was made for her as Sunukkuhkau and another brave grasped her, hard this time, nearly knocking the wind from her. But she fought on, dragging them along in her slow steps. Sunukkuhkau shook her hard, but Isabelle raised the ball high above her head, as tight in her hands as her teeth were clenched together, knowing that he couldn't touch the ball.

"You won't have it," she shouted in his face, knowing he alone could understand her. "I can fight you here, in this game, with your rules." The ball now represented her freedom. "I won't give it to you!"

He grinned, wicked and determined. "Yes, you will," he answered, following his proclamation with a long howling scream.

The scream, more than his words, caused a shiver to snake down her spine.

The whole crowd was crushing them now, surrounding them, but Isabelle remained on her feet with the ball above her head. Then she heard her name being called. She turned her head, saw Sinchi, a little ahead of her, her face glowing, her head nodding, arms long and outstretched. Isabelle reared the ball back and threw it with all her might, going down to the ground now, beneath some kicking feet as the crowd burst away from her and toward the ball.

Sudden hands reached down and snatched her bodily from the ground, placing her on her feet and then stood, blocking her from harm. She looked up to see Samuel saving her from being trampled.

"Did she catch it?" she yelled.

Samuel pointed. "Look!"

Isabelle turned toward the women's goal just in time to see Sinchi cross it with the ball still in her hands, dragging four or five braves behind her, like trailing barnacles on a canoe. She'd done it! They had done it! Isabelle ran with the rest of the woman toward the goal, cheering and yelling and jumping up and down together.

It was the best moment she'd had with these people, and Isabelle let herself feel the joy of it.

---

SHE HAD EATEN so much at the feast that Isabelle didn't know if she could move, much less dance. But the women of the tribe didn't seem to care about that, dragging her with them into the middle of the ceremonial ground, giggling at some mysterious joke that she was once again left out of due to her lack of understanding their language.

It had been a . . . fun day, the first day she'd had brief moments where she had forgotten what they had done, how they had destroyed her family, and she felt waves of guilt roll over her for allowing it. They didn't deserve her happiness, even Sinchi, as they had jumped up and down together, forearms clasped in glee over their victory at the ball field.

She stiffened her body in renewed rebellion as the group of women approached a brave who had always appeared tall and silent to Isabelle. Now though, he drummed, came to life as only music brought out some people, pounding on a round drum cradled against his bare, crossed legs.

"What is it?" Isabelle asked Sinchi, her new best friend it would seem.

The girl had barely left Isabelle's side since their combined feat, eating next to her, always nodding and smiling at whatever Isabelle said, laughing when Isabelle made a face as she ate their food. There couldn't be another woman in the tribe more her opposite—Sinchi was shy, thin, and open-faced, but she'd attached herself to Isabelle's side nonetheless; and, really, what choice did she have but to let the girl follow her around like a new puppy. She seemed innocent enough.

Sinchi made the motions of a chicken, clucking in her throat, her eyes bright with glee.

"Chicken?"

Sinchi nodded, giggling. Would she ever stop this girlish laughter? It was starting to grate. Then Sinchi swayed her hips and took tiny steps to the left and right. Isabelle couldn't help her answering smile.

"Dance?"

"Chi-ken-dace," the girl nodded, so proud she'd made Isabelle understand. Isabelle was just glad someone was trying to speak English instead of the other way around.

The brave started singing, a chant really, to the beat of the drum. His voice was low and rich, his tone clear and full of . . . some meaning. She'd noticed something, living with the Shawnee for a few weeks: This people knew something of music. Theirs was the kind of rhythm that could take over a person's pulse, as it was commanding hers now.

All the women had gathered around the drummer, and then they began to sing with him. She didn't know the song, didn't know their words, but . . . it was happy and made her want to dance. At Sinchi's nudge, she began to catch on, singing along, not knowing what she sang but starting not to care. It was music. It was dance.

After two more songs, Isabelle learned the steps if not the words, then the women suddenly stopped. Eyes aglow, they turned away from their drummer and faced the men, sitting in a tight circle around them. A few giggled, a few looked determined, a few fluttered their hands. Isabelle didn't know what would happen next, but she could feel these women's excitement.

Sinchi rushed over toward her, ready to instruct, as the whole party grew quiet. There was quiet laughter among the men as they whispered together and looked excitedly toward the women.

"Choose," Sinchi said in Isabelle's ear, pointing at the men.

"What?"

"Choose a . . . man." The girl had learned more English than Isabelle had thought, and she decided that she might be a worthy friend after all.

"For what?"

"*Peleewekaawe* . . . dance . . . man to be dance with." And then she was off, running to her choice, a tall young brave with bold features and a long eagle's feather trailing from his hair. She was the victor today, and Isabelle smiled as she watched her slim form run with abandon. Sinchi could have any man she wanted this day.

Isabelle's eyes found Samuel's over the red-orange glow of the firelight between them. He had been watching her, she knew, as she danced with these deerskin-clad women, watching the way she moved, the way she put her own hip-sway into the movements and twirled, arms over her head. She'd caught his glance, known it like the heat that it was, turning, consciously and unconsciously toward him, growing closer, then further, then closer and closer, their eyes locking and holding every now and then.

And now, it would seem, she could choose any man.

She *should* choose Sunukkuhkau; it would be expected of her. But the thought of going to him and extending her hand when she had a choice . . . she found she could not do it. She glanced at the warrior, saw that he was watching her intently, expecting her to turn toward him. Instead, she looked down at her moccasins.

These were *their* rules.

"I can choose anyone," she assured herself as she watched her decorated feet turn toward the only man she wanted. A tiny laugh escaped, and then she quickly smothered it, keeping her head down, watching them make their way toward Samuel.

Nearly there, she raised her head and locked gazes with him, amber and gray-blue colliding. Everyone else faded—all their noise, their watching eyes, their judgments. Her hips swayed as she stepped toward the only man in the world that she would willingly call "husband." Then she smiled down at him as she reached for his hand.

He sat on the ground with the rest of them, legs loosely crossed, his face tilted up toward her, a small growth of beard on his chin and cheeks.

"Will you dance?"

Her token gift, a few blue stones, smooth from the water that ran beside the camp, passed from her hand to his. She hadn't known why the women had gathered these treasures yesterday, but she'd been told to put them in her pocket, and now she understood. It was a token, a payment for the dance. He reached for them, feeling them with his fingers, then tucked them safely within his jacket, rising to his feet while his gaze never left hers.

He took her hand. She noticed how brown his hand had become from the summer sun. Their fingers touched and grasped, the fringe of their Indian dress meshing, but for this moment she would be as the woman she was—English from her mother's side, French from her father's, and American—because that was the future. That was what she had decided she would be.

Samuel uncoiled, rising gracefully to his feet, taking a firmer grasp of her hand, an ownership, a wicked grin on his face that spoke of nothing evil, only more good and a night of dancing under the moon.

She laughed with the joy of it, her throat exposed as only a trusting person would do to a true friend. She clasped his strong hand and led him to their dance.

The drums were loud, pounding in the air around them, resounding in her chest and causing her heart to rise up to match it as they followed the simple steps of the chicken dance. Samuel followed along, she leading, as she taught him with touch and step and nod and glance.

He was a quick learner.

Then he led her into the Virginia Reel, a twirl. Suddenly it didn't matter where they were and what they were supposed to be. It only mattered that they matched one another, step for step, close then far apart. Isabelle was dipped into a backbend, her black hair pooling in the grass, her back bent so that the onlookers must think it would break in two.

They forgot the chicken dance. They forgot everything and everyone. They made the music their own.

Her breath came fast and heavy. She had danced alone so many times, had twirled and writhed and undulated in front of no one save God. Now this. Who could have known Samuel could lead her in something she could never do alone. He lifted her, and she flew. And this native company, this audience, was left breathless watching them.

And they were afraid.

The song ended, suddenly, as if someone had said, "Enough!" But no one had said anything aloud. They had only watched.

Samuel stood beside her, panting. "That was good."

Isabelle raked her long hair from her face, shook it back and smiled, leaning against him. "Yes. The best thing we've shown them yet."

Another drum began to beat. Only this was different. Not as light and fun. More masculine.

Now the men would choose.

This was the Horse Dance.

# 23

The drumming began again. Isabelle stood, not knowing what to do, as the tribe regrouped. The women once again gathered around the drummer. The men faded back into a tight group, watching them, their eyes dark and wide, their lips curved in smiles. A song was sung by the men now. They gathered closer, intention on their faces as they sang to the women.

Then the song was over.

Several of the men were looking at her, making her wary.

Sunukkuhkau approached her. He held out a single arrow with dappled feathers at the end. Looking down, she recognized it; it was from their kill. It was his dance fee.

His eyes were intense as he stretched out a sinew-thin arm.

She wanted more than anything to reject him and his gift, looking around for Samuel and what he might advise. There he was, being detained by a seemingly benign group of friends who appeared to be congratulating him on his skill as a dancer. He looked up, saw her dilemma. His amber-lit eyes were slashes of pain and caution. Then he nodded once, telling her to accept it.

They both knew an ambush when they saw one.

Isabelle had a feeling of being measured. Even though these were their rules, that the woman could pick the man and now, the man the woman, she knew they fully expected compliance. It was part of the deal she had made at the river's edge. She reached out and took the arrow, her head down in every appearance of modest acceptance.

But they didn't know her.

They thought they did, but she was about to prove to them the name they had given her—That You Cannot Imagine. She smiled to the ground, the shadowy grass. She would dance with Sunukkuhkau and, she determined within her heart, they would not know how to reckon it.

The drumbeat was similar to the last dance but stronger, more like a horse, its powerful hoofs beating the earth as it galloped. She'd always loved to ride. She had always made an instant, uncanny connection with any horse she mounted, making this particular beat familiar as though remembering a dream. It beat in her chest now, making her want to ride . . . or at least dance. Isabelle turned and led her enemy to the center of the grassy floor.

She followed their simple steps at first, hearing cheers from the onlookers who had no partner. This was a test. Eyes watched to see if she would hold to her end of the deal. She exhaled a private smile. Sunukkuhkau may fight like no one else, but this was a plane where a man's physical strength did not reign.

This was the realm of grace.

Soon she abandoned the simple steps. She closed her eyes, ignoring her partner, and said quietly, "Be it my last dance, my Lord, I give this to you."

No one understood, nor even heard her simple prayer, but it didn't matter.

She moved to the center of the group, her arms undulating over and around her head, eyes closed. She mouthed a quiet praise, like she had at the river's edge, or in her yard as a child, in the quiet, God-moments of her life. She turned their drumbeat against them.

"Holy, holy, holy is the Lamb. Forever and ever to be praised. No one has gone before You and no other will go after You. The beginning . . . the end . . . the beginning . . . the end," she breathed against their unknown tongue. "There shall never be another like You." She smiled, joy filling her. "There shall never be another like You."

She wasn't dancing with Sunukkuhkau, and he must have known it, for when she finally opened her eyes, he had stopped dancing and was watching her with suspicion of her power . . . as had everyone around them. Once again they didn't know what to make of her wild ways. Once again she held them all enthralled, reflecting God's glory.

A halt was called by none other than the chief. He looked at her askance, as if she'd committed some grave crime. She didn't care. She glared back at him, back at them all, save Samuel, willing them to do something about it.

The chief approached her, motioning Sunukkuhkau over to translate.

"He says you have much power."

Isabelle exhaled a small laugh. "It was just a dance."

"He wishes that you learn a special song and sing it to us."

Isabelle smelled a trap. "I do not know your language. What is this song? What does it say, and what does it mean?"

Her questions were ignored.

"It is a great honor, Cocheta."

The name again. The reminder.

"It is called 'Danna Witchee Nachepung.'"

"Tell him I will sing a song I know for him. In his honor." She bowed at the chief, with all seeming deference. "I will sing 'Amazing Grace.'"

Sunukkuhkau translated. The chief shook his head in defiance, his eyes ablaze as he gazed into hers. "Shawnee now. Sing Shawnee now," he commanded to the grumbles of the tribe.

Isabelle felt the noose tightening. She couldn't sing their song. She knew it. It would be worshipping another god. As Shadrach, Meshach, and Abednego had been ordered to bow to the golden idol in their land, she too was being tested. Her gaze caught Samuel's on the outskirts of the crowd. Would it mean his death if she refused?

He stared at her with determination, then briefly shook his head. He was willing to deal with the consequences, knowing them as well as she did.

She slowly shook her head. "I cannot."

The tribe riled, a ripple of disquiet and fear, friends suddenly become foes. She saw that they still abhorred her, that they abhorred her God and everything that she had in Him. They seemed, now, ready to kill her.

But the chief quieted them with his upheld hand. In a loud voice, he said, "Sunukkuhkau and Cocheta will marry. When the moon is full. And then Cocheta will know our ways."

There was a great cry from the Shawnee, their shrill yelping causing waves of fear to travel up and down Isabelle's spine.

Isabelle searched for and found Samuel's frantic gaze. God help them, now everything was lost.

A sound broke from the trees, a great crashing sound, as

many horses pounded into their midst. And there, at their fore, on a white stallion, was the flame-haired George Rogers Clark.

The Americans had come to rescue them.

---

CLARK'S MEN HAD been waiting among the tree whispers, the rustling of forest leaves and gusts of wind covering any sound they made as they watched from the outskirts of the Shawnee village. They had taken in the moonlit scene with weapons drawn and ready, their breath short and expectant in their chests.

Clark had kept his hand upraised in the quiet stillness, feeling their combined straining to rush forward and affect rescue but holding them back until he fully knew the moment. So they watched, undetected, for a long time, seeing a play as it were, a worship service where an outsider had stolen a heathen stage. They wanted to cheer Isabelle on, many of them knowing the God she worshipped. Most of the men had never met her, and yet, suddenly and completely, they were on her side, eager to battle for her. Isabelle didn't know it, but she had just won another kind of warrior to her side, and they were the loyal sort, the kind who would fight to the death for her.

Clark saw Samuel sitting off to one side watching the dance. Now he understood. He couldn't blame Samuel for his eagerness to lead such a woman and her brother back to Vincennes. She was like no woman he'd ever seen.

He'd left Kaskaskia to personally lead this rescue. Father Gibault and the good doctor Lafont had convinced him that they would lead the conquest of Vincennes. And so, with a few of Clark's best men, he'd allowed them to travel to the fort in his name and secure it, without guns, without a fight, but with a message of peace and hope for the American cause. Not that he hadn't had doubts or sleepless nights over it, but he trusted the priest for some reason that he couldn't quite understand. He was giving up his element of surprise, leaving so much into the hands of strangers.

But right now, Samuel, his friend, needed him.

He was glad to see the man intact and seemingly in good health. Now he would have to decide: Should he rush and attack—take him and this woman by force and surely make enemies of this tribe and others aligned to them? Or should he pursue the path of diplomacy? Everything in him shouted the latter, and yet he knew his men wouldn't be too happy about it. They had been eager finally to engage in a fight, and this scene had no doubt fired them up.

Now Clark sat atop his prized stallion in front of the startled tribe, having seen and heard the moment he'd been waiting for and knowing that if they'd waited one more second something terrible would happen to the woman. So he'd given the signal to charge forward.

Clark held up two belts of wampum—the red of war and the white of peace—one in each hand. He shouted into the clearing, holding them enthralled. "Will the Shawnee choose the side of peace . . . or the side of war?" He bellowed it as a conqueror, as if ten thousand men were at his right hand, as if he could single-handedly take them all, so sure of the rightness of his cause.

Several of the tribe backed into Samuel, fencing him in, but Samuel was a full head taller and just grinned at Clark.

Someone yelped something, and then two younger braves went to flank the chief as he moved forward. It took some time before the old chief made his way to the front of the group. Stopping in front of the white horse, the chief motioned for Clark to dismount. Sunukkuhkau materialized at his side, seemingly to interpret.

"Why would this man bring us wampum?" the chief asked in a croaky voice, which Sunukkuhkau asked in stilted English.

"Do you not know?" Clark demanded in a loud voice. "Are you old dogs slow of hearing? The Americans have taken the British forts. The French are aligned with the Americans. We wish to make an alliance with the native people and bring peace to this land."

The old chief looked askance at the fire-haired man. "We know only that the white man has come into our land, slowly taking our hunting grounds until there is nothing left to fill the bellies of our women and children."

"The white man has many faces, great chief. I have come to show you the face of honesty and truth. Will you hear this face?"

The old chief considered Clark, looking tired and defeated. Finally he nodded. "We will smoke the pipe of peace and council together."

Clark nodded in respect, then directed his men to dismount. They were led, slowly and with much study from the villagers, to a wigwam. At one point Clark came abreast of Samuel and whispered, "I have seen Isabelle, but where is her brother?"

"Julian is dead. Burned at the stake in front of her." Samuel looked square in his leader's eyes. "Whatever deal you make with them, know that I will not leave here without her."

Clark measured the moment, then nodded.

They made their way into the lodge, sitting in a crowded circle of men, about ten braves, some of Clark's men, and Samuel. Once everyone was settled, the chief motioned to Samuel. "You know this man."

Clark nodded. "One of my best."

The chief smiled, showing a few missing teeth in his tanned face. "One of *my* best," he corrected.

Clark nodded acquiescence. "Yes."

The chief seemed to like that. They all waited while a pipe was filled and lit.

Clark began, talking with wide gestures of the American cause, about what he had come here for. His words were solemnly interpreted, sentence by slow sentence, explaining the vast change that was occurring on the frontier. Then Clark motioned to Samuel.

"Samuel Holt is my scout. He was commissioned to me by the Virginia government. If you agree to join our side, you must see that he is mine but on the side of good for both."

The old chief stared hard at Samuel. "He is Patamon now, of the Shawnee."

Clark nodded solemnly, staring at the old man, waiting a long minute in the silence of the curling smoke. Then he said quietly, "He has been Samuel Holt much longer than Patamon of the Shawnee. He is where his heart lies."

The old chief appeared to consider these words, looking at Samuel then back to Clark. "Our way is the old way. Patamon has replaced our dead brother, bringing justice to our fallen and peace to the family of our fallen. He is Shawnee now."

Clark nodded, then argued, "We believe a man can only be truly adopted if he is bereft of family." He nodded to Samuel. "I see the value of such a warrior and that you would not want to lose him as a son. But this man, Samuel Holt, has sworn an oath to my service. He is mine." The last was spoken with authority, with an underlying threat.

The chief pursed his thin lips together. Then, after a long pause, he nodded, "Another then shall have to take the place of our dead brother. Do you have another among you?"

Clark stalled, taking a long drag from the pipe, peering up into the smoke hole of the lodge house. Turning to the chief, he leaned toward him. "There is more at stake here than a dead brother's recompense. You must choose sides in this war between the British and the Americans. We will not make you our harlots as the English would. If you do not choose the side of the Americans, you will lose far more than Samuel. You will lose everything."

The statement was prophetic; they all felt it, as if it were a common fact—so simple, so true—and this kind man was merely pointing it out to them.

The chief looked down into his lap, his old thin legs crossed, his white hair wispy around a tanned and deeply wrinkled face. He nodded. "I can see that Samuel Holt," he used his English name, "is your son." He paused for a long moment, then looked up to Clark. "But Cocheta is ours. She belongs with us."

Clark saw the determination in the chief's eyes, knew a verbal battle lost, and nodded in agreement. "We thank you, for the return of our brother." Clark rose and reached out his hand.

The chief looked at him a long moment, judging that outstretched hand, then nodded again, and shook it. "We will take the white wampum. We will not fight against the Americans."

Clark thanked him, bowing out of the lodge house, his men and Samuel following close behind. Once out into the night air Clark turned toward Samuel. "We'll come back for her. Ransom her."

Samuel shook his head, looking around the clearing, then finally back at Clark. "I cannot leave her here."

"Yes. You can." Clark took a step toward him. "You won't do her any good here. If you go with me, we can raise a ransom. Find a hostage of their people to trade her with, something. Here you will only watch her become more and more their captive."

"You don't know her."

Clark stared hard at his best man. "After tonight . . . I think I do. I know enough to know that she will be all right for a few more weeks. It's her only chance. They won't give her up willingly."

Samuel looked into his leader's bright blue eyes. "We could take her, tonight, by force."

"I can't risk war with the Shawnee, not with so much at stake."

Samuel nodded his understanding. "She will think I've abandoned her. She won't understand."

Clark glared hard at him. "Don't forget why we came here. Your purpose, our mission. I won't risk all that for a woman. Not even . . . such a woman as she." He clapped Samuel on the shoulder. "She is stronger than you give her credit. Did you see what she did during their ceremony? How she turned it against them? And still they didn't dare destroy her. She holds some magic over them."

"That's what I'm afraid of. If she doesn't give in to them soon, or at least pretend to, they will kill her."

Clark smiled at his friend. "You've never been so taken with a woman before, have you? Let me tell you. After seeing what I saw tonight, I don't believe they will harm her. Samuel . . . trust me. Come with me. We will get her back."

"Yes." He looked ashen, so sick to leave her, wondering what she would think of a man who would turn tail and run out, leaving her with the enemy.

# 24

Isabelle woke to the news that Samuel and Clark and the Americans were gone. Her hope for salvation had deserted her on a white horse and night wind.

She had been hurried to bed the night before with the other women, the Green Corn Dance abruptly over. Waking early, hoping for some news, she had rushed out into the summer sunshine to find they had left her there. Alone. With the enemy.

The realization was crushing, like a great weight on her chest, her next breath a forced thought. She kicked at a little stone on the ground, watching it roll over and over in the dirt. She picked it up and stared at it in the palm of her hand. It was one of the blue stones she had given Samuel last night for her dance fee. He had thrown it away.

Isabelle turned toward a sound behind her. Sinchi slowly approached, head down, her big solemn eyes hesitant. Isabelle saw that this woman, this enemy, had tears in her eyes.

"I am sorry for you." Sinchi spoke quietly, knowing the traitorous sentiment for what it was. She looked at the stone in

Isabelle's hand, recognized it, and pressed her lips together, her hand coming up to rest on Isabelle's shoulder.

Isabelle looked into Sinchi's eyes, her own filling to match her friend's. Then she dashed them away and took a bracing breath.

"I am not sorry."

She dropped the stone in the dirt and turned away toward her morning chores. After a few steps away she stopped and looked back over her shoulder. "Thanks," she whispered the only word she could force past the tightness in her throat.

The tears flowed down Sinchi's round cheeks as Isabelle turned and walked away.

---

OVER THE NEXT few days the camp seemed to embrace Isabelle, elevating her chores to those more to her liking, giving her choice food, presenting her with gifts, and Sinchi staying nearby and speaking to her in English.

Sunukkuhkau did not press himself on her, didn't demand that she speak to him or expend herself in any way on his behalf. He was simply there, a quiet presence beside her. Together they would look off into the sunset, feeling the evening breeze, not speaking.

Every day she found little presents from him left on her bed or in her moccasins—a beaded necklace, an armlet of beaten brass, a clutch of downy feathers. She couldn't help her smile this morning as she awoke to a baby bird sleeping next to her bed, its tiny, glossy head tucked under a wing. Upon inspection she discovered that one of the wings was wounded.

She carried the bird with her as she did her chores, careful not to bump it, but not knowing what to do to help. The other women, when she asked, only shrugged and gave her a secretive smile.

She hadn't seen Sunukkuhkau for a couple of days, and as she looked around the camp for him, she was surprised to realize that she missed him. Then, looking at the baby bird in her palm, she felt him come up behind her.

"Did you leave this for me?" she asked, raising her head to look at him.

He looked good, tall and lean, strong muscles in his chest and belly. His face was serious and full of compassion. He nodded. "I found it in the woods, fallen from a high nest. Not ready to fly."

"Will it ever fly again?"

"If you help it."

"I don't know what to do. I have asked the women, but they just shrug. Even Sinchi, who I know understands me."

"That is because they know that the bird was not the gift. The gift is the lesson. I will teach you to mend its wing."

A few weeks ago Isabelle would have dumped the bird in Sunukkuhkau's hands and walked away, but now she did not. She nodded, as solemn as he. "I would like to learn such a thing."

They walked to Sunukkuhkau's lodge house and entered, her eyes adjusting to the dim light after the August sun. She had never wondered before why he lived alone, but now she thought it aloud.

"Why do you live alone, Sunukkuhkau?"

He was turned from her, digging in a bowl of odds and ends. He looked over his shoulder at her and grinned. "You are beginning to know our ways. It is a good question.

"I lived in this house with my wife. Her mother and father died many moons ago, and my family lives with my older brother, so I live alone. My wife was," he made a motion of a round stomach, "when she died of smallpox. We had plans to fill this house with many children."

Isabelle nodded, looking down at the bird in her hands. "I am sorry." She knew where smallpox came from; she knew the white man had brought it into the land. And she *was* sorry for him, for the life he should have had.

Sunukkuhkau motioned for her to sit beside him on the raised pallet that was his bed. Isabelle had no fear of being alone with him in his lodge; he might be a wicked opponent on the battlefield, but the Shawnee had strict rules concerning unmarried women and how they were to be treated. Isabelle knew he would never cross any boundary with her on that score.

She sat beside him, holding out the little bird in her cupped palms. Sunukkuhkau gently propped up the wing, moving the broken part so that it was even with the tiny bone that appeared to be intact. He bent over Isabelle's hands, his breath fanning against her palm, moving slowly and carefully, while the little bird chirped and wiggled in pain.

"You're hurting it," Isabelle complained, but she watched closely, knowing he had done this before.

"A little," Sunukkuhkau said softly. Taking up a tiny stick, whittled clean and white, he placed the stick on the underside of the wing. Holding it in place with one hand, he smoothed the feathers down with the other. "Lay it down," he directed her. "Slow." Isabelle laid the little farthing on the bed. Sunukkuhkau nodded toward her free hand and a thin strip of cloth. "Wrap it around the wing."

With painstaking care, Isabelle wrapped the thin gossamer cloth around and around the wing, tying a tiny knot to secure the loose end to the bandage.

The bird quivered suddenly and went still. She looked up to Sunukkuhkau with alarm. "Is it dead?"

Sunukkuhkau smiled and shook his head. "Asleep. Someday, because of our care, he will fly."

Isabelle stared into this man's eyes, feeling herself fall victim to the spell cast by this scene. His eyes were dark brown, the pupils so black, but there was much to be read in them: strength, heat, a man's heat for a woman, and something else—something that made Isabelle's heart start to pound so hard she wanted nothing more than to run.

This was a trap.

She saw it suddenly, in its full intent. This man wanted her. Whether for love or lust or some power they thought she had, she didn't know. But this touching scene, the little gifts, the salve on her wounds left by Samuel's betrayal—these Indians had seen their opportunity, especially Sunukkuhkau, and taken advantage.

Everything in her wanted to stand and rail at him, to run from him, but she had learned a thing or two in these last weeks. She too could be sly. So despite her certainty of a trap, she lifted her face and smiled at him. A slow smile. The kind that never failed.

He pressed his lips together, watching her, judging her, not easily convinced, so she pressed on. "I do hope he flies someday," she said, and she did, "but it was your care that helped the poor creature, nothing of mine."

Sunukkuhkau wasn't one to praise her unnecessarily. "You will learn, Cocheta."

"Yes," she breathed, staring into his eyes. "I believe I shall."

---

WHO IS YOUR survival?

The phrase repeated itself over and over in her mind as she lay, later, feigning sleep on her cot. She had begun to pray the moment she left Sunukkuhkau's lodge. She prayed with her lips moving, but the words were silent and constant until she found her bed. Then came the words, unbidden: *Who will be your survival?*

She pondered this, turning it over and over in her heart, knowing some key was hidden there. She thought back to her mother, Hope, and her lessons of Christ and His sacrifice, of God the Creator, and how He had fashioned this earth and herself. She had always found sure evidence of His glory in the forest and trees and animals and plants. She supposed there was a father-weakness there as well, a need and desire for the loving, constant presence of the father that she'd never had in Joseph. Besides, she loved hearing the Old Testament stories—the fire, the passion, the risks taken by men and women of faith. They had never failed to inspire her.

Yet Jesus, the son of God, had seemed a foreign person. He taught in parables and riddles, seeming slowly to walk the earth, skimming the sand in His holy sandals through desert cities, pouring water into the dry mouths of the Jews. She understood that His death on the cross had paid her redemption fee, like the dance fee, heaven's golden ticket. But she did not understand the man Jesus. His only ambition had been to lay down everything. To die. And that was something she had never had within her.

*Who will be your survival if you do not die to yourself?*

The words frightened her. What if she was *never* rescued from this place? What if she couldn't escape? She didn't want to give up, lay her wildness, her strength, on a cross like His. But she saw, sudden and complete, that she could not save herself. Her strength had not deterred the enemy; it had only made them more determined to have her.

In that moment, in that minute, Isabelle faced the fact that she was a captive.

It was only a matter of time. The Shawnee would wear her down, wear her out. And she would, eventually, give in.

She turned her head into her pillow and allowed the silent, shaking sobs to overcome her. She had been so close with Sunukkuhkau this afternoon, so close to giving them what they wanted. And she knew, deep in her heart, that if she did, she would never live the life she was meant to live. She would lose everything.

She was on the very edge of losing everything.

Tears coursed down her face, wetting her hair, her neck, her dress, her bed. Tears of grief, tears of turmoil, tears of anger. "I can't do this anymore! I can't do this without You," she breathed, quiet and fierce. "I need you, Jesus. *You* are my survival."

A great heaving occurred in her chest that she tried to still for fear of waking her lodge mates. Tremors shook her, and she was soaked in a baptism of tears. Then, gradually, as the emotion was spent, she quieted, and a deep, unfathomable peace came over her. She wept silently now, breathing it in for a long time.

Then, for the first time since Julian's death, she fell into a deep and dreamless sleep.

# 25

Hope's thighs quivered as she half crawled, half stepped over the huge fallen tree in their path. She looked down at the foot she'd thrown over the log and frowned, thinking the red seeping from the top of her shoe might mean something was bleeding. *Well, that would explain the constant pain.*

Adam Harrison looked back at her, saw the difficulty she was having, and stopped. "Need a rest?" There was concern in his eyes as he walked back toward her. He handed her his canteen as she stretched out a hand for him to help her over. She settled on top of the log and took a long drink.

"I'm afraid so," she said, drinking deeply again. "These legs aren't used to marching."

Adam nodded, looking her over and noticing her foot, the red now soaking through the brown leather. "Hope, why didn't you tell me you were bleeding? Here, give me your foot and let's have a look at it."

Hope leaned down to unlace the shoe. They were stout, sturdy shoes but not made for trekking through the wilderness.

"I only just realized it myself a few moments ago. Is it the shoes, do you think?"

Adam nodded as he watched her slowly, painfully remove the offending footwear. He squatted down in front of her and took the foot in his lap, carefully easing down the stocking. "What you need is a good pair of moccasins."

"Ha! I've never worn a pair of moccasins in my life."

"Well, once you do, you will never go back to wearing clunky, hard leather like this." His hands took firm hold of her foot as he turned it slightly to examine the large welt on the outside edge, a raw and ugly wound bleeding profusely. Pouring some of their precious water onto a handkerchief from his pocket, he gently dabbed at the throbbing sore.

Hope drew in a hissing breath. "Maybe you are right. You don't happen to have a pair of those wonderful moccasins in your pack, do you?" She smiled at the top of his head, his dark hair streaked with gray but still thick and wavy.

"Wish I did, but no. We can get a pair in Kaskaskia for the trip home."

"I have a better idea." She smiled at him, her eyes wide. "Let's buy a horse and ride back."

Adam laughed. "Yes, it's too bad mine had a lame foot. If I'd had more time, I could have rounded one up, but what with the rush . . ." He let the thought trail off, they both knowing that had they not left that very hour, Joseph would have found a more forceful way than threats to keep Hope at home.

---

ADAM COULDN'T BLAME Joseph for wanting to keep Hope from going. He didn't want Hope out in the wilderness traveling like this either; she wasn't conditioned to it. But Adam did hold a deep dislike for the man and couldn't begin to fathom a father who wouldn't go after his children or heed his wife's intuition concerning their safety.

If he knew anything about Hope Renoir, it was that she had the ear of God; and if she thought her children were in trouble, then Adam would do just about anything he could to help her find them.

And why not? He had been in love with Hope from the moment she stepped off the boat onto the muddy shore of the Wabash River. She had laughingly asked if there was an empty house in town because she was heartily sick of sleeping on the ground and would take anything she could get with four walls and a roof.

She was so beautiful that day, standing in the late-afternoon sun, her hair blonde and shining, pulled into a loose knot at the back of her neck. Her eyes, when he finally worked up the courage to really look into them, were pale blue ringed in sapphire. He saw such pain hidden there, such strength, such forbearance and wisdom for a woman her age. He saw a lifetime in that long glance, knowing her better in that moment than any woman he'd ever known.

Beside her stood a gangly, gypsy-looking girl with a glowing face and too much energy, straining against her mother's hand. They watched her together, he and Hope, as she broke free and, with a running start and a mighty leap, her arms outstretched like the wings of a bird, jumped to shore with a whoop and a deep laugh that echoed across the water and their hearts.

Hope ducked her head and laughed. Adam stared in wonder.

The small boy, though—Julian, as he would later learn—clung to his mother's hand, a blend of his parents in coloring with the dark-blond hair of his mother and the olive complexion and dark eyes of his father, eyes that were huge and solemn and saw the world from another place.

They were the most beautiful children he had ever seen.

He had fallen so fast and hard that day that he had yet to recover. Then he met the darkly good-looking Frenchman who was her husband, these children's father, barking orders and pointing impatiently.

*God help me*, he'd thought then and many, many times since. *God, You* must *help me.* Every day, every minute after that, he had repeated it, aloud sometimes: *Hope Renoir is a married woman.*

Now as he looked into her beloved face, seeing the gray around her temples, her hair not quite so bright, the intervening years etched on her face, his heart still lurched within him. He had to look away, down at the injury, to breathe evenly again.

"Rip a long piece of that petticoat off and I'll bandage it up before you put back on that awful shoe."

"And ruin a perfectly good petticoat!" she demanded with a smile in her voice.

"Better than ruining a perfectly good foot."

She shrugged, none of the usual tightness in her smile. "Well, there is that."

She was teasing him, and he could hardly stand the joy bolting through him, gripping his chest in a wave of triumph. He had to turn away to keep her from seeing it, using the excuse of her needing privacy so that she could hike up her skirt and destroy her petticoat. He heard the ripping sound.

"You can turn back around, Dr. Harrison. I have your bandage ready now."

He turned, avoiding her eyes and squatting back down in front of her, trying not to notice the smooth texture of her skin as he gently wrapped the cotton around her foot. Rising, he handed her the canteen again, waiting while she took a long swallow, following it with a quick drink himself, wanting to save as much of the water as he could for her.

Growing brisk and cheerful, he turned them from the intimacy. "Shall we march, my lady?"

"Why of course, dear sir. Was there ever a more beautiful day than this for a stroll through the wood?"

He chuckled, taking her arm, loving the English lilt to her voice, leading them on to what now felt like a casual foray through a glorious park in some exotic location that they fixed in their minds.

Two days later, mid-afternoon on a hot August day, Hope and Adam walked along the shore of the Kaskaskia River to the outskirts of town. She looked tired and dust coated but excited now. After all, her children might be in this place. Adam felt years younger, coming alive in the time he had spent with her.

He only hoped that Isabelle and Julian would be here, in full health and in trouble for worrying their mother so.

---

SAMUEL PACED THE floor of Clark's office. "One hundred and fifty pounds sterling?"

Clark nodded, his lips pressed into a grim line. "That was the redemption price of another female captive a few years ago. Delaware. I don't know what the Shawnee price for Isabelle might be. Perhaps more, if they can even be bought."

"Which seems unlikely."

Clark stared off into the distance. "I don't know. You know I would give it gladly if I had it, but I've barely enough to feed this army. We're living on the credit of the good Francis Vigo. The men are being paid with land to fight, one hundred and eight acres of Kentucky frontier when this is over."

"Maybe I could sell my portion. How much do you think it is worth?" Samuel sank into a chair, his head hanging down.

Clark rubbed his face with a hand. "Not enough. And you don't have the deed yet. With the speed of the Virginia Legislature, you won't have that for months after this campaign."

"I can't just leave her there! You said you would help me." He groaned. "I never should have left."

"I am trying to help, Samuel. I've put out word for any information of important Indian captives, someone to trade her for. I've also written to the tribes as far as five hundred miles away, offering them the red wampum or the white. I fully expect them to be arriving on our doorstep in the next weeks for councils. We could learn something valuable from them that might save Isabelle." He paused, piercing Samuel with his bright blue eyes. "For now, all we can do is wait."

"She will think I have abandoned her." It was said as a plea.

"If she thinks that, my friend, then she does not know you well enough yet."

# 26

The stars sparkled in their brilliance, confident in their name, against a thick, velvet backdrop of unending depths. The horizon met the night with hues of green, real and yet unreal in its facets of green, glowing beneath the moonlight. It was a magical night, and it called to her.

Isabelle rose from her bed of tangled blankets on the cool, damp earth. She sat up, rubbing the tiredness from her eyes, looking up and feeling life pump back into her. Finally she knew she had to abandon sleep and meet the night.

She had begged to be allowed to sleep outdoors earlier that evening. It was a fanciful request, the last request of a maiden the night before her wedding. Sunukkuhkau had backed her up and encouraged the privilege, as long as her sisters slept out with her. The other women lay silent and sleeping now, peaceful in the bliss of an unknown enchantment. Isabelle cast a glance at each of them, her gaze lingering over Sinchi, a true friend, making her smile.

Rising, she slipped into her moccasins, trying not to make any sound that might disrupt their sleep, and made her way into the woods, heedless of danger, conscious only of her need to connect with the same God who had made these stars twinkle loud enough to wake her.

She progressed deeper into the trees, felt the thinner grass of the shady places against her ankles and calves, felt them transition into scrub and bramble and then the prickling of small sticks and weeds. She picked her way to the stream, always drawn to any body of water where the clear reflection of the moon danced across the tiny, windblown waves. Reaching the small stream, the place where they had first tried to wash away the white of her skin, she sank down onto the mud-hardened bank. She picked a long weed and bit into the stem, tasting its bitter sourness, twirling it slowly with her hand, holding it out, examining its leaves in the moonlight. Her lips curved into a contented smile as she drank in the still beauty of the glade. So peaceful, so silent, with the wind blowing gently through her long, loose hair. She closed her eyes and lifted her face, feeling everything, feeling at one with her piece of the world. Since her night of surrender to the Lord, she had known many moments of this overwhelming peace.

She realized with an inner jolt that even though she was still a captive on the outside, something had changed inside, and she was freer here than she'd ever been.

They too had noticed the change, not entirely trusting it or her but wanting to believe that she was beginning to accept her place with them. She didn't consider what they thought; she simply lived, one day at a time, and rested in the knowledge that she no longer had to carry herself, that she knew her survival.

In this newfound place of safety, she found herself thinking a lot instead of always trying to *do* something. She spent endless hours allowing her mind to wander into the past, pick through images as they appeared while she cooked or washed clothes or hunted for berries. When she slept, she slept soundly and contentedly, but she found she needed little sleep these days. Her mind was filled with thoughts and her chest with feelings that she'd never before taken the time to explore. Behind her closed lids at night, she dreamed awake of all the things past and present. Often she saw her father's face, a young face, from when she was a little girl. She lingered over the image, allowing her memory to turn over his features. She smiled, the air whooshing out of her lungs as she realized how much she looked like him. Her dark coloring, her gypsy-slanted eyes and freewheeling heart—those traits had come from him. Other times she remembered him as she last saw him, now older, his face rounder, his hair a little grayer, but his eyes—his eyes still fascinated her. They still held the light of youth. He was still full of a life of chasing rainbows.

Isabelle closed her eyes now, a trickle of a tear seeping out and down her cheek and neck, making her cold where the breeze blew it dry. But it wasn't a sad cry; she was happy to remember her father.

Tonight her mind's eye roved the childlike curves of her brother's face. She saw Julian when he was little, laughing at some silly thing she had said. He had never taken her as seriously as she wished he would, but then he had seen her, seen *inside* her, something everyone else had missed. He had believed in her when she wasn't doing anything great or special or beautiful. He'd loved her at her least lovable.

Her chest heaved with a sob at the thought, the sound skipping over the water's edge, her face pressing into her upraised legs. If only she had known! She would have been kinder. She would have . . . loved him better. "Oh God," she breathed into the still night air, "I miss him so."

She thought back on their best times together, feeling in this moment the need to relive them in her mind. He had been so very different from her, his every thought from some other place of reference, that she wondered how it was that they hadn't hated one another. But they hadn't. If anything, they had clung to each other, enjoying their differences. They were both passionate about what they loved in life. They had lived as children, she saw now, always in the here and now, trying to make whatever that elusive thing was that made them feel the most alive as real and as tangible as possible. With Julian it had been his music, his poetry. With her it had been . . . something to rid her of the restlessness.

Everything in her now stopped in revelation. There were many things that she loved—music, the feel of a heavy gun in her hands and knowledge that she had the ability to use it, time spent with her brother or her mother, those brief moments of connection with her father. And now Samuel, his face when he looked at her, his strength, his matching abilities and that feeling that, together, nothing could stop them.

But something *had* stopped them. She sensed that God wanted to show her more, something bigger than all those things, that if she only asked, He would show her.

"What is it?" she whispered into the dark sky. "What is it?"

The night breeze caressed her face. She could hear the pattering of the leaves as they rustled in the tree above her head. The breeze became a wind, then a strong wind, gusting around her, making her hair fly.

She found herself standing, rising to the challenge to stand against it. Her eyelids fell, and behind them she saw an image of herself dancing on that wind. She was floating upward, her hair twirling around her, colored ribbons in her hair swirling and twirling, covering and then revealing her face and her body. She saw herself becoming as one with the wind, not flying, for this wind didn't move in one direction. No, this wind danced. Leaves whirled about her in a counterclockwise motion, reversing the flow of time, changing now from the dry death of winter to the brilliant hues of fall, then transforming into the strong, sure leaves of summer, going back, back, to the newborn leaves of spring. They danced as she danced, in all the seasons of her life.

Isabelle stood completely still, her eyes still closed as she watched the scene unfolding behind her eyes. "I am to worship You," she breathed, her chest quivering, undone at the way He chose to show her this.

"Isabelle?"

Her eyes were still closed, her heart still in the grip of His presence.

"Isabelle!"

But this was a woman's voice calling her name, a voice she knew so well. She turned, startled, thinking she was seeing another vision.

But no. It was Hope, her mother, running toward her, with two men following close behind.

They ran to her while she just stood there, not believing her eyes. Adam, her mother's friend from Vincennes. Her gaze swung to the other man, knowing him before she saw him.

*Samuel.*

He had come back for her.

She began to sob, a sudden and deep response as her mother's arms wrapped around her.

"Thanks be to God," Hope breathed, smoothing back Isabelle's wild hair from her face.

Samuel then took her deep into his arms and laughed. "Only you would make this so easy. How did you manage it?"

Isabelle looked about, suddenly afraid that the Shawnee would hear and they would all be discovered.

"The stars woke me," she said with a sob and then a laugh. "I didn't know. I didn't think you would come back for me."

Samuel laughed low in his chest. "Then Clark was right. You don't know me well enough yet. But I plan to remedy that, as soon as we can get away from here."

They turned as one back toward Kaskaskia and freedom.

And so Isabelle simply walked away. Out of her slavery, her captivity, her restless running, and into the future of her glorious promised land.

# 27

They walked through the night, not saying much but not panicked either, the four of them feeling a sureness, a peace that they would not be pursued.

Years later Isabelle would hear that the Shawnee had all slept particularly long that morning, that when they rose and saw her gone, they had searched for tracks and found none, that her sleeping partners had not heard anything amiss. They had said that the night sky and the stars had been particularly bright that night and decided among themselves that Isabelle had been caught up, caught away by the God she worshipped, as He was jealous of their time with her and wanted her home. She was truly named, they felt. Something they could never imagine.

But she did not know that now, as dawn lit the sky and they came upon the Kaskaskia River. She only had a certain feeling that she would never see the Shawnee again.

Hope sat on the ground as the men went in search of the little canoe that the farmer owned. The farmer wasn't up and about yet, but they were determined to use one of his boats for passage, Adam saying he would go later in the morning and paddle it back to him.

Isabelle sank down next to her mother and leaned on her shoulder. "You must be tired."

Hope laughed. "Yes, tired but happy this moment." She put her arm around Isabelle's shoulders and squeezed.

"How did you find me?"

"I knew something was wrong, back in Vincennes, so I asked Adam to bring me here. When I arrived, I went to the commander's office. George Rogers Clark. Vincennes has also pledged their allegiance to the Americans. This country is changing fast, Isabelle, and it's a good thing. A great thing is happening here. I can feel it."

She took a deep breath and continued. "Clark wouldn't tell me anything. He would only say that there was a man I needed to meet. That scared me, I can tell you! But I never could have prepared myself for what I learned had happened to my children." She paused, her throat working to control her emotions. "Clark took me to Samuel, and he explained how you had been taken captive by the Shawnee and all he was doing to try and free you." She looked into Isabelle's face. "Did you know he wanted to sell his land? The land he will receive as payment for fighting in Clark's campaign? He was trying to raise money to buy you back."

Isabelle shook her head. "I thought he had left me there."

"He loves you."

They were both silent a moment, leaning into each other's shoulders.

Hope took a shaky breath. "Then Samuel told me about Julian, how he died. I–I didn't know how I could go on, how to save you, but I kept thinking, *I still have one child living*. I wasn't going to let the Shawnee have you, so I convinced Adam and Samuel to go with me and demand you back. We had no weapons—well,

Samuel had a few, but we knew they wouldn't do us any good. And we didn't have any money to buy you or captives to trade you for." She hugged Isabelle tight into her side, crying a little. "But we had prayer, and so we prayed, the three of us, the entire way, to get you back." She let out a little sob. "He answered our plea. He must have known I couldn't have borne losing you both."

Isabelle looked up into her mother's face, her voice low and choked. "I tried to save him. I did try."

Hope shook her head. "This is not your fault, Isabelle. Don't ever believe otherwise."

"But it is. We went on this journey to satisfy something in me."

"Yes, but I let you both go." In a lower tone, gazing off into the distance, she added, almost to herself, "Your father will blame me." She turned back to Isabelle. "And the priest, we could blame him; it was his mission."

"He was only trying to help. As were you. The two of you didn't know what to do with me anymore."

"That is true. If you want to bear the burden of your brother's death, I cannot take it from you. It is something you must decide to lay down and walk away from, never looking back or taking it on your shoulders again. Don't believe the enemy's lies, Isabelle. He would destroy you, and I think," she gazed at Isabelle's face, seeing so much change there, "that you have grown up since I saw you last. You are no longer that straining, unsatisfied girl."

Isabelle's eyes widened, tears pricking again. "How do you know?"

"It is in everything about you now. You have made your peace with God, I think."

Isabelle blinked, two big tears rolling down her face. "Yes."

Hope squeezed her shoulders, tears coursing down her cheeks. "Then there is another thing to be thankful for this day."

"But Julian . . ."

Hope pressed her lips together for a moment and took a bracing breath. Her voice was shaky but firm as she said, "Shall be greatly missed. Every day. But I will grieve him later, when time allows it and I can bring it to my Father's lap." She took another deep breath and stood, brushing off her skirts. "Come, they have found a boat."

The water was still as they crossed the river, the sun of a new day glinting off the surface. They returned to Kaskaskia silently, Samuel grasping Isabelle's hand.

---

AS WORD SPREAD of Isabelle's rescue and how they had simply walked away from the enemy, unscathed and untouched, the town began to turn out in spontaneous celebration. Food appeared as if from nowhere—ham, goose, stew with potatoes and cream, carrots smeared with butter, bowls of freshly picked peas, round and green, baked beans, and hot, fluffy yeast rolls with pie upon pie. Isabelle stuffed herself until, finally, Samuel had to laughingly help her from the table.

Then began the music and the dancing. Unlike the Shawnee drums that had taken hold of her in a strange and disturbing way, this was fiddle music, light and happy, the bow skipping over the strings in tandem with the trilling notes of a flute. Samuel pulled a harmonica from his pocket and joined in.

Isabelle laughed out loud.

"I didn't know you could play that."

Samuel grinned around the instrument and nodded. "There is a lot you don't know about me, sweetheart."

"Tell me something I don't know," she challenged, her chin coming up, a smile in her eyes and on her lips.

He shrugged a shoulder. "Wait and see." He smiled back, still playing. When the song ended, he shoved the harmonica into his pocket and took Isabelle's hand, leading her away from the crowd, over to a small stand of trees. They sat down on a spindly bench, looking out over the party, quiet together, enjoying the scene.

Isabelle saw her mother dancing with Adam and was startled by how happy she looked, her face fairly glowing as she looked up into Adam's face. Different emotions assailed her as Isabelle suddenly realized she'd only seen Hope as her mother and not as a woman. Hope giggled like a schoolgirl as Adam twirled her about. And Adam's face, as he laughed too, was filled with love.

What if the marriage she had watched from a little girl's view wasn't what she had thought? Her parents' relationship had seemed normal enough. But now it hit her like a bucket of cold water thrown in her face that, in fact, it was distant, forbearing. What if her mother should have married a different man?

---

"IS IT HARD?" Samuel asked.

Isabelle's head jerked in his direction. "Is what hard?"

Samuel nodded toward her mother and Adam.

"It's hard that I didn't know," she said. "Maybe I could have done something. Helped somehow."

Samuel shook his head. "My parents' marriage isn't very happy either. I grew up in Virginia, on a plantation. Holt Plantation." Samuel paused to laugh. "My father wasn't very creative when he came up with that one. My mother, she harps on him all of the time, and my father escapes by going to Williamsburg or riding all day to oversee the land."

Isabelle looked up into his eyes. "Is that why you left and joined the Americans?"

Samuel looked away. "One of the reasons, I guess."

"What were the other reasons?"

Samuel shook his head, as if he didn't know the answer himself. "A young man feels a need to strike out on his own, I suppose. I wanted to prove myself . . . prove something to myself."

Isabelle spoke her thoughts out loud. "They were rich, weren't they? Handing it to you without any effort of your own? Do you plan to return someday?"

"No, I don't think I will ever go back."

"But why? Are you not your father's heir? Do you have brothers?"

Samuel shook his head. "I'm his only son. His eldest. I guess my sisters' husbands will run the place after he is gone."

"You turned your back on all that? Your family must have been devastated." She turned toward him. "Samuel, tell me about your life . . . before all this. Before Clark and his army."

"There is nothing more to tell." Samuel leaned back against the giant oak tree at his back and twirled a weed between his finger and thumb. He wondered why he didn't tell her about Sara. Why he couldn't voice any of it out loud. But he found he couldn't get it past the lump in his throat.

Instead he rose and grasped Isabelle's hand. "Come. We are missing the party. And I know how much you love to dance."

Isabelle looked long into his eyes, trying to read something there. Suddenly her hand reached out and touched the cord around his neck. He allowed her to drag it from his shirt, hold the delicate silver crescent moon in her hand.

"Tell me what this is, first. It must mean something."

Samuel looked down at the necklace, too delicate for a man to be wearing but a constant reminder of Sara. He remembered when he had given it to her, the quiet joy on her face as she clasped it behind her neck. He had thought to bury it with her but at the last minute had decided to keep it instead. He'd worn it every day since, thinking of her and their daughter. She must be four years old now. Although he didn't know her, his chest sometimes ached with the feeling of missing her.

Would Sara have been proud if she could see him now? He would never know, but the feel of the metal against his skin made it seem possible.

"Just an old thing I picked up," he said, trying to shrug off the probing. Isabelle would never understand his need of it.

She looked up into his eyes, her lips flattened, her eyes knowing that he wasn't telling the truth. "Can I have it? I think it's pretty."

She was calling his bluff, and he didn't like it. He could either tell her that it meant something to him or hand it over. He reached for it, held its crescent form between his fingers.

"I guess I know how your father felt when you decided to leave," Isabelle said softly, then turned away and walked back toward the party without him.

He just stood there, a part of him wanting to go after her and tell her about Sara, and a part of him not wanting to let go of it. Letting go might make room for something else to get in. And as much as he wanted Isabelle, as rare and glorious as he knew her to be, he didn't seem to have the strength to reach up and rip the leather cord from around his neck.

# 28

Samuel crouched low over his fire pit, taking in the last embers of warmth before dawn arrived and commanded that he move. He hadn't really needed the fire on this warm summer's night, but he had needed reassurance of his self-sufficiency.

A doe was stretched by his right hand, like the last time, except that this doe lay in green grass instead of the brown leaves of autumn. And this time he didn't wake to shrill war cries; there would be no running for a fort with the will and the way to bring them sustenance. No, the good citizens of Kaskaskia would hardly notice his addition to their stores. And the biggest difference was that this time he was running from something far more daunting than an Indian scalping: the memory of a wife he never really knew.

He sat back on the ground, his arms loosely crossed over his knees, laughing at his paltry attempts to be somebody, to recreate a moment in time when he thought he was special. He pulled the necklace out of his shirt and stared at it, hating it but knowing that something in him wanted to keep it close against the warmth of his bare chest.

He studied the trinket, the little indented outline that some silversmith had labored over to effect its particular sparkle. It was a pretty little piece, or so he'd thought when he had seen it in a jewelry shop and bought it as a wedding gift for Sara. He turned it over and saw that it had become tarnished. Probably from all the moisture he'd exposed it to. He huffed with a laugh at that thought. The piece certainly hadn't been created with thought of a soldier's wearing it.

He growled, then looked up. "What do you want from me?" He posed the question to God, to the sky, to the trees and the forest animals. Then he said it again, lower and fierce, this time to his father and his family and his dead wife. "What do you want from me?" He leaned his forehead against his crossed arms and just breathed.

"Nothing feels right anymore," he whispered. "Not going home, not staying here with Clark, not homesteading in Kentucky . . ."

He thought of Isabelle, saw her as she'd been when he first met her, her rifle trained at his chest, her dark eyes flashing fire at him. He smiled, then laughed aloud, throwing his head back. He'd never met a woman more sure of who she was.

He closed his eyes and saw the wolf charging her, saw her dancing under the moonlight, and the heaving dance-like movement when she'd thrust the dagger in the wolf's belly. He gasped, finding tears in his eyes.

Here was one who didn't need him.

Then he saw her broken at the Shawnee camp, collapsed at her brother's stake, rubbing ashes in that foreign but lovely dress, turning it gray and not caring, daring them to do something about it, do something with her. And they had. Not immediately. No, they had staged a long campaign, longing to rein in that spirit inside her. The Shawnee had been patient conquerors.

He remembered the time in camp when he'd called out to her and she hadn't seemed, at first, to remember her name, as if she had begun to forget who she was.

Samuel's face stilled as a single tear slid down his cheek. He hadn't been able to save her then either. Why? God, why? He was Samuel Holt, frontiersmen, sharpshooter, soldier, as strong and capable as men came. He was one of the famed Long Knives. *God, why couldn't I save her from that?*

He grasped hold of the necklace and, with a mighty jerk, tore it from his neck. He held it out, looking at the dangling sliver of moon, as thin as Sara's life had been.

"Why did she have to die?" He dropped his head to his knees, weeping as he never had. "I should have been able to do something. Why didn't *You* do something?"

And there it was: blame. He looked up, his heart pausing at the realization that he had been blaming God. He had spent his entire adult life making himself strong because he no longer believed God was capable.

He exhaled sharply with the knowledge of it. A Scripture came to mind, from his church days, something that hadn't meant anything to him at the time.

*Where You are weak, I am strong.*

The words reverberated through his mind and his heart.

"I am weak," he cried out, his face lifted toward heaven.

"I am so weak."

*Then I am so strong. I AM.*

The words breathed over him like a bath, like a baptism, seeping into every pore.

Samuel shook and sank to his knees before his paltry fire pit. "I'm sorry I blamed you."

*I'm not.*

He heard it again! As plain and as loud as the approaching daylight. He felt completely engulfed in a feeling of love and acceptance.

Looking down at the necklace in his hand, he raised it up to heaven in offering. The pendant swung in the misty light of dawn, the silver glinting, the cord broken. He stood. Braced his legs. Pulled back his arm. The air swooshed around him as he heaved it into the sky. The necklace twisted and turned, the moon flat and glinting in a single shaft of light. Then it fell, far away and into its own grave, a leftover crumb of a funeral supper.

"It is finished," Samuel breathed, watching it disappear, and knowing it was so.

---

IT WAS NIGHT. The night before they were to go back to Vincennes with Isabelle and the books. Such costly books. Some small part of Hope held a bitterness that said she hoped the books were worth it. She hoped they lasted the priest until the end of his days, bringing him as much joy as her son would have brought her.

---

ADAM WATCHED FROM just inside the front door as Hope sank down onto a chair on the front porch of the hotel where they each had a room. Her shoulders began to shake with silent sobs, and he wrestled with going to her or leaving her alone. He reached for the doorknob. She turned as the door opened and creaked.

"I'm sorry. I didn't mean to disturb you." Adam made to go back inside.

"No, please." Hope patted the arm of the chair next to her. "Bear me company."

Adam nodded once and crossed the wide wooden planks of the porch. He sank down into the chair beside her, his knees creaking too, feeling that he was getting older, that a good part of his life was past and spent. He didn't know what to say to Hope. He didn't have a wife or children—only a dream of her and hers. How did one comfort a mother who had lost a son?

Hope reached over and clasped his hand, their intertwined fingers hanging between the two chairs, feeling so right. Now that she'd reached out to him, he didn't know how he was going to let go again.

They sat in silence for long moments, looking out at the silent town, each taking quiet comfort in the nearness of the other. Adam turned his head and stared at her, wanting to memorize this moment for all the moments to come in his life. Her profile was lovely, hair pulled back like a frame. Her cheeks were a gentle swell against the night, her lips lightly held together, her eyes still wet with tears. She was a picture of grace and calm. How that could be only added to her mystery. She was, and would ever be, Hope.

She turned and looked at him, a sad smile on her lips. "Thank you, Adam."

Adam exhaled. "There's nothing to thank me for."

"Yes. Yes, there is. I wouldn't have been able to do this, to get through this, without you."

They gazed long at each other, sharing the pain, the connection between the past and all that had been and the future and all that would never be.

"Hope." He paused. Was it time to say it? Would there ever be a better time than now? "You know I love you."

Fresh tears sprung into Hope's eyes as she gazed into his. It was dark, but her eyes glistened like diamonds, like a million glittering pieces. "I know." She blinked, and a single tear slid down her cheek.

Adam leaned toward her, wiped the tear away with his thumb. He took a deep breath, words tumbling out that he hadn't planned, words of desperation. "You could leave him. We could go somewhere. Start over together."

Hope laughed, a mixed bitter-sad and fearful laugh. "I've thought of it. Don't think I haven't. But he is my husband. I won't be the one to leave."

Adam leaned in further, took her face between his strong hands. "We've waited so long. He'll never leave you. Hope . . . please. I can't go on seeing you and not having you at my side."

"God will see us through this. I can't leave him. It is not right."

Adam leaned closer to kiss her.

She pulled back with a gasp. "No." She stood up. "I'm sorry. . . . If you have to do something, if you need to leave without me, I would never blame you for it. It might make it easier for both of us. You need to find a woman of your own." She backed away from the temptation, clasped her hands together and squeezed, her knuckles turning white. "Adam, you have to let me go."

She turned and left him alone on the porch with a freshly broken heart, one of a hundred such moments he'd felt with her. One of a thousand. Adam looked up toward heaven. "You would think it would be that easy," he whispered, "but I can't do it."

"I will wait."

---

SAMUEL WOKE WITH a start. Excitement filled him as it did when he'd had a dream about some future world, knowing that something grand and unfathomable was coming. He climbed out of bed, slipped into his breeches, and ran his fingers through his long hair. It was time to get a haircut.

Taking a long drink of water, he peered into the small mirror in his room in the commander's offices. He needed a shave and maybe some new clothes, he thought with a laugh as he looked down at the grimy clothes he was wearing. It was a new day, a day to tell Isabelle he'd thrown away the necklace, a day to look his best. With that thought in mind, he scraped some coins off the bureau and headed out into the bright sunlight, toward the apothecary, a man who purportedly could do wonders with shears.

He walked down the dirt street, to the door with the medicine-bottle sign swinging in the breeze above it. He stepped inside, the musty smell of the place hitting him in the face. It took a moment for his eyes to adjust to the dim light.

"Anybody here?"

A man came out of the back, round around the middle with a jolly-looking face. "What can I do for you, monsieur?"

"I'm looking for a haircut. Maybe a good shave." Samuel ran his hand across his prickly chin. "I heard this was the place."

"*Oui, oui*. Sit, and we will see what we can do, monsieur."

Samuel sat in a chair by the window, closed his eyes, and felt the long drape of a sheet being wrapped around him, his hair being pulled free of the collar. "You want it short?" the Frenchman asked.

Samuel looked into the mirror opposite. "Just a trim. Leave it a little long."

The man bent to his work, the *snip-snip* of the scissors working quickly on Samuel's mane.

"You are one of the soldiers, yes? The Americans?"

"Yes."

He hoped this wasn't the wrong answer as the man brought out a straight-edge razor. Maybe this hadn't been such a good idea.

But the man was nothing if not efficient. A hot towel was placed over his face, and Samuel gradually relaxed his tensed muscles, almost falling asleep in the chair. The shave took only moments.

Then a comb was run through his hair again, and a mirror thrust into his hand.

"You like, eh?"

Samuel stared at his reflection in the mirror. He smiled a little. Truly, he looked a new man. A new man for a new day. Today he would ask her. He would ask Isabelle to be his wife. Now for some new clothes.

He handed the man some coins and headed for the trading post. There he pawed through cotton, linen, and buckskin. He finally settled on some fancy buckskin leggings and a loose-fitting shirt that tied at the throat with long, flowing sleeves.

He stepped out the door and swallowed hard. He hadn't felt this nervous on his wedding day! Slapping his hat on his head, Samuel grinned at himself and started for the hotel where his gypsy bride awaited him.

# 29

Samuel made his way across the dusty street of Kaskaskia, hoping Clark wouldn't see him and tease him unmercifully about his new getup. He reached the hotel in no time and pulled open the front door.

At a long counter, he cleared his throat. "I'm looking for the Renoirs. Isabelle Renoir. Is she here?"

The man behind the counter stared at him from little eyes, squinting up from his paper. "The Renoirs? They left about an hour ago. Gone back to Vincennes with the books, you see."

Left? He stared hard at the man. "They left for Vincennes already?"

The man nodded his head. "About an hour ago. They seemed eager to begin the trip home."

"Were they riding?"

The man nodded. "I think they had two horses. One for the books and the other," he paused and shrugged, "maybe for the women to take turns riding."

Samuel stomped from the room. He had missed them! He couldn't believe it. Isabelle had left and hadn't even bothered to say good-bye.

He practically ran to the town stable, digging into his haversack for some money. Did he have on him enough for a horse? No. He'd spent his last bit of silver on clothes, trying to impress her. He turned and ran back to his room at the American offices. Perhaps he could still catch them and be back before his absence was noticed.

In his room he retrieved the worn saddlebag that he always kept with him. Inside was money. Lots of it. He spilled out the coins. He'd never even counted it. Never touched it. He had never told another soul that when he left home his father had given him his inheritance in gold. He hadn't wanted it at the time, had never tapped into it, satisfied with a soldier's grassy bed and slim rations. But there it was, glittering back at him, a small fortune at his disposal. He could have gone anywhere. He could have been anyone with this kind of money. But all he'd wanted was to prove himself.

But now, aside from this trove, he was broke. If he was going to go after Isabelle, he would have to use some of it to buy a horse. He reached for a coin, felt the hard edges of it slide through his fingers. What good was it, he reasoned, if he couldn't use it when he needed it most? He wrestled with his pride and his guilt as he stuffed the golden coins into his sack. Had he thought the Shawnee would accept it, he would have used the money to ransom Isabelle. But this money represented a life he had scorned, the work of a man he hadn't respected or acknowledged.

Back at the stable he paid for the best and fastest horse, not caring that the man was taking advantage of his obvious rush by charging twice what the horse was worth. It didn't matter. Nothing mattered beyond finding *her*.

He mounted, feeling the fight of a new kind of battle rise within him.

*Isabelle. Come back to me.*

He rode out fast and hard, barely registering the greeting of a few fellow soldiers. He didn't spare them a glance.

Samuel made for the woods.

And Vincennes.

---

"ISABELLE?" HER MOTHER said for the third time, a worried look in her eyes.

Isabelle roused enough to turn toward her mother. Hope was riding the horse with the books, a solid, slow-moving character named Blacky, while Isabelle rode a light-brown beauty with quick-stepping ways. Adam walked beside them, a thoughtful look in his eyes as he pushed through the brush for them.

"I'm sorry." Isabelle gave her mother a halfhearted smile. "What did you say?"

"I asked if you were hungry." Hope looked at her in concern. "Should we stop for a noon meal?"

Isabelle shrugged. Food was the last thing on her mind. "If you wish," she managed. "I could eat a little." She couldn't really. But she would try, for Hope's sake, so that her mother wouldn't worry so much.

Everything was different now. Hope was still her mother . . . and yet she was a different daughter somehow. She knew deep within her that if Adam and Hope suddenly disappeared, evaporated into some dream or nightmare even, that she could travel this road alone. She was bereft, but a woman bereft had strengths. A woman bereft no longer loved her own life.

*Oh, Samuel.*

Had he noticed they were gone? What would he think when he heard the news? Would he care?

Her lips compressed as she remembered him clinging to that necklace around his throat. He had his own choices to make. And from all appearances, he'd chosen his secrets over her. Chosen a silver moon that was flat and small over a full-blooded woman who danced in moonlight. She hoped he would be happy with the cold feel of it against his chest each night.

She would have given him everything—her heart, her heat, her life. But he hadn't been able to reach out and take it. So she departed for Vincennes and the hopes of some other future that only God had full knowledge of.

---

IN THE DISTANCE Samuel saw a waving of weeds, fresh tracks all around in the soft earth. Then he heard them. They were loud and being none too careful, making him clench his teeth together. Had she learned nothing from the Shawnee?

"You shouldn't say such a thing, Isabelle!"

"And why not? You know it is true."

They were discussing Joseph Renoir, Isabelle's father. Samuel had only heard bits and pieces about the man. He stopped, quieting his horse, thinking that he sure would like to learn more.

"He is your father. You must honor that, even through his weaknesses. We all have them."

Samuel had edged close enough to see Isabelle look at her mother with fire spitting from her eyes. "Tell me why you married him."

Hope paused and sighed heavily, looking away from both Isabelle and Adam, into the woods. "He made me believe in rainbows."

"Rainbows?" Isabelle scoffed. "What does that mean?"

Hope shook her head, looking down at the horse's ears. "I don't know what it means," she said softly. "I suppose he made me believe that anything was possible. He was my grand adventure." She turned slowly to Isabelle. "You may think I'm just an old woman, just your mother, but there was a time, my dear, when I wanted adventure too."

Isabelle just stared.

"And you may believe you are your father's child through and through, but you are very much like I was as a girl."

Isabelle shook her head in disbelief. "Really?"

Hope laughed a small laugh. "Yes, really. Marrying your father was like running away with the circus. Do you think my parents were happy about it? He was foreign, strange to them, and so volatile. They foresaw the life I would live. But all I saw was . . . a grand adventure."

Adam remained quiet but alert, hearing the answers to questions he'd had for years. Isabelle just looked stunned.

Samuel did his best to remain close but quiet, wanting to see this scene played out until its end. Sometimes being a trained spy came in handy.

There was a long, pregnant pause as they each pondered what Hope had revealed. Then with sudden intensity Isabelle asked, "Do you think it is the same with Samuel? Was he only some grand adventure that I wanted?"

Hope turned and reached out to touch Isabelle's shoulder, a picture of comfort. "I can't answer that for certain . . . but I can say that Samuel reminds me more of Adam than your father."

Adam turned at that. He stared hard into Hope's eyes, and for a moment Samuel read all the pain and loss and yearning that they had for each other.

Hope had married the wrong man.

Just as he had done, marrying the wrong woman.

Samuel looked down at the animal he rode and let the thought settle on him. Logically he had to wonder if Hope would have even met Adam had she not married Joseph. After all, Joseph was the one who'd brought them to this territory. And Adam? He didn't know his story, but it seemed the man had been in Vincennes his whole life. "So how," he looked up and questioned, "could she meet the man she was supposed to be with, without marrying Joseph."

*My ways are not your ways.*

He heard the quiet words, words from Scripture that had been read aloud when he was a lad in church. He hadn't picked up a Bible since he left home, yet some phrases of it seemed to stick with him, rising up as this one did when he least expected it.

"What are Your ways?" he asked as his horse snorted and puffed and seemed to want to move forward. He pulled lightly at the reins, knowing he needed this answer before he could move on, move forward with Isabelle. What if he was only an adventure to her? What if she tired of him? He could never imagine this woman in a cabin in the wilderness bearing his children and looking after the next meal. No, a woman like Isabelle would mean *many* adventures. And he would need to be willing and able to provide and allow them. He wouldn't be marrying a woman who would be content as a wife and mother. And he would have to go into that marriage prepared and determined—yes, determined—that she got that life. He would have to become the protector of it, guarding it and sanctioning it.

He heaved a breath, seeing it so clearly.

He might be her way. But her way in this life might mean his being the one to lay down his life for her. Because, quite simply, her life might be the one that mattered more in the grand scheme of things.

It was a hard truth. Almost impossible in the time they lived in, and he recognized that in his visions of the future he had felt there was less difference between men and women, and he realized that this may be why he'd been given those dreams.

A part of him rose up and said no. He was a man, strong and sure himself! He didn't need a woman to make him into something. He was something all on his own. Just look at what he had done and what he would yet accomplish. Sara wouldn't have demanded this of him. Sara would have, eventually, loved him and bore him children and lived the quiet woman life that his mother and sisters lived.

But he'd abhorred that.

*God. Why? Why show me this?*

*My ways are not your ways.*

It was all he could hear. And he didn't want to hear it. Yet something in him knew it to be true. The prophets of old asked for the scales to fall from their eyes. But seeing eyes, truth-seeing eyes, cut to the core and left one gasping for breath. But the scales had dropped from his eyes onto the muddy path where he stood, and he couldn't put them back.

Isabelle was his grand future. His dying-flesh death was her life. And for some reason the future depended on her being able to do something—something no one but she could do. And he would have to hold her up because there would be times coming when it would be too much for Isabelle to bear alone, she would need him to complete her destiny.

He breathed with the truth of it, coming to terms with it. Breathing in the peace that came with acceptance. Sara and their children would have been a shadow life. Isabelle was full color, full blown. Pain. Ecstasy. Life. Their purposed life. Together.

---

"I THINK SOMEONE is following us," Isabelle whispered to her mother.

Hope turned in her saddle, fear on her face. "Where? Are you sure?"

"No, I'm not sure. I just have that feeling. And I think I heard something."

Isabelle turned in her saddle and peered into the forest.

"Samuel?" she said as he rode out of the trees, looking like he had something on his mind.

# 30

Samuel reined in next to Isabelle's still horse. "You left without saying good-bye," he said, his eyes hard, not masking the pain.

Isabelle swallowed. He looked good. Different but good. He was dressed in fine clothes, his hair neatly trimmed, his beard gone. Her gaze roved the bareness of his face. The lean cheeks and dimples. The broad strokes of his eyebrows, darker than his golden hair. The intensity in his amber eyes as they pierced hers. She took a slow and silent breath.

"I didn't think you would care." She was lying, or hoped she was. She had thought he might, was hoping to hurt him the way he had hurt her.

"When are you going to *know* me?"

She could only stare at him, a tight knot in her throat. Had she misjudged him? "I tried."

Hope was dismounting. "Adam, I feel the need for some fresh water. Didn't you say there was a stream just up ahead?"

Samuel and Isabelle barely noticed them leave the little clearing, so deep was their concentration on one another.

Samuel edged his horse closer. The horses pawed the ground, growing skittish. But Samuel was firm, determined to reach the woman he loved. With a sudden movement he grasped Isabelle's waist and hauled her off her horse and onto his lap. They sat still as his horse sidestepped, getting its footing.

Isabelle felt that she might fall and cried out, but Samuel grasped her firmly and pulled her to his chest.

They didn't say a word. Their eyes did all the talking for them.

Samuel leaned in, his mouth reaching hers. Isabelle felt a small sob break free from her lips as he kissed her like she'd dreamed he would.

"Don't ever leave me like that again," Samuel muttered against her lips.

"But I thought . . ."

"You thought wrong. Don't you know how much I love you?"

Isabelle blinked back tears. "But the necklace. You wanted that more than you wanted me. I know it."

Samuel took her hand and brought it up to his cheek, then lower, to his chest, his heart.

"I may have had a moment's weakness. It represented something, something I'd been hanging onto and . . . I wasn't sure that I was ready to give it up."

"What did it represent?"

"A life lost."

Isabelle shook her head. "If you really love me like you say you do, then Samuel," she reached up and touched his smooth cheek, "you are going to have to do better than that."

Samuel exhaled, nodding once. "You have every right to know. I was married once. She died giving birth to my daughter."

Isabelle's eyes grew round. "You have a daughter?"

Samuel nodded. "Her name is Isabelle, too. But I called her Belle—my little Belle—before I left her, left them all, and rode off to join the army."

"You left your daughter?" She reared back, appalled.

"She was in better hands with my mother and sisters than with me. I wasn't any good to her then. I had nothing to give her."

Isabelle quietly digested this shocking revelation. Then she raised her chin and demanded, "Did you love her, your wife?"

Samuel gazed off into the distance, rubbing Isabelle's waist with his thumb. "In a way. I was nineteen. I didn't know much about love."

"Then why did you ask her to be your wife?"

Samuel shrugged. "My parents and her parents owned adjoining lands. She was an only child, and our fathers wanted us to marry to unite the land."

"But you didn't want that kind of life."

Samuel locked gazes with her. "I didn't know what I wanted. All I knew was that she was pretty, in a pale, frail kind of way. But she didn't want me. She only wanted that life."

"She didn't love you?" Isabelle was sad and unbelieving at the same time. How could anyone not want this beautiful, strong, and capable man?

"No, I don't think she did."

Isabelle took a long breath. Then she put her palms on either side of his face and commanded his full attention on hers, on her eyes. "Then she was a fool of the worst sort. I would have loved you." She blinked the tears from her eyes. "I *do* love you."

He smiled with tight lips, looking like he was trying to hold in the emotion her words stirred in him. Then he crushed her in his embrace, his mouth reaching for hers, their breaths intermingling as their lips made contact.

Samuel pulled back to gasp, "The vows we made . . . at the Shawnee camp. I want to make them good in a Christian church. Will you be my wife in truth?"

She could only nod and stare into the depth of those amber eyes. "It will be as it has been since we first saw each other. A connection that no one can sever. I have been yours since that day you walked from the trees and met the barrel of my rifle." She grinned at him. "I will be yours forever."

Samuel clutched her to him. She smelled the soap on his skin, felt the pliant touch of his lips against her temple, his hand grasping her unbound hair. "I'll not have you staying at home cooking and cleaning, you know," he whispered in her ear, smiling. "The sky might be our roof and the grass our bed."

A laugh escaped her chest. "It sounds perfect."

"I might even make a scout out of you. We might head west and see lands yet undiscovered."

Isabelle nodded. "We will travel."

Then she turned serious, leaning back to look at him. "I want to meet her, you know. We have to go there first. Back to your family and get her. She belongs with us."

Samuel stared at her, a prick of tears in his eyes. "I was hoping you would think so." He paused and gripped her shoulders. "You know if we go back, they will want us to stay. They will want us to pick up that life."

"We will cross that bridge when we get to it. We will sort it out . . . together."

"You would want another woman's child?"

Isabelle nodded. "I want your child. She will be my Belle too."

"Sara must have known something. She asked me to name her that, just before she died."

"Maybe so. I always *did* love that name."

Samuel threw back his head in laughter. "You are one of a kind, Isabelle Renoir! You are some kind of woman."

"Isabelle Holt, do you mean? Because I think we are going to have to rush this wedding."

"Why is that?" He smiled at her again, a smile that welled up and out of him.

"Remember the night at the farmer's house, just outside of Kaskaskia, when we slept together?"

Samuel nodded, looking both eager and afraid of what she might say next.

"Well, I'd like to repeat that night as soon as possible. Only this time, you will not get to turn over and go to sleep."

---

SAMUEL LEANED DOWN to kiss her again, breathing deep, collecting handfuls of her hair in both fists. This woman wouldn't lay there cold and dead as he tried to woo her. No, this woman would woo him.

"Where's the nearest preacher?" his voice rumbled in his chest, almost a purr.

Isabelle laughed. "I think we are halfway between Kaskaskia and Vincennes. My father is in Vincennes, and in Kaskaskia is your friend, Clark. You decide."

"I think I should meet your father." Clark wasn't going to be too happy when he discovered Samuel gone again. But the man seemed to be doing just fine on his own on this mission.

"I'm glad. I think he will like you."

Samuel leaned in for another kiss, which she returned, matching him. She would never be the kind of woman to turn away from the heat of their passion.

Behind his closed eyes he saw Sara, saw her face clearly for the first time in a long time, . . . and she was smiling. She looked pleased. It was as though she was giving him her blessing—a release from heaven's clouds.

---

THEIR REVERIES WERE interrupted by the return of Hope and Adam. They both grinned as they entered the clearing and saw Isabelle atop Samuel's horse, in his arms.

"I guess this means we will be having a wedding?" Hope ventured, happiness in her eyes.

Isabelle nodded from Samuel's arms. "Yes, I believe we will."

Adam handed up a water canteen. "You two look like you could use some water."

Isabelle slid down from the horse. "How soon can you plan a wedding, Mother?"

"I think a wedding can be quickly arranged. We are going to Vincennes, yes? We should have your father's blessing on this."

"Yes. But if he doesn't give it, I will be heading back to Kaskaskia and a wedding with George Rogers Clark in attendance instead."

Hope looked up to Samuel. "Oh, I think he will give it. I think he will be relieved to have a gypsy like you taken off his hands."

She was teasing, but Samuel took her seriously.

"I will need your prayers, ma'am."

Hope nodded and smiled. "Yes, Samuel, you will."

Adam laughed. "If we mount up and ride hard, we can be there in another day, before Samuel has a chance to change his mind."

Isabelle huffed at them. "I am That You Cannot Imagine," she said as she tossed her long, glorious hair over one shoulder. "None of you who know what you can imagine know what you're talking about."

"Like I said," Hope laughed, full joy on her face, "you will need some prayer."

---

THE NIGHT WAS bright, lit by a full moon. A few wispy clouds scudded across its face like spiderwebs caught too high, blown on an errant wind. The breeze gusted against Isabelle's new, hastily made dress, pressing it against her legs as she walked to the church. Her chosen bride's gown was red, sure and loud even in the darkness. Her long, unbound hair blew in her face, making her look like the wild gypsy so many had called her. She didn't care. This was her and Samuel's night, a magical night and hard won. He would love her wild ways, and that was all that mattered.

It was time. Almost midnight. Time for a candlelight wedding.

She opened the creaking wooden door of the church and stepped inside.

It was a solemn, old place, full of the comfort of growing-up memories. As she looked over the assemblage of people, she knew a breaking moment of tears rushing to her eyes.

There were so many people.

She hadn't known. She hadn't known how loved her family was. It seemed everyone she'd ever met, and some she didn't even know, were sitting there, looking up at her, their faces wreathed with smiles.

She caught Samuel's eye as she stood at the back of the narrow, silent aisle. He was standing beside Father Francis, a man whose round, smiling face brought a rise of happy laughter from her chest. How relieved he must be that she had found her purpose, her life's love, the fulfillment of her dreams.

Her father took her arm, his face florid and radiant. Joseph had not only accepted Samuel as his son-in-law; he had taken an immediate liking to him as well. They had spent many afternoons talking and walking, looking over Joseph's business, talking of Samuel's plans, replaying together the hard truth of Julian's death. Hope had been the one to tell him, but somehow Samuel had been the one to recount all the details, to soothe a father's pain. Julian was a hero in the story as Samuel told it. And Isabelle too. Samuel made sure Joseph knew how brave they both had been.

Joseph took the first happy step with her toward her future. Then, halfway down the aisle, in front of everyone, he turned her toward him, kissed her soundly, saying in a loud, jubilant voice, "I love you."

Isabelle nodded once, looking up into his dark-brown eyes, eyes that looked just like hers. "Yes."

"And you will always be my girl."

"Yes."

"And life will bring you things . . . things that you can't yet fathom."

She nodded. Quieter and agreeing, "Yes."

"But you will always be my beloved daughter."

Her face crumpled. "Yes," she breathed, knowing what he was trying to say. Knowing in her heart that, no matter how he had failed, no matter how frail and unable he'd sometimes been, she would always hold a special place in his heart, and he in hers.

Music started, the music she had chosen. It was an old Irish dirge, with bagpipe and flute, that spoke of love lost and then found.

It was time to take her husband.

But she stopped her father from moving forward. She leaned in and whispered into his ear, "And you will always be *mon Papa*."

He nodded, tears forming in his eyes. He knew, just like she knew: They were peas, the two of them.

He took a tight hold on her arm, and they were off again, moving toward the man she loved, toward a future she couldn't wait to begin. They practically danced the rest of the way down the aisle, laughing together. The whole congregation was with them—friends, neighbors, French and English settlers, Indians whom Joseph played cards with—everyone loving him and, now, her.

Isabelle arrived at the altar a little breathless, laughing and crying at the same time. She was thrust into Samuel's waiting arms.

Samuel was laughing and shaking his head at them. "What will I do with you?" he whispered into her ear.

"Love me. Only love me," she whispered back, tilting her head to take in the beauty of his face.

Isabelle took his hands hard in hers and stared up at him with all the meaning of their future shining in her eyes. It was the eve of a new day, a glorious day.

That You Cannot Imagine was joining forces with The Glorious One.

The candlelight flickered, then the air seemed to still as they made their vows. And heaven looked down and smiled. A victory won.

A match made in heaven.

# 31

They arrived at Holt Plantation after weeks of travel by horseback. Isabelle could sense the tension in her husband as they crossed the border into Virginia. The tension had mounted steadily since, until his shoulders were pulled up in a knot hunched over the reins, his mouth drawn into a tight, white line. He practically jumped when she spoke.

"Do you think they will be surprised that you are married?"

"I expect so."

Isabelle laughed, trying to lighten the mood. "But they will love me, don't you think?"

Samuel didn't even crack a smile. "To be honest, I'm not sure they will let us in the door."

Isabelle sighed and gave up trying to cheer him. He was going to be like this until they found out exactly how his family would react.

In the silence she let her mind wander over the weeks since their wedding. With no home to call their own, they had camped under the stars that first night together. Her parents had offered them a roof, but they'd both agreed that they wanted to be alone, beyond the reach of any ears and eyes. They had waited out the congratulatory crowd, then packed up Isabelle's personal belongings and said good-bye to the Renoirs, starting out for Kaskaskia where Samuel would report to George Rogers Clark.

Isabelle had married a soldier, and she wouldn't have it any other way. She would go where he went, even into battle if they would allow her, which she doubted. But she wasn't worried; she would find a way to be with him.

Remembering their first night together brought a grin to Isabelle's face, which she quickly tried to hide by looking down and away from Samuel. He had been so shy at first! And she so curious. It hadn't taken her long to disabuse him of any modesty. With the forest floor as their bed and the night as their walls, they'd discovered that they were well matched as lovers, as in the daytime hours.

Upon arriving in Kaskaskia, they'd sought out Clark together, Samuel telling their story. At first Isabelle had been afraid the gleam in Clark's eye meant an inevitable explosion of temper. But after a token lecture on how Samuel should have confided in him, should have trusted him instead of running off without a word to anyone, Clark congratulated them on their marriage.

"What are your plans now?" he asked, knowing there was more.

Samuel took a breath and plunged in. "I guess we're going back to Virginia. As soon as my service here is finished," he hastened to add. "I was hoping Isabelle could stay here with me until then."

Clark nodded slowly, rubbed his chin in a gesture of deep concentration. "Things are so quiet here. I would hate to detain you.

"What would you think of riding to Virginia on an errand for me? I have packets for Patrick Henry and the Virginia Legislature. We have made many friends among the Indians, and I want him to read the treaties for himself as soon as possible."

Samuel nodded. "I could do that."

Clark grinned. "Then, if you decide to stay in Virginia awhile, that would be all right with me. You have certainly done your duty to your country, Samuel."

"But if I am needed, I will return."

"Of course. This fight has been easier than I expected. All three forts are firmly under American control, and hundreds of citizens and Indians have sworn loyalty to our cause. It is beyond what I had hoped."

"I am glad. I was honored to be a part of it, sir. When do we leave?"

"Give me a day to prepare the documents, then you and your lovely wife can begin the journey home." He turned to Isabelle. "Are you ready for a trip like this, madam? It could be dangerous. It will certainly be long and tedious."

"I think I can manage, sir. Thank you for allowing us the chance."

Clark laughed, looking back at Samuel with a twinkle in his eyes. "You have chosen well, my friend."

Samuel looked at Isabelle and smiled. "I think so, Colonel. I don't believe there is another like her in the whole territory."

Clark barked out a laugh. "Don't take away my hope! There must be at least one more."

Clark gave Samuel a big, shoulder-slapping hug, then turned to Isabelle and kissed her on the cheek. "If he ever mistreats you, you know . . ." His eyes were twinkling again.

Isabelle blushed. "I will know just where to go."

They had spent the following day preparing for the journey—purchasing a strong horse for Isabelle, figuring out how to pack all her clothes on the poor beast, stocking up on food and supplies.

And now they were almost there.

---

"THERE. DO YOU see it?" Samuel's husky voice interrupted her musings.

Isabelle stood up in her stirrups and peered over the rolling hills. There in the distance, on a bluff overlooking the James River, sat a massive stone house.

"Well," Isabelle grinned at Samuel, "may as well get this finished and find out if we are to sleep in that fancy house tonight or back on the trail. I would like to sleep in a real bed for a change."

Samuel laughed. "That doesn't sound half bad."

Over the remaining distance Isabelle kept her awe of the place to herself. Huge trees draped in fall colors lent splashes of crimson and gold and orange onto the ground, like a painting come to life on a westward wind, lining either side of the drive up to the mansion. At the end of this picturesque passage was a three-story house. Fourteen windows in rows of five encircled a huge door framed with ornate molding. Four massive chimneys stood sentinel at each corner of the house, with a light-colored roof lit by the afternoon sun completing the picture.

Samuel led them to a hitching post off to one side of the drive. He dismounted and helped Isabelle down by grasping firm hold of her waist and pulling her from the horse into his arms. A long kiss later—a kiss to remind them that, no matter what, they had each other—they turned and wrapped the reins about the hitching posts.

Samuel silently took Isabelle's hand and led her up the walk to the front door. He raised his hand, hesitated, then knocked.

Moments later the door was opened by a black man wearing a fancy suit. Isabelle suddenly felt every speck of the trail dirt and looked down at her dress, realizing that she wasn't exactly looking her best. "I probably stink too," she accidentally mumbled aloud, causing Samuel to turn toward her and chuckle as the old man exclaimed, "Why, Master Samuel. It's Master Samuel!" His brown eyes lit up, and his lips curved in a big toothy smile. He turned and yelled to the house at large. "Master Samuel's come home! Master Samuel's come home, y'all!"

Samuel was swept inside as Isabelle stood blinking in the foyer.

Feminine voices were raised from the back of the house. Samuel appeared braced for anything. A tall, stately woman with upswept silver hair and dressed in an elegant, pale-blue brocade gown entered the room and stopped short upon seeing him, her hand rising to her mouth.

"Samuel?" She whispered it, the sound echoing off the tall ceilings. "I cannot consider it." There was a slight sheen in her eyes as she came forward and put her arms awkwardly around him. "You have come home, at last." She sniffed once, pulling herself up straight and tall. Turning her gaze toward Isabelle, she asked, "And who is this?" Her gaze swept from Isabelle's dirty hair to her mud-caked boots, making Isabelle really wish she had thought to stop and freshen up before they arrived.

Samuel turned and pulled Isabelle forward, his hand a comforting presence on her low back. "Mother, this is Isabelle. My wife."

"Isabelle? Oh, goodness."

Isabelle dipped a small curtsy. "So good to make your acquaintance, ma'am."

The three sisters rushed into the room, exclaiming over Samuel, chattering like birds in springtime and examining Isabelle much like their mother had. She soon learned their names. Ruth was the eldest and looked very much the spinster Samuel had described her to be. RaeAnn was plumper than the others, the only dark-haired one of the group, with small eyes that studied Isabelle thoughtfully.

The youngest, though, grasped her hand and gave her a beaming smile. "I'm so pleased to meet you. You can call me Betsy. That is what all of my friends call me." A southern drawl warmed her voice.

"Rebecca," corrected her mother in a tone that broached no argument, "stop fawning over the girl. I am sure she is, well, tired from her long journey." She looked around, and a servant mysteriously appeared. "Show them to their room, Lorena. Samuel's room. And bring them food and . . . lots of hot water."

Samuel laughed, leaning over and kissing her wrinkled cheek. "You haven't changed a bit, Mother. It is good to see you again." He seemed relieved. They were to stay.

"And why should I change?" his mother challenged, but there was softness in her eyes as she gazed at the face of her only son. Then she said in a kind voice, "You have changed much since I last saw you."

Samuel nodded agreement. He had left a boy and come back a man. A married man. "Where is Father? And Belle? I would like to see my daughter."

Margaret, Samuel's mother, waved her hand. "Oh, you know your father. I expect he will be home in a day or two. Belle is with her nurse. I will send her up directly."

They were led upstairs, the house as grand on the inside as it was out. Cream-paneled walls graced every room. The glittering chandeliers and wall sconces would make a festive light when night fell. Samuel's room was in perfect order—a pale green and gold counterpane on the bed, dark-green curtains drawn at the wide windows, which Lorena opened, flooding the room in light. There was a simple desk and chair, a large bureau of polished walnut, and a matching armoire. Samuel dropped their dusty saddlebags onto the plush rug that covered gleaming wood floors.

"Good heavens, Master Samuel! You look as dirty as pigs. Where you been all these years? Scaring your momma half out of her wits leaving like you did, not that she showed it. I just know her. And your father," she threw her hands up, "whoo-eee, he was a surly bear for those first months when you didn't come back. We all thought you was gone for good."

Samuel laughed, and it was a hearty sound. Apparently Lorena had spoken to him like this often.

Isabelle felt she'd stepped into another world. This was a wealthy home, a wealthy family with a deeply entrenched life. Her father had been successful, providing well for them in their wilderness outpost. But this—this was different. Real wealth, real power, real culture.

Lorena busied herself setting out an enormous amount of silver on a small table that another servant had carried into their room and set up, followed closely by two chairs. Before Isabelle could blink, there were two settings of China plates, silver tableware, linen napkins, and silver dish upon covered dish with steaming hot, heavenly smelling food. Her mouth started to water, and she swallowed quickly as she stared at it.

"Why, look at that girl! She's fairly starving, she's so thin. You been feeding your wife?"

Samuel chuckled again. "I sure did miss you, Lorena." He laughed, squeezing her tight.

The woman promptly burst into tears and smacked him on his big, muscled arm. "Now look what you've done. Oh!" Then she fled the room, her wide skirts swaying with her hurried steps. "Jonas, you got that tub ready?" they heard her yell as she fled down the hall.

Isabelle sank into a chair at the table and laughed. "She is quite in love with you."

Samuel sat across from her, reaching for a juicy-looking chicken leg. "Yep. My nursemaid as a child. And I can tell you, she's all bark. The girls never could get anything over on her . . . but me?" He held up his little finger. "Wrapped so tight, I could have told her the moon was blue, and she would have agreed."

Isabelle laughed, reaching for the food. There was steamed asparagus, so green and dripping butter she could hardly tear her eyes off it. Three kinds of meat—a whole roasted chicken, sliced honeyed ham, and a thick beefsteak with peppercorns smeared over it. Corn pudding, flaky rolls that melted in her mouth, and some other kind of bread Isabelle wasn't sure of. She took a quick bite, her eyes growing round with delight.

"Good?"

"Oh, yes. This is like nutty pumpkin-apple bread. Mmmmm. Did you eat like this every day?"

Samuel nodded, his mouth full and eyes twinkling at her. "Most days. I guess you will be getting fat if we stay here any time at all."

Isabelle threw a pea at him. "I guess I will." She laughed, drinking of the cool apple cider. "This is the best thing that's ever happened to me."

Samuel leaned over and took her hand, the one clinging to a chicken wing and teased, "The best thing?"

Isabelle turned her head down a little down and to one side. "Well, maybe not the best thing. We haven't tried out a real bed yet."

Samuel groaned and laughed. "I might have known taking you here with me would make it so much better." He paused, looking at her with such love. "I couldn't have done this without you, Isabelle Holt."

"I'm glad you didn't have to." She felt so happy just being with him that it didn't really matter what his mother or sisters thought of her, of them.

A sound at the doorway caused them both to turn at the same time.

There in a white, frilly gown, her hair shoulder length, straight and so blonde it was nearly white, stood Samuel's daughter.

Isabelle heard Samuel's sudden intake of breath.

"My little Belle." He said it so quietly that Isabelle was sure the child did not hear him.

But she had.

And all Isabelle could think of was how opposite the girl looked from her. How the past was meeting the present. And how reconciliation would have to be worked out, somehow, between abandoned relatives and the three of them, this new family.

And always, now, the ghost of a mother who could have been.

# 32

Hello, Father," the child said with perfect diction, dipping into a curtsey.

Isabelle stifled a laugh, remembering how at this child's age she would propel herself into her father's arms and lap when he returned from a long excursion, demanding candy and treats and presents, knowing that she would find them in his haversack or hidden in his curled-up fists. But this child had a pale face, almost as white as her hair, and big, solemn eyes. Isabelle found suddenly a mother's heart, wanting to gather the child up and hold her. But she knew that look of independent pride and so remained still in her chair, her hands tightly clasped to stop any headlong rush. Something told her—some innate reading of another soul—that she must win this heart with stealth and cunning. It would be hard and slow won. But she was determined.

Samuel rose from the table, walked to the little girl, and squatted down in front of her. "Hello, Belle," he said, as solemn as she.

They didn't seem to know what to say to each other, so Isabelle stepped forward, gesturing toward the laden table. "Are you hungry? Would you like something to eat?"

The girl's eyes locked with Isabelle's, and Isabelle saw a flash of pain and resentment. "I don't eat at this hour, ma'am."

Isabelle laughed, not to be put off. "No? Not ever?" She gave her the look her mother used to give her, chin down, eyebrows raised, knowing that such a look somehow, someway impaled the heart and demanded truth.

The girl looked quickly down, turning pink. "Once I went to the kitchens, and the cook gave me a cookie." She looked up at Isabelle. "But I shouldn't have taken it."

Isabelle leaned down, reached out, and touched the little girl softly on the shoulder. "Not such a great sin, I should think," Isabelle said in a sincere voice. Then she leaned in with a conspirator's whisper. "Why, one time, I ate a whole pie in the middle of the afternoon. And," she paused, waiting for the girl's full attention, then finished in a dramatic whisper, "*it came from a neighbor's window*."

Belle's eyes grew round with shock. "You stole it?"

Isabelle laughed, winking at the child. "I surely did. And got my behind switched for that one. But it was an awfully good pie, and later I thought it worth the punishment."

The child didn't look like she believed her or at least didn't know what to make of such a tale.

Samuel chuckled, motioning toward Isabelle. "Do you know who this is?"

The little girl slowly shook her head back and forth, staring at Isabelle like she might sprout horns at any moment.

"This is your new mama."

Belle looked genuinely appalled.

"And you know what?"

Belle looked at her father and shook her head again.

"Her name is Isabelle too."

That really shook the girl. Isabelle was sure she was wondering how someone like her could sully such a grand name.

"But you won't call me Isabelle," Isabelle assured, kneeling in front of the child, locking gazes with those big brown eyes. "I hope, someday, you will call me mama . . . . or *Ma Mère*, as that is what I called my mama when I was young.

She didn't look as if she would ever do anything of the sort but was much too polite to say so, so only responded with a quick nod. Isabelle reached for her hand and brought the girl to the table, seating her in her chair. "I think it's time for me to remove this grime from the road. And you," she looked up at Samuel, "should finish this forbidden mid-afternoon meal with your daughter."

---

SAMUEL WATCHED HER go behind the screen in wonderment. He hadn't known what to think of his Isabelles meeting each other. Couldn't even fathom how they would be together. She'd always said that children bored her. But his wife had seemed caught and intent, willing this child and them to come together as a whole. He found a knot in his throat tightening with the thought of it.

He picked up a clean plate and set it before his daughter, saying, "You can have anything you want this day, Belle. Because today is a special day. Do you know why?"

Belle shook her head, her eyes on the pumpkin bread Isabelle had so enjoyed.

"Today is the day I found my Belle again."

"Are you staying, sir?"

The child was to the point and intuitive enough to get to the root of matters right away. "I don't know," he answered honestly. "But if I go, you will go with me."

She swallowed, gingerly picking up the bread her father had placed on her plate. "Going where? I don't think I would like to leave."

Samuel laughed. "You might not think so. But Isabelle and I go on grand adventures. Wouldn't you like a grand adventure?"

She looked as though the idea had never crossed her mind. Thoughtfully she chewed on the sweet bread. "I don't know. What *is* a grand adventure?"

Samuel laughed with a huff. He found he didn't know how to explain it. "Well . . . I think you might like it."

Isabelle came from behind the screen a few moments later, washed with wet hair and a clean dress on. She was toweling her hair as she walked over to the table. "Belle, if you could go anywhere in the world, where would you want to go?"

Belle's little brow puckered. She was clearly stumped, and Isabelle had to wonder if the child's obvious education had included any geography.

"To Williamsburg, with Grandfather," she finally said.

Samuel laughed, wiping the final crumbs from his mouth. He rose, stretched, and winked at Isabelle. "I think I would have answered the same at her age."

A young woman appeared in the doorway and, spying Belle, scolded her. "You'll ruin your dinner, girl. Come on, now, time for lessons."

Samuel pierced the woman with a stare. "She is sharing a celebratory dinner with her father. I shouldn't take her to task for it if I were you."

The woman nodded. "Yes, sir." But she didn't look like she liked it.

Samuel gave Belle a hug and a kiss on the cheek, then said, "Go with your nurse now. I will see you again soon."

---

HIS FATHER WAS back.

Samuel and Isabelle had spent the previous evening in the company of his mother and sisters, sharing with them stories of his missions over the years. His sisters had asked a thousand questions about his meeting with Isabelle, but he left out most of the details of the Indian capture. Samuel deftly conveyed the tale in a way that made Isabelle out to be a hero. By the end of the telling, they were looking at their new sister-in-law with something between awe and horror. And he'd only told them the best parts.

They had been so sheltered, their lives so different from his.

Now, after a day of visiting the plantation, talking to the overseer, and spending time with Belle, he and Isabelle had escaped to their bedroom, despite the early hour.

Then the summons had come.

His father was home, and it was time. He gave Isabelle a quick kiss on the forehead, reached for the saddlebag of gold, and turned from her. At the door he turned back around. "I'll call you down to meet him if it seems right."

Isabelle nodded, looking forward to the thickly feathered bed. "I understand. I will get myself on my knees and start to pray." She grinned a wicked-looking grin, making him feel that no matter what happened everything would turn out all right.

The walk to his father's library reminded him of many other times he had walked down that hall. Times when he was called to the carpet for some misbehavior, times of import when his father shared some important news of the plantation or the family, times of counsel concerning the business of running such a plantation. Looking back on his younger days, Samuel realized that his father had always included him, had tried to make this life as important to Samuel as it was to him. He had been training Samuel to take possession of it someday.

Now he turned the knob and stepped into the library, his heart beating in his chest like it did when he was rushing into a battle.

Thomas Holt turned in his chair, a smile on his lips. When he saw Samuel standing in the shadows cast by the firelight, his features faltered, then on a rush of breath said, "They didn't tell me it was you."

Samuel was surprised. How could they have kept such a thing from him? His mother's face flashed before his eyes, and he knew that she had planned for and wanted this shock.

"Who did you think was coming?" Samuel asked quietly, walking farther into the room.

His father just stared for a long moment. "She said someone important was here to see me. Someone I had not seen in a long time. I thought maybe Jefferson, or even George Washington himself. It never occurred to me that it might be you."

Thomas stood, poured two stiff drinks and brought one to Samuel, handing it across the abyss that stretched between them.

"I'm sorry."

His father laughed, a short, hard sound. "Sorry for what, son? Sorry you left? Sorry you broke my heart?"

Samuel set the glass on the desk, and nodded. "Yes. Sorry for all that. And sorry they didn't tell you."

His father sipped at his drink. Returning to his chair behind a huge, scarred desk, he sat down. He looked long and considering at his son.

"I heard you were in Washington's army. Distinguished yourself. A corporal, am I right?"

Samuel nodded, taking the seat across from him. "It was a volatile time. It fit my mood."

Thomas smiled a grim smile, sipping again. "Would that I could have gone with you." He stared off into the distance. "I didn't blame you, you know. I understood." A long pause in which Samuel was wise enough to keep silent followed. "I was a young man once, wanted to join the army in the French and Indian war. But we'd only just arrived. And my father wanted the impoverished aristocrat's life. We didn't have time for our country or our manhood. We had a farm to build."

Samuel had never really thought of it that way, had never wondered if his father had wanted anything different from this life he seemed so set on prospering. "I didn't know."

"Of course you didn't. Had I told you, I wouldn't have had a chance of keeping you here. As it was, you were determined to make your own mark. You never wanted mine."

Samuel looked hard into his father's eyes. "I don't want you to think I took it for granted. I wanted to want it. I tried. But after Sara . . . everything opened up underneath me, and I thought—no, I knew—that if I stayed here, I would never be anything."

"Is that why you're back? Are you ready to face it?"

Samuel looked down at the saddlebag of gold beside his chair. He rose, lifted it, and dumped the massive amount of coin, trickling like a waterfall as they cascaded onto the desk. "I am ready to face you."

Thomas stared at the coins, glittering in the candlelight. "You didn't use it." He seemed surprised. And proud.

"A little. I married a woman, a French woman from Vincennes, and I needed a little to get us both back here."

Thomas chuckled and nodded over his clasped hands. "Yes, women will cost you extra." He reached for the gold, lifted up a handful, and let it pour through his fingers back to the desk. "Is she worth it? This blow to your pride." He was smiling, but it was a kind, understanding smile.

Samuel didn't smile back. "I have done many things that I never dreamed I would do to have her. She is worth everything."

Thomas nodded. He looked up at his son in the flicker of the candlelight, reading his son's eyes. "And what do you want now, Samuel? Do you want this plantation? Because I've kept it for you. I won't let some son-in-law inherit what rightly belongs to a Holt, though they plague me to death to do it. Or do you prefer the gold? I will double it since you are married. Women are expensive creatures."

Samuel shook his head. "I don't know. Being back is bittersweet. I have been walking the land. I see it differently now. I know its cost. And then there's Belle."

"Ah, Belle. Now you can't take my only joy from me." He looked serious.

Samuel decided to bare his heart as he never had. He needed this man's advice. "Tell me then. I've married a woman who can outshoot, outtrack, and outfight most men I know. I've married a gypsy who is as at home in the wilderness as she is decked out in finery in a ballroom. The Indians who captured her named her That Which You Cannot Imagine, and there is nothing better to call her. She astounds me at every turn. And then I have a daughter that seems tied up inside. Isabelle would free her of that. I would free her of that. But I know Belle needs stability and a good education. I know now that you love her, and she said to me that her greatest request is to go to Williamsburg with you. You have been more a father to her than I."

He paused, seeing tears well up in Thomas's eyes.

"And I . . . I could run this place. I have remembered how much I loved it in the days I've been back. I could stay here. Make it work. But there would be a part of me, and of my wife, that would long for something else . . . something greater than a secure life could provide.

"Tell me, what should I do?"

Thomas stared off into the flames of the fire, considering. Finally he spoke. "The needs of a young man are different from the needs of an older man, Samuel." He leaned across the desk toward his son. "Do you see this gold?"

Samuel nodded.

"It is not so much. Less than what I am giving the girls for their dowries. I only wanted to make sure you didn't starve." He laughed. "I want them to marry men who have something of their own to give them, and they will. RaeAnn has a beau that will make her very comfortable, if she will come around. And Becky? Becky has her pick of the men around here. She will do just fine." He took another long drink and said thoughtfully, setting the glass on the desk, his fingers wrapped comfortably around it, "From everything you have told me, I think you and your wife should take this gold and live your young lives as you see fit. And then, when you are both older and ready to settle down, your mother and I will probably be ready to hand this place over to you."

Samuel breathed in and out, trying to grasp such generosity.

After everything he'd done. After everything he had put them through, his father only wanted his son to have his inheritance.

"Why would you do that?"

"Because, as you will see with Belle and any other children you have . . . this is what fathers dream of doing. Why do you think I have worked so hard? Why do you think I go out there every day to make this place function and thrive? My father birthed it for me, and I have expanded it for you. Who knows the limits of what you will do for your children? And they for theirs? It is what fathers do."

Samuel was overcome. He could only stare in wonder at the man he had left. "I'm sorry I hurt you."

Thomas huffed. "I understood. After that mess with Sara, you needed to find out who you were. And now that you have, . . . you will make me proud. You already have."

Samuel found himself without words and a throat clogged with emotion. When he looked up, he saw that his father was struggling as well.

"What about Belle?" Samuel finally managed to ask.

"Just . . . give me a few more days." His father looked down at his loosely clasped hands in his lap, then back up at Samuel. "I think I would like to take her to Williamsburg, buy her some candy, show her the sights." He smiled. "Then, if you and your wife need to haul her off into the wilderness or into the great world for a while, why, I think that would be a good thing. Your mother, God bless her soul, has put too much starch in a child of her age. It would do her some good to grow up away from here." He nodded, as if talking to himself. "Do her some real good."

Samuel rose. He went around the desk and touched his father on the arm. "Thank you."

Thomas rose from his chair and took Samuel into his chest with a crushing hug. "I am glad you came back, son. I am so glad."

# Author's Note

As an author of historical novels, the writer uncovers many fascinating facts. Research is like digging for gold. There are so many stories to tell. Stories of great heroes and heroines. Stories of our ancestors. Stories of fellow Americans.

George Rogers Clark was bigger than life. He was one of the men in that time and place who embodied the spirit of courage, had steadfast faith in his mission, and knew a call to greatness.

When Samuel and Isabelle left him in Kaskaskia, Clark was sitting on a ticking bomb. Henry "the Hairbuyer" Hamilton heard of the capture of Vincennes and retaliated with an army of trained British soldiers and American Indian braves.

On October 7, 1778, Hamilton left Detroit, traveled down the Maumee and Wabash Rivers, marching on Vincennes to take it back. Hamilton was easily successful. After all, only a token army under the command of Leonard Helm held the fort for Clark.

What happened next was one of the greatest military blunders of the American Revolution: Hamilton decided to postpone an attack on Kaskaskia and wait until spring, sending his native allies home for the winter.

It was then another hero arose—an Italian trader by the name of Francesco Vigo, a wealthy man committed to Clark and the American cause. He was permitted to leave Vincennes for St. Louis on a supposed trading mission. Vigo kept his word and went straight to St. Louis but on the way back made an inconvenient but important side trip. He headed for Clark with the news of all Hamilton had done and planned to do in the spring.

When Clark learned of Hamilton's victory, it was late January, and winter held a firm grip on the land. Clark realized that his small force could not hold the Illinois posts of Kaskaskia and Cahokia if Hamilton was given sufficient time to gather his forces in the spring. So, being Clark, he boldly decided to move on Vincennes immediately. His letter to Patrick Henry states his conviction so succinctly, that if he failed, "this country and also Kentucky is lost." Clark firmly believed that in gaining the territory north of the Ohio River, they would gain a nation. And if they lost it, they would lose everything.

On February 5, 1779, Clark led one hundred and seventy-two men, nearly half of whom were French volunteers, from Kaskaskia to Vincennes. They marched through flooded country, often shoulder high in water, with freezing temperatures and rain that fell unceasingly. There was never enough food as the hunting parties often came back empty-handed. It took eighteen days to make what should have been a five- or six-day trip. It is a traumatic tale of fortitude and the miraculous. It's the story of the power of one man's conviction and the men who were brave and inspired enough to follow him.

During that harrowing march, Clark buoyed the spirits of the men by taking the lead when plunging into a body of water, singing with them and telling them how they were the greatest of men. As they waded through swamps and streams, the men held their rifles above their heads, their food and ammunition upon their shoulders, and they sang at the top of their voices, their legs quivering with weakness in the freezing temperatures. A drummer boy floated beside them, ever rapping on his drum.

On February 23 the frozen, little army surrounded Vincennes. Clark ordered that the flags be marched back and forth behind the slight rises to convince the British that theirs was an imposing force of six hundred men rather than less than two hundred. Old Testament fighting, to be sure. They opened fire on the fort with such accuracy that the British had to abandon their cannon ports. Two days later Hamilton surrendered. He was sent to Williamsburg as a prisoner of war.

The British never regained control of Cahokia, Kaskaskia, or Vincennes. Later the lands won by George Rogers Clark and his Long Knives were ceded to the United States in the Treaty of Paris in 1783, four long years after Clark's harrowing campaign. The British withdrew from Detroit without Clark and his men ever having to fire a single shot.

Clark's mission had been successful beyond even his wildest imaginings—and this was a man who knew how to dream. The west was opened, and America now stretched to the Mississippi River, the Great Lakes becoming the northern boundary of the young nation.

Like many of our greatest heroes, Clark was not recognized during his lifetime as he deserved. He died on land in Kentucky that he had to fight to possess. The Virginia Legislature would not recognize that Clark personally indebted himself to keep the campaign afloat and refused to pay his war debts. He died in debt. He died in pain.

His was a life spilled out for his country.

There was, however, a well-worn path to Clark's cabin. He received many visitors in his old age. Indian chiefs whom he had made treaties with, men who still admired the tall redhead, remembering him as a man of his word. Men who had followed him and argued with him and heard him and *loved* him. Men who knew what he had done and were in awe of the man named Clark. He was, to the end, a hero to the free landowner of the Northwest Territory and to the new people west of the Allegheny Mountains who called themselves Americans.

My hope is that his courage and faith are being rewarded every day, day after day, in eternity. George Rogers Clark accomplished what he was set on this earth to do, and no one can ask for more than that.

Did I mention he had a brother? William Clark of Lewis and Clark fame. Those boys must have had some kind of parents. Between them, those men carved out a nation from sea to shining sea. I would like to be as inspiring as those parents. I would like to be like those men, pressing on in freedom and courage, rushing headlong and victorious into the glory of God. Only maybe in a dress. One as red and as flashy as Isabelle's.

And dancing.

A gypsy worshipper in a dance song for Him.